"I haven't taken time to be a good friend to you."

There it was again. The goodness in her that she failed to see.

"I can't think of a greater friend than someone who, despite how I broke your heart, would do as much for Milly and me as you have. None of my friends in Ohio would even give me a job."

Silas looked over at her, but Rose's gaze remained focused on the ground. "I did so very grudgingly."

"I know. But you did, which is far more than anyone else."

The moonlight cast shadows over her face, framed by the tendrils that had fallen out of her bun. He let the silence hang between them, and her thoughts, whatever they may be, work through whatever she needed. For the first time since he'd come to Leadville, sitting alone with Rose felt almost comfortable. If only he didn't remember the evenings when they'd sat in the moonlight, laughing, kissing and planning a future that was never to be.

Danica Favorite loves the adventure of living a creative life. She loves to explore the depths of human nature and follow people on the journey to happily-ever-after. Though the journey is often bumpy, those bumps refine imperfect characters as they live the life God created them for. Oops, that just spoiled the ending of Danica's stories. Then again, getting there is all the fun. Find her at danicafavorite.com.

Books by Danica Favorite

Love Inspired Historical

Rocky Mountain Dreams
The Lawman's Redemption
Shotgun Marriage
The Nanny's Little Matchmakers
For the Sake of the Children

DANICA FAVORITE

For the Sake of the Children

HARLEQUIN® LOVE INSPIRED® HISTORICAL

Recycling programs for this product may not exist in your area.

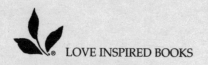 LOVE INSPIRED BOOKS

ISBN-13: 978-0-373-42508-2

For the Sake of the Children

Copyright © 2017 by Danica Favorite

www.Harlequin.com

Printed in U.S.A.

Then Peter came to Jesus and asked, "Lord, how many times shall I forgive my brother or sister who sins against me? Up to seven times?" Jesus answered, "I tell you, not seven times, but seventy-seven times."

—*Matthew* 18:21–22

For my precious Linnie,

As president of your fan club, I'm so grateful for being allowed glimpses into your life. As a writer, I'm really glad your mommy was willing to answer all my questions that began with "What would Linnie say?" I can't wait to see what an incredible woman you're going to grow up into.

Thanks, Kristen, for sharing Linnie with me.

Chapter One

Leadville, Colorado, 1882

The cheerful yellow house didn't look all that imposing as Silas Jones stood in front of its fence for the fourth time that day. Yet he paused at the gate, as he'd done on each of his previous trips, unable to bring himself to open the latch and walk the few steps to the porch and knock on the door.

He turned to walk back toward Harrison Avenue, then over to the boardinghouse he'd been staying in for the past couple of days. Maybe coming to Leadville had been a fool's errand, but he'd had no place else to go. At least not where he could keep his daughter safe from the Garretts.

Smiling down at the little girl in his arms, he gave her a squeeze. "It's going to be all right, Milly. Papa's going to find a way."

Barely two years old, she was too young to understand his anxiety. Or just how much was at stake. Silas took a breath to calm the thundering in his chest. He had no reason to expect that Rose wouldn't hear him out, other than the fact that the last time he'd seen her, three years ago, she was tossing daggers at him with her eyes in church.

He'd deserved those daggers. Actually, he'd deserved far worse, and he knew it. But he'd like to think that deep inside Rose Stone was a compassionate woman who'd understand that he'd had no choice but to break her heart.

Silas shook his head. Who was he kidding? Of course Rose wouldn't understand. He'd jilted her. Not so much in the eyes of the world, since theirs had been a secret engagement, but he'd jilted her all the same. Married the woman his family had picked out for him instead of following his heart and marrying Rose.

She had to hate him.

Which was why he had no idea why he'd come all the way from Ohio to Leadville, Colorado, to beg for her help in saving him.

No, not him.

Milly.

When his wife, Annie, died giving birth to their second child, her parents insisted Silas and Milly stay with them. It didn't take long for Silas to realize that the Garretts weren't intending for them all to be a family, but to take Milly from him. They claimed it was for the best, that a single man wasn't fit to raise a little girl on her own.

But how could a child not having her father when she'd already lost her mother be for the best?

The only solution, of course, was to take a wife. Given that Silas had already married once for convenience, it didn't seem such a leap to do it again. He'd be lying if he said he didn't hope to find love the next time around. But for Milly, he was willing to do anything. After all, he'd come to love Annie in a way.

"Can I help you?" an older woman called out, pulling Silas from his mental debate.

He smiled at her. If he didn't move forward now, he would never be able to. It would look too odd for him to leave after having spoken to someone and then to come back later.

His throat tightened, strangling his ability to speak. Milly squirmed in his arms, reminding him of his purpose.

"I've come to see Rose Stone. Does she live here?"

The woman stared at him like she was trying to decide if he was friend or foe. Her gaze focused on Milly, and like everyone else he'd met on his journey, she softened when she looked at the little girl.

"She does. You come on in, and I'll get her for you."

Silas's feet seemed frozen to the ground. The air was crisp, chilly, to be expected for October, but not enough to render him motionless.

Milly squirmed again. "Down, Papa!"

"It's all right," the woman said. "We've enough children round here that she won't hurt a thing. Most folks expect these young ones to behave far better than they're able to, but we don't pay attention to that sort of thing. Let kids be kids. That's what we always say."

He opened the gate and let Milly down. His daughter immediately propelled herself in the direction of the porch and the waiting woman. Silas shook his head slowly. That girl seemed only to have two speeds—

stop and go. Right now, she was on go, and he could only hope that the woman meant what she said about Milly not hurting anything. The Garretts were constantly chastising Milly for her behavior. As if a two-year-old knew anything about how to behave like a proper young lady.

"Who are you talking to, Maddie?" Rose called from somewhere inside the house. "And what's this nonsense about letting kids be kids? You were just complaining last month to Polly about her children's fingerprints on the wallpaper, and when Uncle Frank told you that children will be children, you told him that they ought to do it in—"

"Oh," Rose said as Silas entered the house. "What are you doing here?"

She hadn't changed a bit, at least not as far as he could tell. She still wore her dark hair piled on top of her head in an elegant way, too elegant for their small town in Ohio, yet it had always suited her. Her cheeks still had a natural rosy glow that accentuated the way her blue eyes shone in the light. Rose had gained a little weight, and her figure seemed fuller, but he'd always thought her just a little too thin.

In essence, she was still as breathtakingly beautiful as she'd been three years ago.

"I was hoping we could…talk."

Maddie entered behind him, holding Milly by the hand. "She is a dear. Makes me miss little Isabella. I do wish they'd come back up from Denver soon."

Rose sighed. "So that's what your change of heart toward children is about. You know Mitch had business to take care of, and you can't expect Polly and the children to stay behind. I'm sure they'll return as soon as they can."

With a quick glance in Silas's direction, Rose said, "Not that it's any of your business, but Polly and Mitch are close friends, like family." The glare she gave him indicated that he was not included in that label.

Though he'd once been.

Maddie smiled at Silas. "What is this little darling's name? I'd be happy to have her in the kitchen with me while you conduct your business with Rose."

"Her name's Milly," Silas said.

"He won't be staying long," Rose said at the same time.

"All the same, I've got a cookie with Milly's name on it in the kitchen." Then she bent down to Milly. "You do like cookies, don't you?"

Wide-eyed, Milly nodded as Maddie took her to the back of the house.

"The only reason I'm not throwing you out is because it would break Maddie's heart not to spend time with that little girl of yours." Then Rose glared at him. "I'm assuming she's yours."

"Yes." A knot formed in Silas's chest. Though he didn't necessarily expect a warm welcome from Rose, this felt wrong.

"Where's Annie?"

The question was a knife in his heart. "She died."

"I'm sorry for your loss."

The coldness in her voice told him she was anything but. Her gaze held little sympathy for him, and while he couldn't blame her, he missed the easy smiles she'd once given him. Did she still smile?

Before he could come up with an appropriate response, a baby cried in the other room.

"I need to take care of him."

Rose turned and walked into the next room, barely acknowledging Silas, and not inviting him to join her. He did anyway.

He watched as she picked up a baby out of a basket. "There now," she cooed, "Mama's here."

Mama.

The knife Rose had been slowly twisting in his heart jabbed him so painfully he thought it might have come out the other side of his body.

She had a child. It had never occurred to him, when he'd found out Rose's address from a mutual friend, that she might be married. He'd assumed that if she'd gotten married, he'd have heard folks talking about it. Then again, he'd had to ask several people to even get her address.

"Your husband is a blessed man." The words felt like shards of glass on his tongue coming out, but he had to say them. Had to consider Rose's happiness in the situation above his own desperate need.

"I have no husband," Rose said coolly, cradling the baby as she turned to face him.

"But the baby…"

"Is my son."

Silas stared at her for a moment. "I don't understand."

With a long sigh, Rose sat on a nearby chair. "We both know where babies come from. There's nothing to understand. I have a child. It happens sometimes."

He'd known Rose to be angry on occasion, but

mostly, he'd known her sweetness. This coldness… Silas didn't know. Nor did he know how such an upstanding young lady would find herself in this situation.

"The baby's father?"

"Is dead. And I wouldn't have married him anyway."

"But…"

Rose made a noise in the back of her throat. "Look. I did something I'm not proud of. For a brief period of time, I turned away from the Lord. I made a horrible mistake. But God, in His mercy, chose to bless me with a child who brings me more joy than I could have ever imagined. Some folks might say that my reputation is forever tarnished, but I am too grateful for this baby to care."

Then she shot him a look deadlier than he'd ever thought her capable of. "And that is all I will say on the matter."

The baby fussed in her arms. "Matthew needs to eat. Say your piece and be gone so I can feed him."

Her eyes darkened with a flash of defensiveness Silas remembered from all the times the other girls at church made fun of her for being poor. No wonder she seemed so different. How often did Rose have to defend herself to the women in this town for having a baby out of wedlock? He'd known, of course, that there were the babies born seven months into a hasty marriage. But he didn't know a single woman from a respectable family who'd had a child without marrying the father.

How difficult her life must be.

Granted, she'd come to Leadville because her brother had discovered a fortune in silver, taking their family from poor relations dependent on an aunt who resented them to wealthy patrons of society. Silas had only been in town for a couple of days, and he'd heard the Stone name bandied about as being a much-admired family. He hadn't heard anything about Rose, but now it made sense.

Perhaps his need of a wife fit more comfortably with Rose's needs than he could have imagined. A husband, even this far after the fact, would quickly raise Rose's standing as a respectable woman.

"My daughter needs a mother," Silas said quietly, slowly, then added, "and it seems your son needs a father."

Rose made a noise in the back of her throat and shook her head. "Please tell me that you did not come all this way, thinking I somehow still held a torch for you and would be grateful for the opportunity to be your wife."

Put that way, his idea sounded even more ridiculous. Three years was a long time, and… Silas let out a long sigh.

"I suppose I didn't think the idea through as well as I should have."

"Clearly." The baby fussed louder, and Rose stood, bouncing him against her body. "He really does need to eat."

The front door opened, and Silas heard the sounds of men talking. He turned and saw Rose's brother, Joseph, along with an older man, enter.

"Silas!" Joseph greeted him warmly. "What brings you to Leadville?"

Rose made an exasperated noise. "He thought that since his wife died, I'd be pining away for him, and would jump at the opportunity to take her place and raise their daughter. Now if you'll excuse me, I need to feed Matthew."

Hearing her tell Joseph only made Silas's plan sound all the more wrong. Why hadn't he considered it on a deeper level? His only excuse was the desperation he'd felt when he'd overheard the Garretts talking about a visit to their lawyer, and how they were going to try to take Milly away from him.

But Rose wasn't giving him the chance to explain. Not when she was already on her way out of the room with the baby.

Silas looked at Joseph, who wore a concerned expression on his face. The older man put his hand on Joseph's shoulder.

"I think we should hear this young man out." The older man held out a hand to Silas. "Frank Lassiter. Joseph is married to my daughter, Annabelle, and I consider the entire Stone family my own. Now have a seat and tell us why you're here."

Frank gestured toward a chair next to the one Rose had vacated. Even at the few feet's distance, he could still smell the rosewater scent she preferred. She used to say that if she was named after one, she should smell like one, too. Silas closed his eyes. He hadn't expected so many of the old feelings to rise up in him again.

Then he shook his head. More of his foolishness.

"I suppose it's like Rose said. My wife died several months ago. I'm doing my best to raise our daughter on my own, but there are circumstances that make it difficult. A wife would help the situation."

"What circumstances?" Joseph glared at him.

Silas swallowed. He supposed he'd done enough to

damage his pride already. Might as well tell them. Besides, Joseph was a good man. He'd left Ohio shortly after Silas married Annie, but they'd always gotten along.

"Annie's parents don't think it's appropriate for a single man to be raising his daughter alone. They were in the process of taking legal action to take her away from me. I thought if I got married again, their argument wouldn't hold water, and I wouldn't have to worry about losing Milly."

"And there were no eligible women in Ohio?" The sarcasm in Joseph's voice reminded Silas of Rose. Only Joseph's tone lacked the bitterness Rose held.

"Rose and I loved each other once," Silas said quietly. "I'd hoped…"

Now his hopes seemed foolish.

"You broke her heart." Joseph leaned forward, staring at him. "How could you think she'd welcome you so easily?"

He wanted to say that it was because, after three years of being married to someone else, of doing everything he could to be a good husband to Annie, that he'd been unable to forget Rose. Not in the sense that he was still in love with her, rather, he had many fond memories of their time together. Surely they could build something on that.

He'd been wrong.

"I wasn't thinking," Silas said instead. "I was so desperate to find a way to keep my daughter that I suppose I didn't consider Rose's feelings had changed."

"You didn't consider them at all," Joseph said quietly. In the one conversation Silas had with Rose after his engagement to Annie was announced, she called him selfish, only thinking of himself and not of anyone else. He'd tried explaining that to marry Rose would have been selfish—his parents' farm was in trouble, but by marrying the daughter of the family with the adjoining farm, it could be saved. But now, he wondered if perhaps her words were true.

"I didn't mean to be selfish." Silas ran his hands down his face. "I truly just wanted to do right by my daughter. I never meant to cause Rose any pain."

Frank nodded slowly. "I can see that. But it seems to me that two folks marrying to solve a problem only ever creates more problems. Rose deserves a man who considers her happiness above his own, and you deserve happiness, as well. So let's figure out a way to help you besides you marrying our girl."

Rose couldn't believe what she heard as she reentered the room.

"Why haven't you gotten rid of him?"

"Now, Rose," Uncle Frank said gently, "Silas is here because he needs help, and it is our Christian duty to do what we can for him."

"He needs help because he's a lying snake." Rose glared at him, then turned to her brother. "Please tell me that you aren't part of this scheme."

Joseph gave an unapologetic shrug. "If it weren't for Silas's father giving me work on their farm when they could ill afford it, I wouldn't have had the money to come to Leadville, and then we wouldn't have the life we do. I owe him a debt."

"Which was canceled the day he broke his word to me about getting married."

She hadn't expected, even after three years, that it would still hurt to think about how, the day after she was supposed to meet him to run away to get married, his father had announced in church that Silas was marrying Annie Garrett.

Granted, she'd been over an hour late for their meeting, but Silas knew how hard it was for her to get away. Why hadn't he waited for her? How long had he waited by the old oak tree before he'd gone over to the Garrett farm and had pie with Annie? Had he even come?

For as long as she'd thought about those questions, they should have easily been on her tongue to ask him. But the truth was, as much as they hurt, the answers didn't matter. He'd married Annie, not Rose.

"I'm sorry," Silas said quietly. "What I did to you was unforgivable. But I hope you'll let me make amends."

"Amends?" Tears stung the backs of her eyes, but Rose willed them to stay in place. Silas didn't deserve the satisfaction of knowing how many tears she'd cried over him. "I hope you don't think that your offer of marriage can possibly…"

Silas shook his head, looking so mournful that Rose almost felt bad for being harsh with him. "I spoke in haste. I was wrong to assume…"

Then he straightened, squaring his shoulders. "The truth is I need a wife so Annie's parents can't take Milly from me. I saw how you cared for your siblings, for the other children in church. You're the only person I would trust Milly with."

Fighting to keep her composure, Rose took a deep

breath. Of course this wasn't about rekindling their flame. Everyone knew Silas had married Annie for her farm. Now he wanted to marry her to give his daughter a mother. A glorified nanny, only with marriage.

"I see," she said slowly, looking at Joseph to see if he, too, understood that this was just another selfish maneuver that would only lead to her heartbreak—again.

He followed her gaze, nodding at Joseph, who nodded back. "No, you don't. My first marriage, though I have nothing to complain about, lacked the kind of love a man and a woman ought to share."

Then, with a darkness in his eyes Rose had never seen before, he said, "Joseph and Frank reminded me that I shouldn't settle for that kind of marriage again. I deserve better, and the woman I marry deserves better."

With a long sigh, Silas brought his attention back to Rose. "It was wrong of me to come here, thinking that marriage to you was the answer to my problems. I sincerely apologize for any heartache it might have caused you."

Rose's stomach twisted. What did Silas know of the heartache he'd caused? She'd finally found a way to live in peace with her broken heart, and now he had to come to remind her of all the mistakes she'd made.

"And," he continued, "I apologize for the way I broke your heart back in Ohio. It was wrong of me to court you in secret, knowing my father and Annie's father were in negotiations over our marriage. I thought…"

Another dark look crossed his face, and for a moment, Rose thought he might actually be in physical pain. But just as quickly as it came, the expression left.

"Well, I don't suppose it matters what I thought. No

matter how I justified it then, looking back, I had no right to trifle with your heart. My only excuse is that I truly believed my intentions were honorable. I never meant to hurt you. I'm sorry."

Real regret sounded in his voice, and as much as the anger churning in Rose's gut wanted to tell him that all of his justifications meant nothing, the weight of Uncle Frank's gaze on her reminded her that her sins made her no better than Silas.

"I suppose that we all do things that are wrong, justifying them with all kinds of excuses, when deep down, we know that we shouldn't." The ache in her belly started to subside, and Rose took a deep breath. "I've made my own share of mistakes, but Uncle Frank is constantly reminding me that the Lord loves and forgives me anyway."

She squeezed her eyes shut, taking a deep breath. Oh, she knew what she was supposed to do here. Forgive Silas. That's what Uncle Frank preached about constantly—loving and forgiving others. She'd thought it hard enough to forgive Ben Perry, the father of her child, an outlaw who'd only been using her to get his hands on her family's fortune. But she had. It had taken so much prayer, so much time reading her Bible, but it wasn't until she held little Matthew that she understood that she couldn't possibly hate someone who'd given her such an incredible gift.

Her family had forgiven her for the scandal she'd brought upon them by running away with an outlaw. They'd forgiven her for the scandal of her child born out of wedlock. Even when members of the church had left the congregation because they were shocked that

Uncle Frank would not condemn Rose for her behavior, her family had stood by her in love and acceptance.

Rose didn't feel like forgiving Silas. No, she felt like raging at him for how deeply he'd hurt her. How that hurt had made her do unspeakable things, hurting those she loved. Her insides churned, reminding her of how his abandonment had left her raw and empty.

But how could she be a hypocrite, and deny him that which had been offered to her so freely?

Rose took a deep breath. "I forgive you, Silas."

Saying the words should have made her feel better, but they didn't. All the years she'd dreamed of him crawling back to her, saying how sorry he was, it didn't change any of the pain in her heart. Uncle Frank had told her that sometimes forgiveness meant acting on it long before you felt it, but in Rose's case, she wondered if she would ever feel that particular emotion.

Forgiving him might be the right thing to do, but it didn't ease the pain in her heart. It didn't make any of the things that had happened any better. And even though everyone else in the room looked relieved at Rose's words, they only made her feel worse.

Uncle Frank had told her that forgiveness was a process. That when Jesus said you had to forgive someone seventy times seven, He meant it almost literally, because some things hurt so much that you had to keep forgiving, even when it hurt, until the pain went away. If that were the case, then Rose supposed she had another 489 more times to go.

Please, Lord, help me. I don't know if I'm strong enough to have to keep forgiving Silas. Not when my heart hurts so very much.

Rose's only consolation was knowing that, now that she'd said the words, to Silas, and in front of her family, Silas could return home, and continue with his life. And Rose could do the same.

Chapter Two

Rose's words sounded hollow, fake. Like they had when her Aunt Ina would ask her to do something, and she didn't want to do it but knew she had no choice but to obey. But she'd said she forgave him, and Silas had an equal obligation to accept.

"Thank you," Silas said quietly, wishing it could be like the old times when he could tell her that he knew she didn't mean it and that he understood. But they no longer had the kind of relationship where they could be so honest with one another.

"Good, good." Frank clapped Silas on the back. "I told you it would all work out. Now that things are settled between you and Rose, we need to figure out how you're going to keep that beautiful little girl of yours."

Silas turned to look at him. "I don't understand."

Joseph chuckled. "Ah, my friend, you really had no idea what you were getting yourself into when you told Frank of your situation. I've yet to see him let anyone leave without a reliable solution to their problems."

Rose let out a long sigh, and the pained expression

on her face made Silas wish he'd never come. He'd wronged her; she'd forgiven him, but it seemed that his presence only rubbed salt into her wounds. Silas truly hadn't intended to hurt her. Hadn't dreamed that he'd be causing her this much pain by reentering her life.

"It's all right," Silas said, looking at Rose. "I'm sure we'll manage just fine."

"None of that." Frank clapped him on the back again. "There's no sense in going it alone when you have others willing to come alongside you and help. You have too much at stake to let your pride intervene."

Silas had thought he'd already given up much of his pride just coming here. Facing Rose and realizing how much damage he'd done, it wasn't pride that made him want to leave, but an earnest desire not to hurt her anymore.

Milly came running into the room. "Papa!"

Her little voice made any indecision he might have had disappear. No, he didn't want to hurt Rose, but his actions now weren't about her. Rather, they were about a small child who needed him.

Silas scooped her up in his arms. "Were you a good girl?"

"An absolute darling," Maddie said, smiling. "I don't think I've met such a well-behaved young lady. She just sat at the table, proper as could be, and ate her cookie. She even let me wipe her hands and face without so much as a whimper."

That, of course, was the Garretts' doing. They believed that children were to be seen, not heard, and worked very hard at training Milly to be perfectly quiet and obedient. Annie had been the same way. As much as he regretted not loving Annie fully, Silas had often wondered if Annie harbored any romantic feelings toward him. Most times it seemed as though marrying Silas was one more of Annie's acts of obedience to her parents.

"I'm glad she behaved for you," Silas said, ruffling his daughter's feathery blond hair. Though he'd seen other parents at church lament how their little ones misbehaved, he wished his own daughter would take life into her own hands sometimes and throw the kind of tantrum that meant the Garretts hadn't completely broken her spirit.

Milly leaned into him and let out a contented sigh. Then Silas turned toward Frank. "I'm willing to do whatever it takes to keep my daughter. What do you have in mind?"

It wasn't Frank, but Joseph, who answered. "How's your father's farm doing?"

If Silas hadn't been facing arrows of all kinds shot in his direction since arriving here, he might have felt the agonizing pain of this one. Instead, it was just one more dig at the wounds he carried.

"Gone." Silas swallowed the sour liquid rising from his stomach. "My father died shortly after I married Annie, and the Garretts absorbed the farm. Now that Annie's gone..."

He didn't want to finish the sentence. Marrying Annie had cost Silas everything. With her death, the loss had been just as complete. Meeting Joseph's eyes, he said, "The Garretts are already arranging the sale of the farm so they can move to town. Robert Garrett's health is failing, and he can't work the farm anymore.

That was supposed to be the reason for my marriage to Annie. But now, the Garretts think it 'isn't seemly' for me to remain in that capacity."

"What are you doing to support yourself?" Joseph's question stung, mostly because only a few years ago, the situation had been reversed. Joseph, willing to do anything to support his family, and Silas, looking for ways to help him.

"Anything I can find. The Garretts have made it hard for me to find work anywhere back home, which is part of why I left. I've been doing whatever honest work people offer me to get by."

"I'm sure your lack of regular employment is one of the arguments the Garretts are using to take Milly away from you. They can provide a better life for her than you can." Frank's words were a bitter reminder of the battle ahead.

"Milly doesn't need anything fancy. Food, clothes, a solid roof and a father who loves her. I just wish the Garretts could see that."

His voice caught when he said that, making the words come out less forceful than he'd intended.

"All the same," Frank said, "you'll stand a better chance of keeping your daughter if you have a good job. Joseph?"

"I'm always looking for help at the mine. If I recall—"

"You can't be serious!"

Silas had almost forgotten Rose was in the room, but her outburst was enough to remind everyone that he wasn't the only one affected by the discussion happening.

"Now, Rose, dear…" Frank's voice was gentle, and Rose's eyes filled with tears.

"I know." Her shoulders shook slightly. "I'm supposed to forgive him and move on. But surely that doesn't mean he needs to work in the mine."

An impossible situation. Silas closed his eyes and sent a quick prayer heavenward that God would help him find a way to do the right thing by both his daughter and Rose. Then he turned and looked at her.

"I wouldn't want to put anyone out. Perhaps your brother could recommend someone who might have work for me."

Joseph shook his head. "None that would give you a fair deal. It's a hard life up here, and most folks will take advantage of you, given half a chance. The Lord blessed me greatly, and it's only fair that I share those blessings with the people who made it happen. I'm not saying that to boast because the only reason I have anything to boast about is because of the great mercies of the Lord. I can't in good conscience let you work anywhere else."

Then Joseph brought his attention to Rose. "And you know that's the truth. Would you see a man with a young child taken advantage of? What would you want for Matthew?"

He didn't wait for a response from Rose, but Silas could see the emotion playing on her face. She was at war with herself, knowing the truth of Joseph's words, but not liking it. Silas didn't like it much either, but having known Joseph most of his life, he knew that Joseph was a fair man. A good man. And he'd be lying if he said he wasn't looking forward to working for him.

"You'll come work for me," Joseph said. "I have a baby girl of my own. Catherine. The joy she brings me...well, I would do anything to help another man keep that for himself."

The defeat on Rose's face almost made Silas tell Joseph he'd find another way. But he couldn't. Not with the little girl tugging on his shirt.

"Down!"

"It's all right," Frank said. "She won't hurt anything in here. We have enough children in the parlor that we've put away everything a child might damage."

More reassurances, like the ones Maddie had given when they'd first arrived.

"Thank you." Silas put Milly down. "The Garretts were always particular about letting Milly run around. I suppose I'm still figuring out what's reasonable for her."

Milly made a beeline for the sofa where Rose sat. The expression on Rose's face went from dejection to horror as Milly raced toward her. But what could Silas say? Don't sit next to the lady because you're the daughter of the person she hates most in this world?

Just before she reached Rose, Milly stumbled on the edge of the carpet, sending her sprawling into the sofa.

Before Silas could react, Rose jumped up and pulled Milly into her arms.

Silas couldn't see Milly's face, but he knew she was trying to decide whether or not to cry.

"There now, you're a big brave girl, aren't you?" Rose cuddled Milly in her arms as she sat back on the sofa. "Do you see why we don't run in the house?"

The light blond head bobbed in agreement. Rose continued cradling Milly as though she'd forgotten whose child she held.

"Did you have fun in the kitchen with Maddie?" Rose brushed Milly's hair with her fingers, and Silas realized as Rose seemed to examine the little girl intently, she was making sure Milly wasn't injured.

Rose kissed the top of Milly's head. "Not even a bump."

Milly wiggled in Rose's arms. "I sit big chair."

The smile Rose gave his daughter reminded Silas of why he'd thought Rose would make a good mother. There was a compassion within her that seemed to understand instinctively what a child needed. Deeper than that, though, was that her heart seemed to flow with a never-ending love for children.

Rose relaxed her hold on Milly and allowed the little girl to scoot over to the unoccupied portion of the sofa. Milly preened as she adjusted herself to a comfortable position, her little legs not even reaching the edge of the seat. Milly smiled, a wide grin flashing a mouth full of baby teeth.

"I big girl," Milly declared, her gaze sweeping the room.

She'd never been allowed to sit on the sofa in the parlor at the Garretts' home. They'd told Milly little girls weren't allowed in the room, and she spent most of her time confined to the nursery.

"You sure are," Rose said, giving Milly an affectionate pat. She turned her gaze to Silas, finally looking at him. "I don't think she was injured in her fall."

It hadn't occurred to Silas that Milly would have

been hurt, but he smiled at Rose all the same. "Thank you. I appreciate your kindness toward my daughter."

"Of course. She's a sweet girl." Rose's expression softened further, and as Silas studied her face, he realized once again what a difficult position he'd put her in.

Back when they were courting, they used to talk about the family they'd have together. Silas had always said he wanted a daughter with dark hair, like Rose, but Rose had always insisted that she wanted a son who resembled him.

Why had he spoken such foolishness? Oh, he'd meant the words when he spoke them. Had fervently wanted them to come true. But he'd known what his father wanted, what his family needed. He'd hoped and prayed that it wouldn't come to the eventuality of his marriage to Annie, but it was all for naught.

He never shared any of this with Rose, never gave her the option of protecting her heart. All this time, he'd justified his actions by saying he'd only been lying to himself. But as he watched her interact with the little girl he once told her they'd have together, his heart ached. He knew that he'd lied to her, as well.

Rose was grateful when Matthew's cries gave her an excuse to leave the room. Ordinarily, his fussiness would have frustrated her. Little Catherine had started sleeping through the night ages ago, but Matthew staunchly refused to sleep for more than a couple of hours at a time. She yawned as she picked him up out of his cradle. Usually, she just kept him with her because it hardly seemed worth the effort to continue going up and down. But today, with her emotions racing all over the place, taking care of her son gave her the respite she needed.

"There, now, sweet fellow. Mama's here." She picked him up and cradled him against her. She hadn't been lying when she'd said that having Matthew made up for all that she'd gone through, all the wrongs that had happened in her life.

Even now, when the brief pause in her routine gave her body room to remind her how exhausted she was, Rose still wouldn't change any of it.

Would her life be different had Silas gone through with his plan to marry her?

Undoubtedly.

But as Matthew smiled up at her, Rose couldn't imagine wanting that life anymore.

Matthew settled in her arms, and she thought about the little girl she'd held only a short time before. Milly. Silas clearly loved her the way she loved Matthew. As hard as she tried, she couldn't make herself continue to hate him.

Forgiveness.

No, she didn't feel it in her heart. In fact, she still wanted to rail at him and tell him of all the hurt she'd experienced as a result of her broken heart. But that wasn't the way of forgiveness. It wasn't the way of Jesus.

Although it didn't say so explicitly, Rose knew that the part where the Bible talked about leaving everything behind for the sake of following Him also meant letting go of her old grudges. Including the one she had against Silas.

Easier said than done.

But with the Lord's help, she'd keep trying, not for

his sake, because he didn't deserve her mercy, but because of the mercy that had been given to her.

"Rose?" Maddie appeared in the doorway. "Frank was hoping you'd rejoin them in the parlor. I believe they want you to be a part of the discussion."

Rose nodded slowly, adjusting the baby in her arms. It seemed that God wanted her to keep facing this, to keep dealing with the pain and the hurt until it went away. So be it.

"Do you want me to take Matthew for you? We could go outside in the sun for a while. It might improve his disposition."

The concerned look on the older woman's face wasn't meant as a criticism, but an honest offer of help. Everyone in the Lassiter house had taken turns up with Matthew all night in hopes that someone could get him to sleep. His fussing would be a distraction in the room with the others, but Rose couldn't bear to give him up. Not when he served as a reminder that every wound, every moment she suffered, and yes, every mistake, was worth it.

"I'll be fine." She adjusted the baby in her arms as she handed him his favorite rattle. It would keep him occupied for a short time at least.

Maddie pursed her lips disapprovingly, and she was probably right to do so. But Matthew wasn't fussing now, and Rose needed the comfort of the baby in her arms.

She carried him to the parlor, where everyone seemed to be in cheerful conversation. Uncle Frank had found a doll for Milly to play with, and the little girl seemed content sitting on the sofa snuggling the toy.

"Sorry to keep you waiting," Rose said, taking the seat she'd vacated next to Milly. She expected her heart to twist at the sight of the little girl, but when she'd held Milly in her arms, all she could think was that Milly was like any other child, in need of a few cuddles and some love. As much as Rose still found it difficult to even look at Silas, her resentment didn't seem to carry over to his child.

"Who dat?" Milly asked, poking the baby.

"This is Matthew, my son."

"Ma-few," Milly said, tugging on his leg. "We pway."

Rose smiled. "He's too little to play. But if you wave the doll in front of him, he might smile for you."

Milly dangled the doll in front of Matthew, making funny noises. Matthew giggled.

"He yikes me!" Milly beamed.

"He does," Uncle Frank said, a tender tone to his voice. While Joseph's daughter was a happy baby and seemed to giggle and smile at everything, Matthew was of a more choleric nature. Everything made him cry, and a smile was hard-won. To make her notoriously cranky son giggle required a combination of timing, patience and skill.

Even Joseph nodded approvingly. "I think this will work nicely."

"What will work nicely?" Rose stared at her brother.

"If Silas comes to work for me, he'll need someone to take care of Milly."

"No," Rose said flatly.

"I'd ask Annabelle, but she was hoping to visit her aunt Celeste and show off the baby. Since her last trip was cut short…"

Because of her. That's what Joseph was implying. They'd been on an extended honeymoon trip, but when news of Rose's indiscretion reached them, they'd returned home. Annabelle had said that it was because she was feeling poorly due to the baby she was expecting, but Rose knew better. They'd come back to deal with her.

If Rose continued in her insistence to not take care of Milly, they'd postpone this trip, as well. Because of her. Again.

Joseph and Uncle Frank exchanged a look. Probably in frustration over their belief that Rose was being difficult. That's what everyone thought after all. Rose was the difficult one, always wanting her own way when it went against what the family thought best.

"Perhaps Mary…" Frank suggested.

Rose's eyes burned. Though she and her sister were getting along much better these days, it always hurt to know that Mary was still viewed as the dependable one, and Rose the difficult one. How she tried to be as perfect as her older sister. But oh, how she failed.

Joseph shook his head. "I can't ask that of her. She's so close to having her own baby, and she's already agreed to take care of our other siblings while we're gone. It seems too much to add in one more child to the mix."

"I thought you were bringing them?" Frank said.

Joseph sighed. "We were going to, but they would miss too much school, and while Daniel doesn't mind, Evelyn and Bess were furious. Nugget wasn't pleased with the prospect, either."

With both of their parents dead, Joseph had taken on

the primary responsibility for caring for their younger siblings: Evelyn, fourteen, Helen, thirteen, Daniel, ten, Bess, seven and Nugget, five. As the next eldest, their sister Mary often helped, as well. Rose did what she could, but since her scandal, it seemed like no one ever asked her anymore.

Sometimes she felt guilty for not doing more, but every time she offered to take one of her siblings or do something for them, they rebuffed her efforts.

And here they were, faced with a problem, asking for Rose's help, but Rose was being difficult. They didn't need to say it. Rose could tell by their expressions.

"I'll do it," Rose murmured.

Uncle Frank frowned. "It's all right. I'm sure we can find someone else. We haven't even asked—"

"I said I'll do it," she said, a little too forcefully, perhaps, since everyone stared at her.

"I don't want to put you out," Silas said, looking at her so forlornly that she felt guilty for not receiving him more warmly.

The truth was, Rose *was* being difficult. Years ago, when they'd all sighed at how difficult she was being, she'd felt misunderstood and angry that no one saw her side of things. Now she could recognize that she was exactly what they thought her to be. The difference was, they still didn't see the heartache she was trying to heal from.

Matthew giggled again. Milly laughed with him.

Would it be so bad to have another child around? One who made her son smile when so few could?

Even Rose could admit that the only reason she said

no was her anger toward Silas. Why should she help him when he'd hurt her?

But that wasn't the way of forgiveness. She'd said the words and made the commitment to forgiving him. Which meant she couldn't act out of the anger, no matter how deeply she felt it.

Why did this have to be so hard? Why couldn't she have just said the words and Silas have been on his way, never to cross her path again?

Because something deep inside her told her that forgiveness didn't work that way.

Rose looked at Silas, giving him the best smile she could muster. "It's all right. I don't mind. Matthew seems to be entertained by Milly, so I'm sure they will enjoy each other's company."

"And that's something," Joseph said, grinning. "I don't think he's gone this long without fussing since he was born."

Rose sighed. She'd like to have argued with him, but he had a point. The ladies at church said he was the most contrary baby they'd ever met, and the most unkind ones said it was no wonder, given the circumstances of his birth.

With a *thwap*, the doll Milly had been waving in front of Matthew hit him on top of the head. Matthew began to wail.

Milly began to cry, as well. "Was assident."

"It's all right," Rose said, patting the little girl with her free hand as she tried to soothe her son with the other. "I know it was. He'll be fine."

Then she stood, bouncing him and patting him in the way that sometimes got him to calm down. Red-faced and fists pounding, Matthew seemed completely uninterested in being comforted.

"I'm sorry," Rose looked apologetically at Silas. "It truly wasn't her fault. Matthew is just overly sensitive."

She looked over at Milly, who clutched the doll to her chest. Her light eyes were full of unshed tears.

"It's all right, Milly," Rose said again. "Matthew's tired, that's all."

The accompanying sighs from Joseph and Uncle Frank both said what she was feeling. Matthew was always tired. Just as they all were.

"He never sleeps," Rose told Silas by way of explanation. "Just an hour or so here and there. Everyone says he'll grow out of it, but for now, we're all doing the best we can."

"Can I try?" Silas held out his arms. "Everyone used to have difficulty getting Milly to sleep, but I always could."

She should say no. At least that's what the stubborn side of her said. But her arms were so heavy. So tired. And her practical side needed a break.

Rose handed the baby to Silas.

Matthew continued to wail.

Silas held him to his chest, tucking him tight against him. "Do you have another blanket for him?"

She grabbed one of the blankets from the side of the sofa. Silas wrapped it around the baby, pinning his arms to the side.

"He doesn't like to be swaddled." Rose gave a sigh. The first thing everyone tried with Matthew was swaddling him, and it only made him angrier.

True to form, his already-red face grew brighter, and his wails louder.

Silas loosened the blanket and began rocking him gently, whispering things that Rose couldn't hear, that Matthew probably ignored. His cries were too loud for him to hear anything. At least that's what Rose figured. But as Silas pressed Matthew against his chest, continuing to murmur whatever he'd been murmuring, Matthew began to quiet.

Then Silas sat, unwrapped the baby and played with his legs, rubbing his stomach. "His stomach hurts," Silas said.

Rose sighed. "I know. Everyone says it's gas, and he'll grow out of it. But peppermint water does nothing for him."

Silas nodded. "I know, little fellow. It's rough, isn't it?" Looking up at Rose, he said, "Rub his stomach like this. It'll help."

"How do you know?"

"Experience."

Matthew stopped crying. His big eyes stared up at Silas, watching him.

"And the Garretts don't think you can take care of your daughter?" Rose watched him, transfixed. No one had ever been able to get Matthew to calm down. Even the doctor, who'd tried every remedy he knew, hadn't been able to make Matthew's tummy troubles go away.

"Men don't know anything about how to take care of babies." He used a baby voice as he smiled down at Matthew. "But we know that's not true, now, don't we?"

Silas returned his gaze to Rose. "This is going to sound crazy, but stop drinking milk, and eating anything made with milk. I'm fairly sure that's what's making Matthew's stomach so upset."

"Milk?" Uncle Frank sounded surprised. "But that's what babies need to be healthy. We've been making sure all of our mothers get extra to pass on to the babies."

Rose couldn't help but sigh. She wasn't fond of milk, but at every meal, someone was pressing an extra glass of milk into her hand, telling her it was good for the baby.

"It's good for most babies, but some babies can't tolerate it. Milly was fussy as a baby, and I remembered my mother talking about how when I was a baby, someone told her to stop drinking milk, and it would make me less fussy. It worked for me, so I asked Annie to give it a try. Milly stopped being so fussy."

Then he let out a long sigh. "One more battle with the Garretts, I'm afraid. I don't give Milly milk, even now. The Garretts make her drink a big glass every day. She's done a lot better now that she's away from them."

Rose looked down at Matthew, who'd fallen asleep in Silas's lap. He seemed content, and Silas still rubbed his stomach. Rose memorized the motion. If nothing else, she could try it on him herself.

"I don't know if you remember," Silas continued, "but I don't drink milk. I never acquired the taste for it. That's why my mother always kept goats. We'd drink their milk, eat their butter and cheese, and it never bothered me the way cow's milk did. People always thought we didn't have cows because we couldn't afford them, but the truth was, goat milk always suited us better."

Actually, she did remember. Aunt Ina had invited Silas over to supper one night, and she'd poured everyone the half a glass of milk she allotted them once a week, and Silas had surreptitiously given it to Rose. At the time, Rose had thought he was being generous in letting Rose have the extra, but now she understood.

"When you gave me your milk, it was so you didn't have to drink it."

Silas shrugged. "Partially. But Ina was so stingy with her portions of everything. I knew how hungry you were. I'd seen you slip a piece of meat to your brother, Daniel, and your roll to your sister, Bess. It didn't seem fair that you always went without."

"Well, we have plenty now." Rose gave half a smile. "But I thank you for noticing when no one else seemed to care."

That's what she'd loved about Silas. He'd cared for her once. When they'd meet for their secret picnics, he'd always brought a basket of food, inviting Rose to eat all she wanted. When the girls at church had taunted her about her worn ribbons, Silas would have a new one for her. He'd brought them eggs, telling Aunt Ina that one of his mother's customers didn't need any this week, and he didn't want them to go to waste.

If it weren't for Silas's generosity, and that of a few others, Rose was certain they'd have all wasted away from her aunt's stinginess.

"I meant what I said about watching Milly for you," Rose said quietly. "I've been so focused on my heart-break that I'd forgotten about our friendship. Joseph is right. You and your family were good to our family when so many people ignored our plight. It would be wrong of me to turn my back when you need our help."

Comprehension flittered across Silas's face, and

Rose's shoulders felt lighter, like some of the load she'd been carrying had been taken off. She'd never admitted to her heartbreak. Never told Silas that he'd hurt her. Only attacked him. But in acknowledging the feelings that had trapped her for so long, Rose finally felt like she could breathe in his presence without it hurting so much.

They were different people now, leading different lives. But if Rose kept focusing on how much he'd hurt her, the pain would never leave. She took a deep breath. Focusing on the good things, and the reason she should help him—that would be the key to moving on. The key to finally forgiving Silas once and for all.

Chapter Three

They'd found a comfortable rhythm over the past few weeks. Uncle Frank had insisted that Silas and Milly stay with them. A boardinghouse was no place for a small child who needed to run and play. With Joseph and Annabelle's house next door and Mary living with her husband, Will, nearby, the Lassiter house had plenty of room for Silas and his daughter.

The perfect arrangement, except that as much as Rose tried to feel more positive toward Silas, the everpresent ache in her stomach when he was around never seemed to dissipate.

Even knowing he'd been right about the milk didn't seem to ease the trouble in her heart. Rose tucked the blanket around her sleeping son, grateful that she'd gotten Matthew and Milly to take naps at the same time in the afternoon. She'd have two hours all to herself.

In the beginning, she'd used nap time to catch up on her sleep. But now that Matthew was sleeping through the night, Rose wasn't as weary.

As she closed the door behind her, she saw Silas coming up the stairs.

"What are you doing home so early?"

Silas gave an easy smile, the kind that had once left her breathless. Now it gave her a different feeling, an old ache like what Maddie often described as her joints acting up when the weather moved in. It wasn't that she still had feelings for him, Rose told herself. They were different people now.

Silas answered, "Your brother asked me to visit some of the smelting operations in town. He's not sure we're getting the best deal we could be, so he wanted me to look into it. I thought I'd come here for some lunch and to say hello to Milly."

She hadn't remembered Silas to be much of a man of business. In truth, she hadn't known all that much about him, other than he helped run his father's farm. The more Rose examined her heart and her romantic follies, she realized how she'd always rushed headlong into what she'd thought was the perfect relationship, without giving the situation much thought at all.

That was the most acute pain she felt when he gave her those beguiling smiles. How great a fool she'd been.

"I didn't realize you were such a businessman," Rose said, giving him a smile to cover up the tumultuous thoughts in her head.

"My mother used to say that if it hadn't been for my negotiating skills, Pa probably would have lost the farm a lot sooner." He gave a wry grin. "Guess it didn't matter so much in the end."

"I'm sure it gave him great comfort to have still had some claim to the farm until his death."

Silas nodded slowly. "That's what Ma said. I shouldn't be too hard on myself for how things turned out."

Rose's heart softened as she remembered Mrs. Jones. "How is she? I can't believe I haven't asked after her until now."

"She's well. Moved in with her sister, Bertha, after Pa died. I know she'd help me if she could, but they're barely getting by as it is. I wouldn't want to make things harder on them than they already are."

A frown furrowed his brow, then disappeared. "I've sent them some money to cover what I borrowed to get here, but I hope to send more to help them out once I get things settled with the Garretts. The lawyer Frank recommended is good, but he doesn't come cheap."

It was on the tip of Rose's tongue to offer to help, but she knew it would only offend Silas's pride. He was already upset with her because she'd bought a few new dresses for Milly. She'd been unable to resist when she'd seen them displayed at the dressmaker's. Clothes for baby boys simply weren't as adorable as they were for little girls. It had been a pleasure shopping for Milly. Not so much when she'd had to face Silas's anger as a result.

Instead, Rose brought the conversation to the case. "Any progress with the Garretts?"

Silas shook his head. "We haven't approached them yet. My lawyer is waiting to put a few things together first. He'd like to have everything in order so they have no ground to stand on."

"But surely they don't? You're Milly's father. You have a good job, a good place to live…"

"I'd like to think so. But with the money and influence the Garretts have back in Ohio, we want to be sure."

A commotion downstairs drew Rose's attention. "Would you mind coming down with me to see what's happening? There usually isn't any trouble, but with Uncle Frank off visiting parishioners and everyone else off at work, I don't want Maddie to have to handle things on her own."

"Of course." Silas had already turned toward the stairs before the words finished leaving his mouth.

In the entryway stood an older couple whose faces Rose immediately recognized. The Garretts. She paused, her feet stuck to the last stair like it was coated in thick, deep mud.

Maddie, who had let them in, gave Rose a nod, then glanced in the direction of the back door. The family's signal that she was going for help. And with the way the Garretts were lit up, they were going to need all the help they could get.

"I demand to see my granddaughter," Mrs. Garrett said, her nasal voice echoing in the foyer.

"She's sleeping," Silas said, looking back in Rose's direction.

Rose nodded and stepped forward as Maddie slipped out the back. "Yes. I've just laid her down. She won't be awake for at least an hour."

"What does that doxy have to do with my granddaughter?" Mrs. Garrett's icy expression told Rose that she knew of Rose's circumstance. Usually, it didn't bother her when people looked down on her for her sin. She knew what she'd done, knew it was wrong and knew that God had forgiven her.

But Mrs. Garrett's censure brought her back to the

shameful place where she once could barely hold her head up in church.

"Rose is my nanny," Silas said, his tone equally cool. "And she's doing an excellent job."

"Is that so?" Mrs. Garrett's hard glare shot Rose straight through the heart. "A woman of her morals—"

"Will be an excellent influence on my daughter. Rose spends a good deal of time volunteering for the church's many charitable endeavors, and it warms my heart to see her teaching the children from an early age to care for others who are less fortunate."

Silas's defense of her made Rose's heart do a funny flip-flop. Not in the way his smiles used to, but something deeper. Something that said he saw her for who she was. While her charitable works were no secret, she also didn't shout them from the rooftops. As much as she had grown and changed as a result of her pregnancy and having Matthew, Rose had never felt compelled to announce those changes to the world. Rather, she'd hoped people would see how differently she lived her life.

"That may be the excuse you give everyone else, but we know differently. That Jezebel was chasing after you in Ohio, trying to steal you away from our Annie when you'd already been promised to her. Had we not switched churches, I'm sure she'd have tempted you to forsake your marriage vows. And now, here she is, living in a den of sin, and you're right in the middle of it. If you think we're going to let our beloved granddaughter be raised in such a place…"

As Mrs. Garrett paused to take a breath, Uncle Frank came in through the back.

Breathing hard, Uncle Frank held out a hand. "Welcome to the parsonage, Mr. and Mrs. Garrett. I wish you'd have let us know you were coming. We would have had someone meet you at the station." Uncle Frank gave a bright smile, but his eyes were dark, angry. "At the very least, we would have had tea ready for you. Fortunately, Silas and Rose kept you entertained so that Maddie could fetch me, and now she's preparing a tray for us all. Please, won't you join us in the parlor?"

He gestured toward the parlor, and Mr. and Mrs. Garrett exchanged glances.

"This is the parsonage?" Mr. Garrett looked around.

"Why yes," Uncle Frank said, smiling as he saw the confusion written all over their faces. The Lassiter house was much larger than the average home in Leadville, and though it was nothing grand in comparison to Ohio standards, many people questioned how a preacher could live in such a fine place. "I suppose it's a misnomer since the church doesn't pay for it. My father left me a goodly inheritance, and I've never drawn a salary or asked the church to pay for anything. More money for the church, you know."

He gave an indulgent smile as he sat in his favorite chair. "Do sit down and tell us about your trip. I imagine you must be eager to see Milly, but we wouldn't want to disturb her nap."

The Garretts looked as baffled as Rose felt. Silas said he was waiting to contact them, yet here they were. Though Uncle Frank gave a few subtle signs of not being pleased they were here, he acted like this was a social call instead of an attempt to take Milly from her father.

"We heard Rose had run away to a den of sin," Mr. Garrett said, looking around.

Rose's stomach churned. She should have known that word of her troubles had gone back to Ohio, but why would they think she was still mired in that lifestyle? Why hadn't word of her repentance also gotten back?

She sighed. Most folks just wanted to see the wrong in a situation, not the good. Not the redemption.

"Rose is a vital part of our ministry at Leadville Community Church," Uncle Frank said smoothly. "I'm surprised you haven't heard of it."

His defense of her only served to put sour expressions on the Garretts' faces. "We're only concerned for Millicent's well-being."

"*Milly* is just fine," Silas said, emphasizing Milly's name. From the twitch in his jaw, Rose could tell this was a fight they'd had before.

Maddie entered the room with a tea tray, busying herself with serving everyone, but Rose caught the watchful way she regarded the Garretts.

"You can hardly blame us, worrying the way we do," Mrs. Garrett said firmly. "You ran away in the middle of the night, sneaking off with our only grandchild with no word of where you were taking her. A man with no means, and no experience raising children. If it hadn't been for our investigator, we'd have no idea where to find her."

Mr. Garrett pulled a paper out of his pocket. "This here's from our lawyer. You'll find the terms quite generous. We just want Millicent safely home."

Rose watched as Silas read the paper. His face turned

red as he examined its contents briefly before tossing it back at the Garretts.

"You want me to *sell* my daughter?"

Mr. Garrett smoothed the paper. "I wouldn't call it, selling, precisely. Merely financial consideration for your trouble. As you know, we can give Millicent the best of everything, and we want you to have a token of our gratitude for allowing us the opportunity to give her the life she deserves."

The skin on Rose's arms prickled, and she rubbed them, despite the room being quite warm. Even the cup of tea Maddie pressed into her hand before leaving the room did nothing to stave off the chill. She'd known the Garretts to be self-serving, but this seemed to be going too far.

"Milly deserves a life with her father," Silas said, standing. "I won't allow you to take her from me."

Silas couldn't believe the gall of the Garretts to offer money for Milly, as though she were a prized horse. But that's exactly what she was to them. Hadn't they done the same with Annie? Dangling her and the farm out for the highest bidder? Had it not been for the clear stream that flowed on the Jones farm, Silas wouldn't have been considered for the prize of their daughter.

What would Milly's life be like, paraded around in frilly dresses, expected to act in accordance with their wishes? They might be selling the farm, but what price would they eventually put on Milly's hand?

Silas's stomach churned.

"Now, Silas," Mrs. Garrett said in the sickeningly sweet tone that he'd always hated. "Do you think you're giving Millicent any kind of life, with you working in a dirty mine all day, exhausting yourself? You're not really raising her, now, are you?"

Then she glared at Rose. "And I will not have my granddaughter cared for by a doxy."

"That's enough," Silas said, clenching his fists as he raised his voice to the older woman. If she'd been a man, he'd have punched her. "You have no right talking about Rose that way. You don't even know her. She does an excellent job watching Milly, and I won't hear you slander her character that way."

"She did have a child out of wedlock, did she not?" Mrs. Garrett said in such a condescending tone that Silas felt the blood rushing to his hands. Violence never solved anything, but it was tempting.

"Yes, she did," Frank answered, using the same calm tone he'd used during the entire time the Garretts had been there. "And while it's easy for us all to cast stones at such a blatant sin, not one of us is so pure that we can. Rose has done an exemplary job of turning her life around, and I am sure we can all learn from her example."

Silas saw the shame flash across Rose's face until it settled on her cheeks as a faint pink. Her lips moved slightly as she briefly closed her eyes. She was praying. The Rose he'd known had gone to church, of course. They all went to church. But this Rose seemed to be deeply aware of her connection to God, and as the others discussed her behavior as though she wasn't in the room, she took the discussion where it belonged—in prayer. Silas himself hadn't even developed a close relationship with God until recently. Until circumstances, and needing to be a better man for his daughter's sake, had made it clear that living his life without the Lord was no way to live at all. Perhaps becoming parents had changed them both.

The Garretts, however, didn't have the same reaction. Mrs. Garrett pursed her lips in the disapproving way Silas had come to dread, and Mr. Garrett patted her hands.

"That may be so, Preacher," Mr. Garrett said, "but why should our dear, sweet Millicent have to suffer for Rose's sin? We are prepared to give Millicent a good home, where those living under our roof have never strayed from our good Christian values. Silas means well, but he can't give Millicent the life she deserves."

"How, exactly, does Milly suffer because of Rose's sin?" The question was out of Silas's mouth before he thought about it. Before he could consider that he'd be opening up Rose to more criticism.

Mrs. Garrett snorted. "I would think that's obvious. I can't see any of the respectable families receiving Millicent when she's older because of Rose's influence. And how will she make a proper match guided by someone who clearly put the cart before the horse?"

"Milly is two," Silas said quietly. "She needs to be thinking about being a child, not finding a husband. And as for being received by the respectable families, kindly remember that the Stones are one of the most respected families in Leadville, aligned with the Jacksons of the Jackson banking empire, of which I'm sure you've heard."

The Jackson name was prominently displayed on many buildings in town, their bank being the primary source of funding for many of Leadville's business endeavors. They were also at the very top of Leadville society, patrons of most major charities, and though the Garretts had likely only been in town a short while, they would recognize the name.

"It's true," Frank said, nodding. "I don't hold much for ranking people according to their importance in society, but I've always been appreciative of how well-received our Rose is. Naturally, Milly accompanies Rose when she goes visiting. I'm sure you'll be pleased to know that Milly gets along very well with all the other children."

The Garretts did not look pleased. Rather, they looked like someone had just told them the tea they'd been drinking had been laced with arsenic.

"Indeed," Rose said, smiling. "And since you are so concerned with her spiritual welfare, let me assure you that she is learning to say her prayers, and I spend time every day reading Bible stories to her."

Frank nodded. "We also have family Bible time every night. But do tell me, what does your spiritual practice look like? I always like to hear ways we can deepen our relationship with the Lord."

The ashen color on both Garretts' faces brought a smile to Silas's face. He shouldn't gloat, but having lived in that household, he knew that their spiritual practice was limited to church on Sunday and prayers at the evening meal. And they usually gave Milly her evening meal in the nursery, not with the family. In essence, they'd just countered the arguments the Garretts had made against Milly remaining where she was.

Truth be told, having the disparity in their spiritual

lives pointed out made it more important than ever for Silas to raise Milly. The Garretts were very good about making sure everyone knew how charitable they were, but the miserly way they counted every penny they gave, unwilling to give beyond what they thought was their obligation, stood out in stark contrast to his time in a household that cheerfully gave everything they could.

Mr. Garrett coughed. "I suppose what you're doing is sufficient. But that doesn't change the fact that Silas is hardly qualified to raise a child. How can he be, when he's not even there?"

Feeling stronger, braver, Silas gave him a hard look. "Does that mean you've dismissed the nanny you hired to care for Milly?"

Mrs. Garrett shrank back as she glanced at her husband. If it was wrong for Silas to have a nanny, then shouldn't it be equally wrong for them?

"She is not just a nanny," Mr. Garrett said. "She is teaching Millicent proper etiquette and deportment, and as Millicent gets older, will also give her her regular school lessons. Miss Bertrand is also helping Millicent learn French. Our little darling will be quite the accomplished young lady."

Mrs. Garrett's eyes gleamed. "And what accomplishments will Rose teach her? Nothing we want her to learn, I'm sure."

Rose stiffened, then adjusted her posture as she regarded the Garretts with such a regal expression that Silas almost felt sorry for them.

"I understand that you're grieving your daughter, and Milly is your only remaining connection to her. And so I forgive you for your grievous insults against my character when you know nothing of it. You are correct in that I cannot teach her French. However, there are a good many things she can learn from me. For example, when Milly first came to us, she did not know how to share with the other children. Now she cooperates well with others, and mothers such as Emma Jane Jackson are delighted to have Milly over to play. That is an accomplishment anyone would be proud to have."

Silas noted the way Rose emphasized the Jackson name. Though Emma Jane wouldn't have minded, he could see the way it pained Rose to have to use her friend as a connection to prove her worth. Especially because Mrs. Garrett's eyes widened at the mention.

"Yes, grief is a terrible thing," Frank said slowly. "And I can see how it must be hard to have lost your only child. I, too, know the pain of losing one's children. Fortunately, while my wife and four children went to be with the Lord, I have one remaining daughter, Annabelle, and her little girl, Catherine, brings me more joy than I could have imagined. It must have been terrible to think you were losing little Milly, too."

Silas stared at him. Just whose side was he on? Rose caught Silas's eye and gave a subtle shake of her head. She seemed to be telling him to trust Frank.

"Which is why I'm sure Silas will agree with me when I tell you that you are welcome to visit Milly anytime. In fact, we would be delighted to have you come for supper tonight. You can see for yourself how Milly has progressed, and then, afterward, you could spend some time playing with her here in the parlor."

At Frank's friendly smile, Silas understood. He was offering them time with Milly, offering them a chance to have a relationship with her, but in a way that still left Silas in control.

"Surely she's in bed by then." Mrs. Garrett's horrified expression matched her tone of voice.

Frank gave her another pleasant smile. "Of course not. The evenings are valuable family time, and we consider Milly part of the family."

The Garretts exchanged glances that said they were none too pleased with the arrangement, but they had no room to complain. Though they weren't leaving with what they came for—Milly—Frank had offered them the chance to spend time with their granddaughter. Silas had to admit the older man was far more reasonable than he would have been.

"What time is supper?" Mr. Garrett asked, his face pinched in an unpleasant expression.

"We eat at six," Frank said, standing. "I'm sure you have other business to attend to, so we'll look forward to seeing you then."

The dismissal was as polite as a dismissal could be, and a weight seemed to fall off the entire room. Even the Garretts appeared to be relieved at having a reason to go without having to continue with small talk that was unlikely to be polite.

"Thank you," Mr. Garrett said, giving a curt nod as he led his wife out of the room.

As the door closed behind the Garretts, everyone seemed to let out a collective sigh of relief.

Maddie reentered the parlor, wiping her hands on her apron. "I thought those guttersnipes would never leave." Then she looked at Frank, disgust evident on her face. "I suppose you've probably invited them for supper."

His smile was the only answer she needed as she groaned and went back into the kitchen, muttering about the indignities of her work.

Then Frank turned to Rose. "I apologize if my invitation will force you to suffer further insult, but I think it best we at least put on the appearance of cooperation. We don't want Silas to be accused of not allowing them to see Milly. As long as we appear to be perfectly reasonable in our efforts, they'll have a hard time convincing a judge that Milly should live with them."

She nodded slowly. "It's all right. I've heard far worse." Then she turned to Silas, her forehead knotted with concern. "Do you think they'd go that far?"

He wished he could take away the lines littering her forehead. "They were talking to a lawyer in Ohio about it, so I would imagine that they'd be pursuing it here if they had to. I imagine there will be quite a few things they don't like about the situation, as if what they voiced wasn't enough."

The old familiar heaviness settled on him again. "Nothing I do for Milly is going to be good enough for them. Though they were pleased by our marriage, even when Annie was alive, they were constantly critical. Annie always meekly agreed. They expected me to, and it irked them that I never did."

Frank patted him on the shoulder. "We know differently. Milly couldn't have asked for a better father than you."

High praise from a man who seemed to be everything Silas hoped to be in a father.

"It's true," Rose said softly. "You're quite wonderful with her. I don't know of any father so involved in raising his children as you."

Then she gave a small chuckle. "Well, except Joseph, Will, Jasper, Mitch and Uncle Frank, of course. But they're family, so I suppose I'm biased."

Sobering, she regarded him with a serious expression that seemed so much less like the Rose he knew, and like a completely different person. "I know it hurts your pride, but if it would smooth things over with the Garretts, I would be happy to help you pay for an actual nanny to care for Milly. The two of you shouldn't have to suffer for my mistake."

A dull knife tearing at Silas's insides wouldn't have hurt as much as the mournful expression on Rose's face. With the way her family and friends supported her, he hadn't given much thought to the way those outside the circle must still treat her. Granted, he'd once thought that marriage would be a perfect solution for both of them, as a means of saving her reputation. But that was before he'd seen how well Rose got by on her own. She didn't need him or any other man to save her.

"I stand by what I told them," Silas said, looking her square in the eye. "Milly couldn't have a better example of how to lead a good Christian life than you. It's as Frank said. You made a mistake, but who doesn't? We're all going to mess up sometimes, so she needs to know that what you do afterward is what makes the difference."

Rose nodded slowly like she'd heard those words before. "All the same, if it would make things easier for you to keep Milly…"

"None of that, Rose." Frank put his arm around her.

"This is just like when we had people asking me to re-sign as pastor because you live here. There will always be bullies pursuing their own agendas, what they think is right, but without the grace the Lord asks of us. If you give up taking care of Milly just to appease the bullies, it'll make you that much more susceptible to the next round of bullies who want to come after you. There will always be someone wanting to take you down. Stand strong in your faith, and it will all work out."

The doubt creeping along her face made Silas wish he could reach out and hold her, to tell her it was going to be all right. But he didn't have that right. Even when he'd been courting her, when he'd held her and told her all the things he wanted to do for her, all the things he'd felt for her, he'd been wrong to be so free with his heart when it wasn't his to give. It was wrong of him to ask her to entangle hers.

Now, with them both free to finally love one another, such comfort and intimacy still wasn't right. They were different people who didn't know each other anymore. If they'd ever known each other at all. The Rose Stone he'd fallen in love with was a bold, sassy woman whose smile lit up every room. Her flirtatious glances had made him feel every bit a man. But that was before he knew what it meant to be a man. Before he knew what it meant to honor the woman he loved.

He hadn't honored Rose back then. If he had, he never would have messed with her heart. He would have been honest about the situation between his family and Annie's family. He wouldn't have stolen all those kisses that didn't belong to him.

In truth, the biggest problem with all the things the

Garretts said against Rose was that they were pointing their fingers at the wrong person. Silas had been the one to behave dishonorably toward Rose. And though Rose had never spoken of her time with the outlaw who'd fathered her child, from what Silas had heard, that man had dishonored her, as well.

Seeing how selflessly she'd been willing to give up Milly for Silas's sake, Silas realized something he hadn't seen in Rose before. Every time he thought he had a glimpse into her heart to see who she really was, he found a depth he hadn't known existed. And the more he examined his own heart, he found how grossly unworthy he was of such a woman.

Though it pained him to make such an admission, the real reason he was grateful Rose hadn't accepted his proposal was that in all the trials people saw as being her flaws, she'd come out too strong, too good, and a man like Silas simply didn't deserve her.

Chapter Four

Rose cradled Matthew against her as she helped Milly finish dressing.

"Won't it be nice to see your grandparents again?" Motioning for the little girl to turn around, she tied the sash at the back of Milly's new pink dress into a pretty bow.

No one could fault Rose for having a poorly dressed child in her charge, but as Rose gave Milly a final once-over, she made sure that every detail was as it should be. Most days, Milly's appearance wasn't so tidy, not after playing in the yard and spending time with the children from the church. But tonight, with the Garretts coming to dinner, she wanted Milly to look her best.

"There now, aren't you as pretty as a princess?" Rose smiled at Milly, who scowled.

"I pway wif da kids."

Rose stood and held out her hand for Milly. "Tomorrow. Emma Jane has promised to bring over Moses and baby David, and if Mary is feeling up to it, she's coming over with Nugget."

"I yike Nugget." Milly's eyes shone. "And Moses. Him's baby yike Ma-few, but him's more fun. I teach him to walk."

Rose couldn't help the warmth that filled her as Milly continued chattering about the many attributes of Moses Jackson. Barely a year old, Moses was still very much a baby, but he could keep a two-year-old better entertained than little Matthew. Emma Jane had privately teased Rose that perhaps Moses and Milly would end up married. Wouldn't that be something to tell the Garretts? The supposed impossibility of finding Milly a decent husband under Rose's care had already been solved.

Rose smiled again. But of course, both women had agreed that the children should be free to choose their own spouses. Emma Jane had been forced to marry Jasper, her husband, to prevent scandal, and though the couple was now deeply in love, the Jacksons had already promised that their children could marry whomever they wanted.

Which was why, as Rose looked down at the little boy sleeping in her arms, she felt no unhappiness at her unmarried state. Several men had offered, with there being so few unmarried women in Leadville who weren't occupied in the world's oldest profession, but Rose couldn't see herself saddled to a man who merely wanted a wife. Men up here were lonely and desperate, and she wasn't lonely or desperate enough to take advantage of that fact.

Even Silas's proposal hadn't been tempting. Not when she'd seen the deep love shared by the couples among her close friends and family. Perhaps it was wishful thinking to hope that Rose could someday have it for herself, especially with all the mistakes she'd made. But having made those mistakes, Rose was no longer willing to settle for anything less than an honorable man who loved her with his whole heart and would love and court her the proper way.

"Come, now," Rose said, holding out her hand to Milly. "Let's go downstairs to wait for your grandparents."

Milly took her hand, and they made their way downstairs, Milly skipping as best a two-year-old could. She'd seen the older children at the mission and had begun mimicking their actions. The somber little girl who'd come into their household now seemed to radiate joy.

As they reached the bottom step, Milly caught sight of Silas and ran toward him. "Papa!"

He picked her up and swung her in his arms, then held her tight as he kissed the top of her head. Though she'd watched this scene play out between them at least once a day, it still never failed to melt Rose's heart.

How could anyone think that not having Milly with her father was the best thing?

A noise came from the parlor, and Rose turned to see the Garretts standing there, with matching sour expressions covering their faces.

"Such a ruckus," Mrs. Garrett said. "Surely you don't let her run so wild all the time."

"Ah, but what is a home without laughter?" Uncle Frank gave a pleasant smile as Silas stiffened.

Rose hated seeing the expression on Silas's face. He'd said that they constantly criticized them, but until now, she'd wondered if he'd been exaggerating. Their comments about Milly running wild made it clear that, if anything, Silas had been generous in his descriptions of life with the Garretts.

He set Milly down. "Say hello to your grandparents, Milly."

The smile disappeared from Milly's face, then she turned and ran to Rose, burying herself in Rose's skirts.

"I'm sorry," Rose said, patting Milly's head. "She's usually not so shy. I can't imagine what's gotten into her."

"He's already poisoned her against us." Rose recoiled at Mrs. Garrett's harsh tone.

"I'm sure that's not it at all," Rose said as she knelt in front of Milly.

Focusing her attention on Milly, she said softly, "What's wrong, my sweet? Your grandparents are here. You want to have a nice visit, don't you?"

Tears filled Milly's eyes. "I want to pway."

Rose hugged Milly close, careful not to disturb Matthew in her arms. So far, he'd been quietly watching everything around him, but she wasn't going to risk making him fuss. "Tomorrow."

Then she smiled at the Garretts. "She's sad because the Jacksons invited us to stay for supper, and we obviously couldn't. She adores little Moses Jackson, so it's disappointing for her not to get to stay and play."

"Do you dine with the Jacksons regularly?" Mrs. Garrett's question reflected her snobbery, as though she didn't believe the close friendship Rose had mentioned.

Uncle Frank laughed. "Sometimes I don't know who is eating where. Our families have become so close that it seems like either one of us is at the Jackson mansion, or one of them is over here."

Then he turned to Silas. "Which reminds me. Henry gave me some papers for you to look over for Joseph. Don't let me forget."

With another chuckle, he brought his attention back to the Garretts. "My apologies for bringing up work during a social call. With Joseph out of town, Silas is handling a good deal of the mining business on his behalf. We've been very impressed with Silas's skills. I'm sure you're pleased with how well he'll be able to provide for Milly."

Rose was fairly certain Silas already knew about the papers Emma Jane's father-in-law had asked Uncle Frank to deliver, but it gave him the opening to subtly let the Garretts know that one of their main arguments against Silas raising Milly had been defeated. However, the scowls they wore said they wouldn't be giving up so easily.

"Yes, but at what cost?" Mrs. Garrett said, her voice sounding deceptively pleasant. "Millicent, come, let me take a look at you."

Carefully balancing Matthew, Rose gave Milly a tiny push in her grandmother's direction. "Go on now, give her a nice big hug."

Milly obediently walked forward, holding out her arms, but Mrs. Garrett turned aside. "You may kiss me on the cheek."

Rose's heart hurt as Milly did as she was bidden. All the joy that she'd gotten used to seeing in the little girl's eyes seemed to have disappeared. Rose would admit that her dislike of Annie Garrett had largely been because of Silas, but even before that, she'd always thought Annie cold and unfeeling. Now, though, watching Milly methodically kiss her grandparents on the cheek with no warmth and no hugs, Rose felt a little more sympathy toward the other woman. Perhaps the unfriendliness Rose had always sensed was more about Annie's discomfort than about her disdain for others.

For all the things Rose could find fault with in how she was raised, the one thing she was most grateful for was how, at least until her mother became ill, their home was filled with laughter, hugs and affection. And now that they were here in Leadville, that love had seemed to grow stronger as their family grew. Part of why she didn't regret not having a father for Matthew was that between her brother, Uncle Frank, and all the other men they considered family there was always a man in the house holding his arms out to her boy.

For Milly, a little girl who'd lost her mother, there were half a dozen women with warm laps and plenty of room to cuddle her.

But somehow, Rose knew that these arguments were not likely to sway the Garretts. Rather, they would find fault in the generous hearts Rose was grateful to call family. Some were her blood, but others were friends they loved as such, and she knew she could count on them all, no matter what. She pressed a kiss to the top of Matthew's head. After all, without them, there was no way she'd have been able to raise her son and walk through town with her head held high.

Maddie entered the room, an expression of longsuffering firmly planted on her face. "Supper is ready."

* * *

Silas held out his hand for Milly. "Come now, let's eat."

At least the Garretts were prepared for this break in their tradition since Frank had already explained to them that they ate as a family.

As they were seated at the table, Mrs. Garrett paused, looking pointedly at Maddie. "You let the help eat with you?"

"Maddie is the housekeeper, yes, but we also consider her family," Frank said calmly, taking his seat.

"And the baby?" Mrs. Garrett looked over at Rose.

"Of course." Frank held out his arms for Rose to give him the baby. "We take turns holding him, so Rose has a chance to enjoy her food. As I mentioned this afternoon, this is important family time, and we take it very seriously. Now, let's bless the meal so we can enjoy Maddie's fine cooking."

Silas bit back a grin at the expression on Mrs. Garrett's face. She looked like she'd just been told they were going to eat live toads. And for her, the struggle of sharing a table with people she considered beneath her was probably just as real.

Frank gave the blessing, and it warmed Silas's heart to hear Milly's emphatic, "Amen!" at the end. She loved to "pway" as she called it, and the way she used the same word for praying and playing made Silas smile every time. In the few short weeks they'd been here, Milly had grown to love the Lord in a way he hadn't experienced until adulthood.

The Garretts, of course, did not look impressed at Milly's cheerful ending to the prayer. They didn't see what a gift it was for her to so joyfully live out her faith. All they cared about was her obedience. He'd asked Annie about it once, how she saw her faith, and her answer had made him wonder if she knew Jesus at all.

He looked over at Rose, who was patiently cutting Milly's chicken for her. It wasn't fair to compare the two women, but he couldn't help wonder if Milly would know the Lord as deeply without Rose's influence. Rose's daily reliance on the Lord inspired him in ways he hadn't expected. He'd been crazy to think that they could so easily pick up where they'd left off in Ohio. Especially now that he knew there was so much more to Rose than he'd ever thought.

"Now, tell us, Mr. and Mrs. Garrett, how are you enjoying our fine city? Have you had time to take in any of our exciting entertainments?" Frank smiled at them before stabbing a piece of meat.

"I can't imagine there'd be anything we'd find amusing in this lawless place," Mrs. Garrett declared, frowning at her plate. "Gunshots at all hours, drunkards in the streets—why, even at your supposedly finest hotel, the Rafferty, do you know that there was a woman of the night right in the front lobby?"

Mr. Garrett patted his wife's hand. "There, now, it will be all right. We shan't be here long, just long enough to convince Silas of his folly in bringing our precious girl to this horrible place."

And there it was. Another reminder that as reasonable as the Garretts tried to sound, underneath, the only thing that would satisfy them would be to get their own way. Which meant taking Milly back to Ohio with them.

"I'm sorry to hear you have such a poor impression

of our fine city," Frank said, patting his lips with a napkin. "The Tabor Opera House is famous for its entertainments. I can't say that I ever saw finer productions, even when we were living on the East Coast."

Then he turned to Rose. "And your involvement with the women's charities. I understand you have a good number of teas, socials and even balls, do you not?"

Rose smiled. "Indeed we do. Mrs. Garrett, I think you'd be pleasantly surprised at how similar our society is to what you're used to back in Ohio. In fact, I daresay you'll find things here to be even more advanced in some ways. Some of the homes are getting electricity, and you may have heard of Alexander Graham Bell's fantastic invention, the telephone. The Jacksons, of whom you've heard us speak, recently installed one themselves."

Then she turned to Silas, shaking her head. "And don't you go encouraging Joseph about getting one. I heard you and Jasper conspiring, but Emma Jane says it's an awful nuisance, ringing at all hours."

Silas couldn't help his grin. Jasper had told him that both his mother and Emma Jane objected to the device, but he could see where it would be quite useful communicating with the mine without having to go back and forth continually. The mine was nearly an hour's ride away, and that was just for a man on horseback. With a wagon or buggy, it took even longer.

"A telephone, you say." Mr. Garrett's eyes twinkled. "I was just reading about it on the train ride here. I noticed many homes have gaslights, and I will admit that the bathing rooms at the Rafferty are the finest I've ever seen."

"But the lawlessness!" Mrs. Garrett set her fork down. Not that she appeared to have taken a bite. She'd spent the entire conversation disdainfully pushing around her food with her fork.

Frank gave a wry smile. "I will admit that there is still much work to be done in that area. But the numbers in our church are growing, and our Mary is married to the finest deputy I've ever had the privilege of knowing. I'm confident that soon, you won't find a safer place to live than Leadville."

Mrs. Garrett gave a snort. Whether it was out of genuine disbelief at the state of the town, or a refusal to consider that Leadville wasn't as bad as she wanted to believe, he didn't know, but it was a good reminder that she would be ill-inclined to see anything positive when it meant not getting her own way.

The conversation came to a lull, with the only sound the clinking of forks and knives on plates. Maddie had outdone herself, high praise considering her meals were always delicious. The tender chicken hardly needed a knife to cut it, and the flaky biscuits melted in Silas's mouth.

The front door opened, and Evelyn, Rose's younger sister, entered, followed by the rest of the Stone children, Helen, Daniel, Bess and Nugget.

Evelyn paused when she noticed the family at dinner. "I'm sorry. I didn't realize you had company."

"It's all right, Evelyn, come in." Frank gave a welcoming smile. "What brings you all here?"

"Could I speak with Maddie in the kitchen, please?" Evelyn said, twisting her hands as she spoke.

Nugget pushed in front of her. "Mary's baby is coming!"

"Nugget!" Milly jumped out of her seat and ran toward the other girl, wrapping her arms around her. "You come to pway wif me?"

Milly's words seemed to be all the encouragement the rest of the Stone children needed to incite chaos in the otherwise calm dining room. Everyone began talking at once, and when Silas glanced over at Mrs. Garrett, her face was turning redder than the cherries in the pie Maddie had waiting on the sideboard.

Maddie dabbed the napkin on her lips, then stood. "I'll be getting on then. Rose, you don't mind finishing up, now, do you?"

"Of course not." Rose gave a smile, but something in her eyes told Silas she was less than pleased at the prospect. "Did you all eat?"

"Just some soup and bread," Daniel grumbled. "And it wasn't very good. Mary did something funny to it."

"Daniel Stone!" The tone of Rose's voice brought a halt to the ruckus. "She probably wasn't feeling well on account of the baby getting ready to come. You should be grateful she made you anything at all."

Then she turned her attention to Milly. "And you, young lady. You're not finished with your supper, so it's back to your seat to eat the rest, or you'll go to bed without any pie."

And the Garretts thought Rose incapable of caring for Milly. His daughter gave her a sheepish look and quietly mumbled an apology, then returned to her seat.

As Maddie bustled toward the door, she paused. "You

all be saying prayers for a safe and easy delivery, now, you hear?"

The room's occupants murmured their agreement, and Maddie was off. Silas gave a quick, silent prayer for Mary and the baby, but before he even said, "Amen," Frank had begun praying out loud.

Frank's prayer wasn't anything fancy, or even long, but Silas found his throat tightening at the older man's words. No one had prayed for them when Milly was coming, and certainly no prayers had supported them during Annie's long and challenging second birth. He'd been sitting alone in the kitchen when the midwife had come in, shaking her head and wringing her hands in her apron. He'd gone to inform the Garretts, but before he could open his mouth to speak, Mr. Garrett had shaken his head. They already knew.

He stole a look at the older couple. Were they having similar thoughts? Of an impending birth that had ended in disaster?

Lord, I don't know why You took Annie and the baby. But please, spare this family from the pain I've been living.

Silas couldn't help the silent prayer bursting from his heart. And yet, he also found himself asking the question that God had never answered. Why?

Why had the Lord seen fit to let them have Milly, but take Annie and the next baby? And why, when Milly was the only thing Silas had left, were the Garretts so intent on taking her?

He thought he saw the light reflect off a tiny glistening drop in Mrs. Garrett's eye as Frank said, "Amen."

The reminder of his own grief hit Silas in the gut.

Of course the Garretts were grieving. Frank had made mention of the other couple's grief several times since they'd visited. For the first time, Silas realized he hadn't given their feelings the significance they deserved.

Milly was all they had left, too.

The rest of the meal passed with chatter between the Stones and Frank about the coming baby, but the Garretts remained subdued. Silas couldn't bring himself to join in the chatter, not with the thoughts simmering in his heart. Nugget had found a seat next to Milly, and the older girl quietly entertained his daughter as she ate. The Garretts couldn't find fault in Milly's behavior, or how easily Rose fell into the position of making sure everyone's needs were taken care of.

Once they were finished, Frank calmly stood. "I apologize that our meeting didn't turn out as planned. Perhaps another night..."

Though Frank's attention was on Rose, Silas stood, as well. "No need to put Rose or Maddie out to prepare another meal for company. If the Garretts and Rose are agreeable, I think it would be acceptable if they wanted to visit with Milly for a couple of hours either in the morning or in the afternoon, whichever fits best in the household schedule."

The words weren't as hard to say as he'd thought they'd be. He'd spent so much time in a contentious battle with the other couple, yet the idea of winning no longer appealed to him. Granted, he'd tried, back in Ohio, to keep them all together as a family. They'd forced his hand by shutting him out of the family business, then making it virtually impossible to find honest work. Worse, they'd made it difficult for him to spend time with Milly, saying it interfered with the household routine. But with the reminder of how much they'd all lost, he'd do what he could to minimize their pain.

"I typically do my visiting in the afternoons," Rose said quietly, "but if the mornings don't work for you, I'm sure we could come to an agreement."

Mrs. Garrett didn't smile. Didn't show any emotion at the idea of being able to spend time with Milly. Instead, her scowl deepened. "We weren't planning on staying in Leadville."

"But we are." Silas kept his tone firm, calm. "I have a good job, good friends, and Milly is becoming part of the community. I'm happy for you to spend time with her for as long as you are here."

"Thank you," Mr. Garrett said without glancing at his wife. Usually, he deferred to her, but as the other man cast a longing look at Milly, Silas realized once more how little credit he'd given them for their desire to spend time with their granddaughter. As much as he resented them for trying to take Milly from him, hadn't his actions in taking his daughter to Leadville been the same?

Milly was fortunate to have so many people who loved her. If only they could figure out a way to equitably distribute their time with her so everyone got the chance to love Milly.

Chapter Five

After the Garretts had left, Silas couldn't lose the melancholy that filled him, despite the excitement in the air over the impending birth. Even Milly was running around the parlor with Nugget, happily singing, "The baby is coming," over and over. Of course, she really had no idea what was going on, but it didn't matter to his little girl. In this room was everything he'd ever hoped to give his daughter. A family who surrounded her with love and joy.

Completely the opposite of the oppressive feeling in the Garrett home.

So how did he include the Garretts, who thought the laughter and tomfoolery happening now was completely inappropriate? He could just imagine the sour expression on Mrs. Garrett's face if she could see the way the children were running around the room.

As if Frank understood the nature of Silas's thoughts, he clapped his hands.

"Now, children, I'm sure the baby won't be coming for some time now. So let's all say a final prayer for a safe delivery, then you can go upstairs to get ready for bed. Rose is already up there and she can tuck you in."

Rose had gone upstairs to feed Matthew, and judging from the hall clock, it was well past bedtime.

After a quick prayer, Silas held his hand out to Milly. "I'll take you up, sweetheart."

"No!" Milly crossed her arms. "Want Nugget."

He should be angry at his daughter's defiance, especially knowing that the Garretts would disapprove. But how could he not smile at how quickly Milly had bonded with the other girl?

Nugget reached for Milly's hand. "I don't mind. I like Milly. She makes me not so lonesome for Caitlin and Isabella."

Frank gave the girls an indulgent smile, then turned to Silas. "Isabella, that's Mitch and Polly's little girl, is a little older than Milly. Caitlin is Polly's younger sister, and she and Nugget are best friends. They're all in Denver right now, but hopefully you'll meet them soon. The two of them are thick as thieves, and they take turns mothering little Isabella like she was their personal baby doll."

Then he hugged the two girls. "And I know when they return, you'll be the best of friends."

"Nugget my fwiend," Milly said, looking up at Nugget with such adoration Silas knew that there was no way he could compromise on ever letting his daughter leave this place. So how could he convince the Garretts of that fact but still give them a relationship with their granddaughter?

"There's always room for more friends." Frank ruffled Milly's hair as he released the girls from his embrace.

The other children brushed past him and went upstairs. Silas held out his hand again to Milly. "How about we both tuck you in tonight?"

"I sweep wif Nugget." She still didn't take his hand. Naturally his daughter wanted to sleep with Nugget.

Though the Stones, as well as the other families connected to Frank, maintained their own households, there was a sense of fluidity among them all, and it was common to have different children sleeping in different houses. Even with tonight's disruption, the children knew exactly where to sleep in Frank's home. They'd done it often enough.

The lack of routine might be troubling to some, particularly the Garretts, but Silas thought it was good for all the children to have so many safe places to go and family members looking out for them.

"You can sleep with me," Nugget said. "But don't you think your papa should still tuck you in?"

Milly appeared to consider the words. "Papa pway wif me?"

Her insistence on having Nugget with her rather than him didn't matter in light of those words. Until coming to Leadville, his daughter had never asked him to pray with her. Prayer wasn't as big a part of their lives back in Ohio. And maybe, just maybe, that was the key to getting the Garretts on their side. Not just praying for them to do what Silas wanted, as had been his selfish prayer until now, but praying that they would come to know the Lord with the same added depth he'd found since coming here. And that they could all, as a family, find the right solution for everyone having a relationship with Milly.

He followed the girls up the stairs to the room Milly shared with Rose and Matthew. Milly was afraid to sleep by herself, so Rose had insisted that Milly stay with her. But the little girl paused at the door.

"I sweep in big room wif da kids." Milly looked up at him with huge, hopeful blue eyes. When the other children stayed at the Lassiter house, they slept in an attic room with enough beds for all the children. Silas had often envied the children their ability to be so close. What would it have been like, sharing a room with siblings, cousins and relatives, sharing confidences and each other's company?

Nugget grinned and headed toward the attic stairs. "I'll watch out for her."

Milly didn't wait for his answer as she scampered behind the other little girl. By the time Silas arrived in the attic, Milly was already bouncing on the bed she and Nugget would share.

"You know better than to jump on the bed, Milly." He tried to give his daughter a stern look despite the joy in his heart. The sense of camaraderie she had with the other children made every sacrifice worthwhile.

"All right, everyone," Rose said, coming up behind him. "Let's all get into bed and say our prayers."

Silas watched as she went from bed to bed, giving each of her siblings a quick hug, then murmuring something quietly with them. He hadn't been wrong in his previous estimation that Rose was good with her siblings. He'd always admired how well she cared for them back in Ohio when she and Mary shared the duty of raising their younger siblings once their mother died. Granted, they lived with their aunt, but Ina had been a hard woman, caring only about how she could put the Stone children to work.

He knelt beside Milly's bed, then gave his daughter a hug and a kiss, whispering a soft prayer of God's love over his daughter.

"I wuv you, Papa." Milly squeezed him hard around his neck, filling him with warmth and love. Though he should be used to the gesture by now, it never got old to be reminded of how far he and his daughter had come.

"I love you too, Milly."

Then Rose arrived at the bed. "Good night, Nugget."

She gave her youngest sister a hug and a kiss, then did the same to Milly. "And to you, too, my sweet. May you both have sweet dreams blessed by God, and may He keep you safe in His arms. Amen."

Milly gave Rose the same tight-necked squeeze she'd given him. "I wuv you, my Rosey."

Milly was Rose's sweet. And Rose was Milly's Rosey. How could he have any greater blessing than a woman who loved his daughter so?

She returned Milly's sentiment, then gave her another kiss.

"Good night, everyone."

Rose turned to the door and indicated he should follow her. Together, they descended the stairs, not speaking until they had returned to the parlor.

"You're really excellent with them, you know that?" Silas smiled at her as she sat and picked up her knitting.

"Thank you." Rose didn't look up or smile back. "I do my best, but I know I'm not nearly as good as Mary or Annabelle."

The one thing that hadn't changed for the better with

Rose since their time in Ohio was her lack of confidence in herself. She used to be bold, almost brash, and she never failed to tell people what she thought. Folks used to call Rose wild, but he'd loved her free-spirited approach to life. Now she seemed almost a shell of that person.

"Why do you put yourself down? I don't know many sisters who would so lovingly care for their siblings. What's changed you? Years ago, you would have accepted my compliment, then fished for more."

Rose set her knitting down. "I'm not that girl anymore."

Before he could quiz her further, Frank entered the room, carrying a tea tray. "No need to get up. I just thought I'd bring some refreshments since you're sure to be up all night waiting for news. I have to finish working on my sermon for Sunday, so I'll be in my study. But I'm here if you need me."

Frank set the tray down on a table.

"Thank you," Rose said, smiling up at him softly. "I know I should get some rest, but I don't think I can sleep until I have word of Mary and the baby."

He returned her smile. "She was the same with you. I know you two don't always get on, but never doubt the depth of her love for you."

Rose nodded slowly, a meek agreement when Silas could see the sadness in her eyes. Old Rose would have argued, or at least expressed what he saw on her face. But this Rose said nothing.

As though Frank understood, he left the room, not commenting on Rose's attitude, but mumbling about his upcoming sermon. Silas, too, wished he could ask Rose, but he'd already been bordering on conversation too intimate for people no longer romantically connected. It wasn't right for him to dig deep into her heart when he couldn't be the man to claim it.

Rose hated the distance that sprang up between them after Frank left them alone in the room. But there was nothing she could say that wouldn't open her up to the scrutiny she'd worked so hard to avoid. The truth was, years ago, she'd been vain, selfish and resentful of not having a normal life. She cared for her siblings, yes, but not with a cheerful or loving heart. Rose had been angry, bitter, and it was only to show off for Silas that she'd seemed otherwise.

The girl he knew didn't exist anymore.

And while she knew that God had forgiven her for her sins, she wasn't so sure her family had. Despite her best efforts to bridge the gap, and her earnest desire to be closer to her older sister, Mary still seemed to hold herself at a distance from her. Though the younger siblings respected Rose's authority, they still came to her with trepidation.

Silas seemed engrossed in the Bible Frank had given him. Frank believed strongly in the idea that everyone should have ready access to God's word, and he constantly gave away Bibles to anyone who had need. It warmed Rose's heart to see Silas making use of that generosity. In all their courting days, she couldn't remember Silas ever reading the Bible for himself. Then again, neither had she. One more way the years had changed them. Any fondness they might still have for one another was based on shadows of memories that had no place in the here and now.

The stairs creaked, and Rose looked up from her knitting. Her younger sister Helen, wrapped in a giant shawl, hair mussed from tossing and turning, stood there.

"Is the baby here yet?"

Rose shook her head and patted the seat next to her. "There's no use in staying up there and disturbing the others. Frank made some tea, and though it's probably lukewarm, you might find it soothing."

Helen nodded slowly. She got herself a cup of tea, then sat in the chair farthest from Rose, letting out a long sigh. "It didn't take so long with Annabelle's baby, or yours."

"Every baby comes on its own time," Rose said, ignoring the pang at the thought of how long Matthew had taken. She hadn't wanted to bother anyone any more than she already had, so she hadn't told anyone about her pains until they'd become unbearable. She didn't know how far along in her labor Mary was, or at what point Mary had told everyone the baby was coming. Even with that information, she couldn't tell Helen much more than she already had.

Then Helen turned her attention on Silas. "I heard Milly's mama died having a baby."

"Helen!" Rose gave her younger sister a sharp look. Granted, Silas was practically family but they'd already gone too far in discussing things of a delicate nature in front of him.

"It's all right." Silas closed his Bible, then smiled at Rose's younger sister, his eyes lined with something that looked like pain. "She did. But Annie had a weak constitution, and after Milly was born, the doctor suggested she not have more children."

Silas's voice cracked slightly. "But Annie was bent on Milly having siblings. She didn't want Milly to be an only child, the way she and I had been, and she thought…"

Though he wasn't openly weeping, Rose heard the tears in his voice. "She thought the family ought to have a son to carry on the family name."

Then, as though he could turn his grief off as easily as one blew out a candle, Silas shook his head. "Mary is strong and healthy. You don't need to worry about her."

So many things Rose wished she could say to Silas, to give him comfort at the reminder of what he'd lost. But they no longer had the kind of closeness that would allow it, and it would be a bad example to her younger sister to seem too emotionally invested in a man who was not to be her husband.

But Helen didn't seem to understand the silent cues Rose was sending. Instead, she asked, "Are you sad that you don't have a son to carry on the family name?"

"Helen. We don't ask people such personal questions." Rose's voice was sharper than she intended, but the thing Rose regretted the most in her past actions was how her boldness in speaking of things that people didn't talk about in polite society harmed her family's reputation. She'd always been too quick to speak her mind, branding her an indiscreet fool, and when her sin with Matthew's father came to light, society sniggered behind their gloves, saying she deserved it for being such a flighty girl.

Now Rose did her best to temper those qualities which society deemed so inappropriate. And she'd hoped that her younger sisters would learn from her example.

Only Silas didn't seem as horrified as Rose felt. Rather, he gave the lazy, indulgent smile that had so often made her want to kiss him. In the past, of course. Now she knew better.

"It's all right, Helen. Though Rose is correct that we don't usually ask that sort of question in general society, you're among friends, and I don't mind answering."

Helen looked at Rose like she might stick her tongue out at her, but thought better of it.

"My teacher says I'm impertinent. But I say, how am I supposed to learn if no one answers my questions?"

Silas grinned. "You sound an awful lot like a certain young lady I used to court. I hope you never lose that spirit."

He looked at Rose with those final words, as though he disapproved of the changes in her life. But he had no idea how much the spirit he so praised had gotten her in trouble.

"And in answer to your question," Silas continued, "no, I'm not sad I don't have a son to carry on the family name. Milly is more than I could have ever hoped for in life, and I can't imagine feeling any differently about a boy."

Helen straightened. "Joseph says the same thing about Catherine. And Will says he doesn't care if they have a boy or a girl. But if you all are so happy about having girls, then why don't we girls have the same freedoms as boys?"

Not this again. Rose closed her eyes and said a silent prayer for patience with her sister. Everyone had this conversation with Helen on a regular basis. And, once upon a time, Rose herself might have pursued the same line of thinking. She could even remember arguing that men visited houses of pleasure all the time with no consequence, so why were women held to a higher standard? But that was before her one indiscretion in that regard. Was it fair that men were not shunned for their loose ways as Rose had been? No. But it was the way of the world, and Rose wished she'd paid more heed to the lectures in propriety and deportment she'd been given.

Silas had the nerve to laugh. Not just a chuckle of amusement, but a full-on belly laugh.

"It's not funny," Helen said, her eyes flashing with fury. "My sister is having a baby, and could die, and no one will tell me anything about it. I heard her crying before we left, and she was in pain, and Will wouldn't let me see to her. If this is what having a baby is like, no wonder it's all such a big secret. I certainly don't want to have one."

Her raised voice must have disturbed Uncle Frank's sermon preparation because he entered the room, looking bemused.

"What is all this commotion?"

Rose let out a long sigh. "Helen is expressing her frustration about a woman's limitations."

Frank's smile bolstered Rose's confidence. He, too, had been the victim of Helen's many speeches about the unfairness of people not answering her questions.

"I just want to make sure that Mary isn't going to

die!" Tears burst out of Helen like one of the mighty explosions in the mine.

Rose got up and gathered her sister in her arms. Though Helen usually fought such gestures, she allowed Rose to hold her tight. "There aren't any guarantees. Not in having a baby, not in walking down the street. You know that."

Wishing she could give Helen some comfort, and hoping she wasn't saying the wrong thing, Rose said softly, "Having a baby hurts. That's why Mary was crying. I believe I screamed a time or two, the pain was so bad. But once I held Matthew in my arms, the pain didn't matter anymore. I would have gone through that and more a thousand times over for him."

Then she hesitated, aware that there were men in the room. When their second to youngest sister, Bess, was born, they'd been alone with their mother, no one around to help, and Rose had been tasked with minding the other children while Mary helped their mother give birth. Once it was over, Mary explained the details of what happened to her, including her very rough knowledge of how the baby came to be in the first place. Rose had known much of it from watching their animals on the farm, but somehow the knowledge of what happened between a man and a woman had comforted her. Of course, neither their mother nor Mary had mentioned the temptations and pleasure that went along with it, and sometimes Rose wondered if they should have.

"I'm sorry if our discretion has upset you," Rose said softly to her sister. "I think it's hard to know what is and isn't right to tell you."

The truth was, much of Rose's troubles came out of a

lack of openness between herself and Mary. She would have had fewer problems had she only had someone to confide in. Who would answer her questions honestly.

Rose pulled away and looked Helen in the eye. "I'm sorry if I've seemed too hard on you. I just want to keep you from making the mistakes I have. But I realize now that the harsh answers I received were what drove me headlong into trouble. So I promise to do a better job of answering your questions."

As if he was trying to encourage Rose after having to listen to her long-ago rants about how no one wanted to talk to her about things that were real, Silas gave her a gentle smile. Now, just as he had then, Silas understood. A disconcerting thought since she wasn't sure she was ready to give him any more space in her life than he already had.

Then she brought her attention back to Helen. "But you have to promise me something. You can ask me anything, but you'll only ask me in private, and whatever I tell you will be kept just between us."

Helen nodded slowly. "But what if Evelyn wants to know? We tell each other everything."

Born barely a year apart, Helen and Evelyn had a closeness that Rose had often envied. Though Evelyn was the elder, she'd always been much more timid than Helen, and Helen often spoke for her sister.

"Then you should tell her to ask me. I'll offer her the same promise I gave you."

Helen regarded her suspiciously for a moment. "Why are you now willing to do this?"

Rose glanced quickly at Silas, wondering if he knew the role he played in her life. "Because Silas's comments comparing you to me made me realize that many of my troubles in life would have been avoided had I only had another woman to confide in. I felt very alone from the time I was around your age, until…"

Rose sighed. Sometimes she still felt that alone. Even among the other women in their group, it seemed like she sat on the outer edge, not within the circle.

"Well." She smiled away the painful thought. "I'm willing to be there for you if you'll let me."

"But you had Mary," Helen said.

Rose shook her head. "Mary and I were never close. When we were children, it was always her and Joseph. They were as inseparable as you and Evelyn, perhaps even more so. I tried to join in their games, but they told me I was too little, or I wouldn't understand. When Joseph left to come to Leadville, Mary and I were virtual strangers, and we never confided in one another. We assumed a lot about the other and were often wrong in our assumptions. It didn't promote a healthy sisterly bond."

And maybe that was why Mary hadn't asked Rose to come with Maddie. It had hurt that her sister hadn't wanted her, particularly as it seemed like all the adult women had been present for Matthew's birth. She longed for them to want her, but perhaps they simply didn't want Rose.

"But you're better now," Helen said, hugging her. "You and Mary never fight anymore."

Even though Rose didn't agree with Helen's assessment, she hugged her sister back. Maybe someday she and Mary would be close, but for now, she'd accept the privilege of being able to guide her younger sisters the way she wished she'd been.

Fortunately, Rose was spared from further dissection of her heart by the front door opening. Maddie entered the room, pulling off her bonnet.

"It's a girl. Mother and baby are well, and you've never seen a man happier to be a father than Will. It's not proper, but he refuses to leave Mary's side."

The older woman shook her head. "Folks these days. No one seems to know their place in this world. But I suppose it's about time men started doing more to help their women with the little ones. Not sure who came up with the fool notion that we have to do it all, but at least some people got it right."

Helen giggled, but Rose just smiled. She was used to Maddie's rants about the world not being what it ought, and how despite her seeming resistance to that difference, Maddie was always among the first to accept the changes. Maddie had been the first to recognize that Rose might be expecting, and though it had taken the rest of the family time to get over the shock, her love and support of Rose had been unwavering. Rose had never felt that Maddie was ashamed of her.

"Does the baby have a name?" Frank asked.

Maddie made a noise. "They say they want to get to know her first to see what fits. I'm just hoping it's not something weird from Shakespeare like she was talking about last week. Hamlet. Who names a baby Hamlet?"

Then she turned and regarded the rest of the room, her gaze settling on Helen. "What do you think you're doing still up at this hour? The baby's here. Now go to bed."

Helen turned back to Rose. "Why does Maddie always get to speak her mind, but not me? Why do I have to ask you privately?"

"Because I have forty more years of living behind me than you do, young lady. I suppose I know a little something more about living than you do, and until you have the experience to back that mouth of yours up, you'd do well to close it more often.

"The rest of you ought to think about going to bed, too." Maddie looked expectantly at Rose. "With all these extra mouths to feed, I'll be needing help with breakfast."

"Of course." Rose gave her a smile, then turned her attention back to her sister. "Get some rest now. We'll talk more tomorrow."

The party said their good-nights and Rose went to put away her discarded knitting. When she turned to clear up the tea things, she noticed Silas still in the room, watching her.

"Did you need something?"

"I just wanted to say..." He shifted awkwardly, almost as though he thought he'd be treading on dangerous ground.

She smiled at him, hoping to encourage him to say his piece and be done with it. While she wasn't tired, and therefore not in a hurry to go to bed, she also wasn't sure she wanted to open herself up to the deeper conversation they'd so far successfully maneuvered around. With everything she'd discussed tonight, her heart was too fragile to open it up to him, but she wasn't sure if, given the opportunity, she'd be able to resist.

Silas had been the one she'd confided in years ago when she'd had no one else. Here she was, feeling vulnerable, and the temptation to share it with someone, even though it would be inappropriate, was too great.

They might not be the same people they'd been, and any romantic feelings she might have had for Silas were predicated on circumstances that no longer existed. Yet Rose longed for that previous closeness. Until tonight, she hadn't realized the depth of her loneliness and what her actions had cost her. But to share with Silas and confide in him didn't seem right, not when she knew she was no longer the woman he remembered. Which meant Silas wasn't that same man, either.

So where did that leave them?

Chapter Six

Silas hated the tension between them. He knew Rose was trying to keep a respectable distance, and in light of what he'd learned about her this evening, he could understand. But he was tired of so much going unsaid, not just between them, but in life in general. Helen had the right of things in questioning why people couldn't simply speak their mind. It had been one of the qualities he'd once admired in Rose, and he found her restraint almost painful.

"Earlier, you dismissed my compliment about how wonderful you are with your siblings, but from where I stand, you just gave Helen a very precious gift."

Rose smiled softly. "Only because you reminded me of how like her I used to be. I know you think it's an admirable quality, but I alienated a lot of people with my frankness. People equated my loose tongue with loose morals. The wonderful qualities you saw in me, they were only because it's what I wanted you to see."

Rose picked up the tea tray. "In truth, I was selfish, vain, and only cared about my own happiness. I did what I had to do with the children because it was the only way to keep Aunt Ina happy, which was the only way I could sneak off to meet you."

She looked at him with eyes so full of guilt he found he couldn't meet her gaze.

"And I sneaked off to meet you because you were the one escape I had from a life I hated. I was lonely and miserable, and you were the only person who saw me as being worth something other than cheap labor."

The catch in her voice made him look at her. Really look at her. Though he heard shame in her speech over her past actions, there was nothing in her posture to indicate its presence now.

"I know differently now. The worth God has given me is greater than anything I could have found with you. I used you, Silas, to ease a pain only God can. Don't put me on a pedestal, because I don't belong there."

She started to move past him, but he stopped her, grabbing the tray. His fingers brushed hers as he did so, and though he didn't want to, he remembered the feelings that had once sparked between them.

"Let me take that."

It was a good thing he'd already had hold of the tray because she jerked her hands away like she'd been burned.

"If you like. I'll still need to wash up, though. Maddie hates even a single dirty dish in the sink when she starts breakfast."

"Many hands make light work." He should have probably let it alone, should have gone upstairs to bed.

But he'd always had a certain fascination with fire that, even now, couldn't be doused.

Rose hurried past him, and he followed behind, keeping his pace slow and steady. They both could use some breathing room, though he wasn't going to completely give up on his mission.

Most of the changes he'd seen in Rose were for the better, but he despised how utterly shattered her confidence seemed to be. Though she claimed she accepted God's forgiveness, she didn't always live like it. Rather, she acted as if she was still serving out her penance for the shame she'd brought on her family.

As Rose washed dishes, Silas grabbed a towel and started drying.

"Thanks." Rose smiled at him. "I'm sorry if I seemed cold in there. I just don't know how to…be…with you anymore."

"Just because we no longer have a romantic connection doesn't mean we can't be friends."

Rose handed him another dish to dry. "I suppose. But sometimes I feel like the things I say to you are too personal, and it's not appropriate. However, when I leave things unsaid, it seems just as wrong."

Silas sighed. He'd never been good at hiding anything from Rose—except, well, Annie, and that hadn't turned out well for them. Not that he thought that he and Rose had a future. She was right in that they were different people now, and while he'd like to think they'd both grown in ways that made them better, it didn't mean they'd be better together.

"I feel the same way. I know what I did back in Ohio hurt you, and I know things aren't the same, but you're the only person I've ever really been able to talk to."

The admission hurt, not so much because he felt

bad at his reliance on Rose, but because while kissing her had always been nice, the intimacy he missed most was that of their friendship. She might think herself unworthy, but the truth was, she'd grown to be far more worthy than he. He wasn't sure he could be deserving of Rose, even if he wanted to be. He'd hurt her, tried to use her, and yet found himself the recipient of her grace. Sure, she'd said she'd used him back then, but hadn't he had the same motivations? Not the same situation, but he'd been just as desperate to connect with someone he thought understood him. He'd just left out the one piece of information that would have driven her away.

Rose handed him the last dish, then wiped her hands on the apron he hadn't noticed her put on.

"You want to sit on the back porch for a while? I've got too much nervous energy to sleep."

Had she heard him? Or had she been too lost in her own thoughts to understand?

"I suppose it's better than tossing and turning for the rest of the night."

He followed her to the back porch, where they sat, listening to the sound of the wind as it ushered in what would likely be a storm.

"I feel bad that tonight has been more about me and my family," she finally said, looking over at him. "I wanted to say something after dinner when you got so quiet, but I thought it probably wasn't my place. Then when Helen asked…"

Rose let out a long sigh. "You said I'm the only person you've ever been able to talk to, but I feel bad because I haven't done much listening. I've been so focused on my needs and how I've moved on with my life, that I haven't taken the time to be a good friend to you."

There it was again. The goodness in her that she failed to see.

"I can't think of a greater friend than someone who, despite how I broke your heart, would do as much for Milly and me as you have. None of my friends in Ohio would even give me a job."

He looked over at her, but her gaze remained focused on the ground. "I did so very grudgingly. Had it not been for Joseph and Uncle Frank, I'd have thrown you out."

"I know. But you helped us anyway, which is far more than anyone else."

The moonlight cast shadows over her face, framed by the tendrils that had fallen out of her bun. He couldn't read her expression, but he knew that in her mind, she was still trying to diminish the good he saw in her.

Still, he let the silence hang between them, and her thoughts, whatever they may be, work through whatever she needed. For the first time since he'd come to Leadville, sitting alone with Rose felt almost comfortable. If only he didn't remember the evenings where they'd sat in the moonlight, laughing, kissing and planning a future that was never to be.

Could a person be in love with a memory? Knowing it had no bearing on present reality and that the people involved no longer existed?

As much as he'd come to respect and admire Rose, he didn't like the way she always turned the blame back on herself and refused to see the good in the person she'd become.

Rose looked over at him. "I've been trying to find a way to bring the conversation back around to this, so I suppose I should just say it."

Taking his hand in hers, she said, "I'm sorry our family's joy has been a reminder of your pain. I've never offered my sincere condolences for your losses."

Silas squeezed her hand. "Thank you. I wasn't expecting to have the memories come back like that."

The empathy lining her face reminded him of how easy she'd always been to talk to.

"What you told Helen in there, about Annie…"

"They blamed me." Silas swallowed to ease the tension in his throat. "The Garretts said if I hadn't been so desperate for a son, their daughter would still be alive. Sometimes I think that's why they're trying so hard to take Milly away. To punish me for killing their daughter."

"I thought you said it was Annie's idea."

"It was. But when a person dies, you can't say it was their fault, so you find someone else to blame." He let out a long breath. "And it wasn't Annie's fault. I wish you'd gotten to know her because she wasn't all bad. Just lonely, and her parents were so controlling. She once said that maybe if she'd had siblings, her parents wouldn't have needed to be so hard on her. But they had all their hopes pinned on her, and she could never measure up."

"Sounds like you loved her." Rose's voice was gentle, not judging, almost like she was trying to understand.

"In a way." He looked over and realized they were still holding hands. The right thing to do would be to remove his hand from hers, but having the physical comfort of another human being felt too good to let go.

"When we got married, I knew I had a choice. I could be miserable and resent not getting to choose my wife, or I could find a way to get along with her. I think she loved me about the same. Just two people trying to do right by each other when they hadn't been given a choice. Sometimes I think having another baby was Annie's way of finally choosing something for herself."

Silas tried shrugging off the memory of Annie's joyful face as she told her parents about the baby, then how quickly it fell at their horrified reaction. They'd immediately turned their ire on him, saying he was a terrible husband for forcing her to carry another child. Annie had said nothing. Just stood there, tears streaming down her cheeks.

Could he let Milly live a life where the only choice she'd be allowed to make for herself would be the one that killed her?

Rose squeezed his hand. "You never said, was it a girl or a boy?"

"Another girl." Silas sighed. Even in that sacrifice, poor Annie hadn't been able to get what she wanted. "People said I should be glad it wasn't a boy, but I don't see how that would have made a difference. I lost a child, and there's no greater pain than that."

"Losing your wife?"

Silas shook his head. "No. Annie didn't deserve to die. And I didn't want her to die. But I didn't love her the way I love Milly. I don't miss her the way I miss that baby."

"What did you name her?"

Silas stared at her for a moment.

"They said it wasn't proper."

"Nonsense. She was still your daughter. You have the right to recognize her as your child and grieve her loss."

Rose covered their already-entwined hands with her free hand. "At the mission, we see women from time to time who've lost a child. Here, despite all of our modern conveniences, life is still harsh, and for many, loss is a part of it. Uncle Frank taught us to help them grieve. Just because you're a man doesn't mean you don't hurt, too."

He couldn't have stopped the tears even if he'd wanted to. No one, in all of the conversations following the deaths of Annie and the baby, had told him that it was acceptable to mourn his daughter.

"These things happen," they all said, acting as though it were no different than losing a chicken or a cow. No, a cow had more value than his child.

As for his wife, people alternated between expecting him to throw himself in her grave or to immediately find a new one. The Garretts wanted to take his only living child as a replacement for the one they'd lost.

But nowhere, in any of that, had anyone recognized that Silas had a need to grieve his loss.

Silas untangled his hand from Rose's, then wiped at his face with his sleeve.

"Thank you for acknowledging something that no one else seems to understand."

"You should talk to Uncle Frank. He knows what it's like to lose a wife and children."

Silas nodded slowly, understanding that while Rose was willing to give him some comfort, she also wanted to be sure to leave appropriate space between them. Which brought him back to his earlier resolve regarding the Garretts and the role Rose played in his life.

"I know the Garretts lost, too. That's why I was so agreeable in letting them have time with Milly. I've been so focused on my feelings and fears that I hadn't considered their losses, as well."

He stared down at his hands, missing the softness of Rose's skin against his, but knowing it was for the best. "It's hard. I know I need to be more charitable in letting them spend time with Milly, but I also can't have Milly growing up the way Annie did."

"So find a way to compromise."

"I will." He gave Rose a sidelong glance. "But that's going to be a hard thing to ask a future wife."

A tiny rumble of a laugh filled his insides. It was almost ridiculous to consider remarrying. "Not that there are many wife options here, but it would be nice to share my life with someone. Like I said, life with Annie wasn't all bad."

"I'm sorry I couldn't have accepted your proposal." Rose's tone was light, but then she let out a long sigh.

"Back when we courted, I thought the butterflies in my stomach were all the things that made it love. Then I met Matthew's father, and I quickly learned that those butterflies might actually be moths. Eventually, what you thought was love tears little holes in your soul because you mistook pretty words for something else."

Rose shifted, straightening her skirts to cover her ankles more fully. "But I know better now. I don't have to settle for doing my best by someone. And there's more substance to love than butterflies. The kind of love I want is the kind of love I see with Joseph and Annabelle, Will and Mary, Jasper and Emma Jane, Mitch and Polly. And I won't settle for less than that."

Silas had already been ashamed of how he'd treated Rose and how he'd thought she'd be so willing to accept the shabby proposal he'd offered. But now, with her heart laid bare to him, he felt like a complete heel for offering her anything less than real love. She deserved that kind of love, even though he wasn't the man to give it to her.

Then Rose looked at him with so much tenderness he thought he would combust from the absolute warmth in her gaze. "You deserve that kind of love, too. I know it's tempting to remarry for the sake of Milly. But here she has plenty of family to make up for her lack of mother. So don't pick someone to marry for the sake of convenience, but wait for the right person. A perfect match for you and Milly."

"Frank said the same thing to me about not settling for marriage only for the sake of my daughter."

Rose nodded. "He's taught us all a great deal. I don't know what any of us would do without him."

Silas almost didn't recognize the wisdom in Rose's eyes. Not so much because he'd failed to grasp the wisdom, but because the source was so unexpected. Never, in all their courting days, would he have called Rose wise. Once again confirming what different people they'd become. It had been folly to think they could just pick up where they'd left off. Rather, all he had to rely on was an acquaintance upon which he could hopefully rebuild a friendship.

Chapter Seven

The next morning, Rose found herself too busy to talk with Silas before he left for work to see how he felt after their late-night conversation. She shouldn't be worried about his feelings so much, but she'd opened up a wound, and it only seemed right to make sure he wasn't still bleeding. If only it didn't tear at the aches in her heart.

She'd understood when he said that she'd been the only person he'd ever been able to talk to. He'd been the same for her. And though he disagreed with her at times, particularly about her culpability in what had gone wrong in her life, he never did so in a way that made her feel small. Unlike everyone else in her life.

"When can we see the baby?" Helen's question rose above the din of the children cleaning up the kitchen.

Rose had told the children that after breakfast, they'd see about visiting Mary, but Uncle Frank hadn't yet returned from making sure she was up for guests.

She'd convinced the children to do the dishes, but now she had no more excuses left.

So what, then, was she supposed to do with a group of rowdy children who'd been eagerly waiting to meet their newest family member?

"Want baby Ma-few!" Milly tugged at her skirt.

At least appeasing Milly would be easy enough. She was too young to understand that there was another baby besides Matthew.

"Why don't you check on him? But be very quiet."

He'd wake the second Milly opened the door, but he needed to wake up now or else he wouldn't take his afternoon nap. Now that he'd finally started sleeping, Rose had been taking care to keep him on a schedule that allowed the family to have some sort of routine. A nice change from how things had been since his birth.

Life almost felt normal.

A knock sounded at the front door. With Frank at Mary's, Maddie had gone to the mission to make sure they had everything they needed for the day.

Rose wiped her hands on her apron and answered the door. "Hello." Rose smiled at the Garretts. "I wasn't expecting you."

"Silas said we could visit with Millicent in the mornings, did he not?"

Mrs. Garrett's tone was more brusque than usual, and Rose wished she'd been more welcoming instead of questioning their presence.

"Yes, of course. Please, come in. Have you breakfasted?"

Mr. Garrett nodded. "The hotel does a very nice one in the mornings."

"They do." Rose gestured toward the parlor. "When we first arrived in Leadville, we stayed at the Rafferty for several weeks, and I must say, it has the finest restaurant in Leadville."

"It's passable," Mrs. Garrett grumbled.

"I will own that nothing beats home cooking, and I certainly wouldn't trade any of the meals we share here for what the Rafferty has to offer, but at least it's not terrible."

Rose didn't know why she bothered trying to defend the hotel, especially since Mrs. Garrett merely harrumphed at her words. But Mr. Garrett nodded, and his face lacked the hostile expression that seemed to be plastered to his wife.

"Why don't you have a seat and I'll find Milly for you. We're still in a bit of an uproar this morning, with Mary having her baby last night."

The Garretts didn't comment as Rose led them into the room. With a heavy heart, she remembered Silas's concern that they were still grieving the loss of their daughter and grandchild. Perhaps their hostility was borne more out of their pain than out of her original assumption that they simply weren't nice people.

She turned to them and gave them what she hoped was a compassionate look. "I'm very sorry if our family's happiness brings up painful memories for you. I want you to know that you have my deepest condolences over your loss. Annie was a lovely woman."

A few weeks ago, she would have choked on that last sentence. In truth, Annie had been very pretty. And though she would have never described the other woman as being a nice person, after hearing Silas talk about her, Rose felt more kindness toward a woman who did the best she could with a life she probably didn't want. Besides, Annie had been Milly's mother, and Rose owed it to Milly to find good to share with the little girl.

"I would think you'd be dancing in the streets, now that Silas is free to marry you," Mrs. Garrett snapped. "You have him. Why must you keep Milly too?"

The words stung, mostly because a couple of years ago, they would have been true. Sometimes having to face the person you used to be was the hardest part about becoming someone new.

"Silas and I aren't getting married," Rose said quietly. "I harbor no ill will toward him or Annie for their marriage. From what Silas tells me, they had a good life together, and for that, I'm very grateful to Annie."

As the words tumbled out of Rose's mouth, she realized the truth that resided in them. Without Silas's marriage to Annie, neither Rose nor Silas would be the people they were now, and there was nothing on earth that could induce Rose to want to go back to who she'd been.

"Rosey!" Milly came tearing into the room. "Evewyn won't let me hold Ma-few!"

Rose caught the little girl in her arms. Just as she could not regret the mistakes that had led to Matthew's birth, she could not ask to change anything that led to having Milly in her life. How was it possible to love another human being not related to you so quickly?

"Slow down, Milly. I'm sure Evelyn will let you have your chance. But first, say hello to your grandparents. They're here to visit with you."

Milly turned and glared at them. "I no want visit. I want to pway."

"We're going to see the Jacksons this afternoon. But you must behave yourself and use your best manners with your grandparents. They've come a long way to see you, and they miss you."

Her lower lip jutted forward as she appeared to consider Rose's words. Last week, Milly hadn't been allowed to play with Moses one afternoon because she'd gotten in trouble.

Milly took a step toward her grandparents. "You pway wif me?"

Mrs. Garrett looked horrified. Mr. Garrett looked confused. If what Silas had told her about the older couple's interactions with Milly was true, they probably had no idea what it meant to play with a child. What had the couple been expecting would happen in a visit?

Kneeling beside Milly, Rose said, "I don't think they know any of your games. But I'm sure if you get your storybook, they would love to read a story to you."

Milly turned to her grandparents. "You wike stowies?"

The older couple looked perplexed, but Milly didn't wait for their answer. She ran out of the room to get her book.

"I hope that's all right," Rose said. "You can certainly do whatever activity you like with Milly, but I thought I'd break the ice with something I know she loves."

Mr. Garrett nodded slowly. "Thank you. I don't know much about such young children."

Mrs. Garrett glared at him but said nothing.

Milly returned, carrying her favorite book, a worn primer meant for teaching early readers their ABCs.

Though Milly was far too young to learn her letters, she loved hearing the rhymes over and over. Most of the family had grown tired of reading it to her because she wanted to hear it so much.

"Dis one." She handed the book to Mrs. Garrett, who looked at it distastefully.

"It's tattered. Surely you teach her to take better care of her things than this."

Rose took a deep breath to deflect the criticism. "It was that way when she got it. I believe it was one of the pastor's from his childhood. He and his wife spent many years living in mining camps, teaching people how to read. Many hands have touched that book."

"Really?" Mr. Garrett looked perplexed. "Why would a man of God spend his time teaching people to read?"

"People in mining camps live such a transient existence, following the gold or silver to the next discovery. Many places don't have a church or even a preacher. Uncle Frank wants people to be able to read God's Word for themselves, so that when there isn't a preacher available, they're still able to study it."

"Extraordinary," Mr. Garrett said as Milly clambered onto his lap.

Uncle Frank's plans were extraordinary, which was why they were spread so thin at the mission. Uncle Frank didn't think it was enough to simply feed, clothe and shelter those in need. When they'd been given an old barn to convert into space to use for the women displaced by the brothel fire last year, Uncle Frank set up classes and activities designed to help the less fortunate better their lives. The family helped out where they could, of course, but they had more people wanting to take reading classes than they had teachers.

Rose spent a good amount of time there herself, not that she'd share that information with the Garretts. After all, the children Milly played with at the mission were children of the lowest parts of society. In Rose's estimation, still good playmates, but likely not anyone the Garretts would approve of.

In some ways, the mission, or at least the need for it, was Rose's fault. When she'd run off with Ben, at the time thinking him a respectable man, he'd brought her to The Pink Petticoat, a notorious house of ill repute. He'd promised Rose that it was only temporary, but she soon learned that Ben was a liar, and she was held prisoner. Will, Jasper and Mary had to rescue her, and they accidentally burned the place down in the process.

The town saw the destruction of such a place as a blessing, one less house of sin. But for the working girls, losing all of their belongings in the fire as well as their livelihood was devastating. Though some found work in other establishments, Uncle Frank used the fire as an opportunity to give the ladies a chance at a new life.

Sometimes, Rose felt like it was all her fault—the lives ruined by her selfishness. She'd told Uncle Frank, and he'd merely told her it was as in Genesis, that what had started as something bad, God used for the good of saving so many lives. Their previous lives might be over, but God brought something better to them.

What good was God going to bring out of all this? Mr. Garrett had put his arm around Milly, patiently reading the words she pointed to. But Mrs. Garrett still wore the expression of someone who'd spent too much time sucking lemons. Would she allow Milly to add some sweetness to her life?

Helen entered the room, carrying a tea tray. "I saw you were busy with guests, and Maddie isn't back from the mission yet, so I thought I'd help out by bringing refreshments."

"Thank you, Helen, that's very kind." Since their talk last night, Helen had been more helpful than ever, and it seemed like, for the first time, her sister wanted to partner with her to make things run smoothly.

Then Rose turned to the Garretts. "Shall I pour, or would you prefer I leave you to your leisure?"

"You may go," Mrs. Garrett snapped, dismissing Rose as though she were merely a servant. And, she supposed, given that she was Milly's nanny, that is exactly what she was to the older woman.

But how else was Mrs. Garrett supposed to treat her? Rose thought back to the older woman's angry accusations and how she thought Silas should just give Milly to them. To see Rose as a legitimate person who loved and cared for Milly as her own meant that taking the child away wasn't the right thing to do. Rose shook her head. No. As much as she loved Milly, she had no part in the conflict between Silas and the Garretts. Milly wasn't hers, and she had no claim in Silas.

But still, Milly wasn't like a person's favorite horse, which could easily be replaced. She was a human being, and she'd already burrowed her way into hearts that would be devastated if the Garretts took her away.

Which was why, despite Mrs. Garrett's unkindness, Rose would do everything in her power to help everyone get along, and for the Garretts to see that this was

Milly's home. Though she didn't relish the idea of entertaining the cross old woman for the rest of her life, the only way to make everyone happy was for these visits to go smoothly.

Silas trudged up the steps to the Lassiter house after what had ended up being too long a day at work. It had been tempting to sleep at the mine, as he'd done on occasion, but though his body was weary, his heart was even more so. He'd left this morning before Milly had risen, and though she'd be asleep now, he wanted to at least look at her beautiful little face.

Acknowledging his loss to Rose had served to make the deep love in his heart for Milly even stronger. What he most wanted to do was hold his daughter and cherish the fact that he still had her.

The house was mostly dark, but when he entered, Silas heard a noise in the parlor.

"Hello," Rose whispered, gesturing at the bundle in her arms. "Matthew is having a rough night, but I finally got him to sleep. Busy day and too much activity, I think."

"Oh?" He leaned against the doorjamb. "What happened?"

"The Garretts had a visit with Milly this morning, and then Emma Jane was feeling ill, so instead of going to her house, we spent the afternoon at the mission, which was a good thing, because I hadn't realized how shorthanded they were. But that changed Matthew's routine, and he spent all evening fussing."

Rose yawned, closing her eyes briefly. Even in the dim light, he couldn't help but notice how, despite her exhaustion, she still looked lovely. Her hair was down, but in a long braid that fell over the front of her shawl. Though Matthew was wrapped in a blanket, Silas could see his head resting on her bodice. So charming, the scene could be a painting gracing the halls of the finest museum.

"How did the visit with the Garretts go?"

Rose opened her eyes as she gave a wan smile. "As well as can be expected, I suppose. Milly brought them books to read, which Mr. Garrett did in earnest, but Mrs. Garrett spent the whole time alternating between looking cross and complaining. They're coming back tomorrow, though, so perhaps it will get easier once we've established a routine."

"I'm sorry this is so difficult for you. I just don't know what else to do. Giving them time with Milly seems like the right thing to do, but—"

"It is the right thing to do." Rose shifted her weight in the rocking chair. "Mrs. Garrett said some very unkind things to me today, about my being glad Annie is dead, and I realized that you were right when you said that they're grieving."

She looked up at him, her gaze settling on his face. "I'm not glad that Annie is dead, and I would not have wished her fate on anyone. I just thought you should know that."

"I would have never thought that of you. Mrs. Garrett was wrong to accuse you."

It seemed unfair that Rose had to be the one to deal with Mrs. Garrett's hostility. Not when it was Silas who deserved it. He shook his head. No, he didn't deserve it, either. But the older woman was hurting, and she needed someone to blame. Even if it wasn't right.

"I know. But she has no other outlet for her grief."

Silas's chest warmed, and he felt a smile curl his lips. "Funny, I was just thinking that. I appreciate your willingness to see past the barbs for what they truly are."

"It's what's best for Milly."

"I agree."

Rose yawned again, then rubbed her eyes with her free hand.

"You should go to bed."

She shook her head. "Every time I lay him down, he wakes up crying. But he likes being held like this, so I'm just going to spend the night here. We've done it enough times. Milly's upstairs with Nugget again, so she'll be fine without me."

Matthew made a sound and Rose adjusted the blankets around him. "He's so sweet. I think he's having a good dream. His little lips are moving, and he has a smile on his face."

She pressed a kiss to the top of the baby's head. Something in Silas's heart swelled. How could Rose not see what a wonderful person she was? He'd never met a more loving woman when it came to children. Even Annie, whose love for Milly he never doubted, had never seemed so full of the kind of joy Rose possessed when she was with the children. Even when she was so obviously exhausted.

"You're a good mother," Silas said, wishing he could go into the room and brush his lips against the face of a woman so serene that she seemed almost unreal.

"Thank you." She smiled softly. "It's been a hard day, and I appreciate the encouragement."

"What else happened?"

Despite his wish to go to bed, Silas slipped into the room and sat in one of the chairs.

"Milly threw a fit because we didn't go to Emma Jane's to play with Moses. Daniel got in trouble in school for fighting with one of the boys. Nugget and Bess wouldn't stop arguing. Maddie was no help because with all of the family either indisposed or traveling, she was at the mission all day. Uncle Frank had an emergency in one of the mining camps to tend to, and he's not even back yet."

Her voice sounded weary, resigned. She hadn't sounded so dejected since their time in Ohio. Back then, all he'd ever done for her was listen, though when things were really bad, he'd find a way to send a basket of food to the house. It hadn't been much, but he'd done his best to ease her burdens. Even though things weren't the same between them, he'd still like to help her now.

"I'm almost afraid to ask about Helen and Evelyn." He kept his tone light and was rewarded by a soft smile on Rose's face.

"They were a big help, actually. My talk with Helen last night seems to have brought on a deeper willingness to cooperate on her part. Usually, she's the one arguing about why things have to be done a certain way, but she was wonderful in doing everything I needed. So how was your day?"

Silas looked at Rose. "Long. We had a piece of equipment break, and I couldn't leave until it was repaired so they could start work again first thing in the morning."

"Is fixing equipment your job?"

"No. But making sure everything runs smoothly in your brother's absence is. It's important that I be there to oversee something like that, so the workers don't think he's an absentee owner, the way some of the mine owners are. There, the workers take advantage."

Rose nodded thoughtfully, like she understood his words, or was at least trying to. "Isn't that what Polly's father does?"

"In part. He knows the mining aspect well, but managing the operations gets to be too much for him. That's why Joseph separated the jobs and gave this one to me."

"That makes sense," Rose said. "I know Polly's father wanted to spend more time with his family, especially now that Polly is married."

When Annie had been alive, they'd never had conversations like this. Mundane things, really, but they'd never given each other details about how things had gone in their lives. He'd ask about her day; she'd say it was fine, and then they'd switch places. Sometimes he'd come home to see Annie with eyes puffy from tears, but he'd always accept her answer that she was fine.

Now that he thought about it, she'd never actually asked how his day was, just said, "I trust your day was fine, as well."

They shared the same house, same bed, interacted politely enough, but neither knew what happened in the other's daily activities.

Yet here was Rose, not only asking about his day but listening to what he had to say, digging deeper into the details. He might have once been able to settle for the peaceful coexistence that happened with Annie, but this small conversation with Rose had him longing for more.

The heavy thud of boots sounded on the porch. "That'll be Uncle Frank," Rose said, adjusting the baby's position again. "I forgot to mention, we left plates warming for you both above the stove."

A long, stressful day and still Rose had time to think about taking care of his needs. True, it wasn't just him, but Frank, as well. In some ways, Rose had been right about her past. He hadn't known her to be so considerate as to go out of her way to care for others. It hadn't mattered to him back then, but he found that now, seeing this side of her, it did, quite a lot.

"I see you're still up." Frank poked his head into the parlor.

"Matthew was restless, and Silas just got home himself. I was just telling him that there's food in the kitchen for you both."

Silas watched the tenderness flicker across the older man's face. "Do you want me to take him for you so you can sleep for a bit? I'd like to eat, read my Bible and relax for a while before I go to bed."

Frank's face was lined with exhaustion, and though Silas imagined that he probably did read his Bible every night before bed, he knew the offer of taking Matthew was more for Rose's sake than anything else.

"It's all right." Rose yawned again. "He hasn't wanted anyone but me tonight. I think he senses all the changes and just needs his mama. We'll sleep here tonight, and it'll be fine."

Her eyes fluttered closed, then opened again. "Now you both go eat and leave me in quiet, so I can rest.

The children are bound to be up early tomorrow, and Maddie's already said that she's needed at the mission again."

Silas had felt like a heel for not making the same offer Frank had, especially since now she'd for sure not accept. But at least there was something he could do.

"Why don't you sleep in tomorrow? I'll get up with the children, and among us, we can figure out breakfast."

"That's a fantastic idea," Frank said. "I don't have anything in the morning, so I can help. I assume Milly's in the attic with Nugget, so we can move the rocking chair up to your room so all the noise doesn't wake you when everyone gets up."

"That's very kind, but..." Rose let out a long sigh. "My duty..."

"You've done plenty. But you also need your rest. We need you, Rose, but if you're exhausted, you're of no use to us." Frank's voice was gentle, full of the concern of a father.

"I insist," Silas added. He might not fully know this new Rose anymore, but surely she was still the stubborn fool who would argue to death when it came to her pride. "You've been so good about helping me out and haven't taken any time for yourself."

That was one thing that hadn't changed about Rose. As much as she told people how selfish she was, he'd seen how much she sacrificed herself for the benefit of everyone else. Even in the dim light, he could see the circles under her eyes. Why hadn't he noticed them before?

Silas walked toward Rose, then held out his arms. "Let me take Matthew. I have a way with him."

As though she were too exhausted to argue, she gave him the baby, then stood. "Thank you."

Frank came around and took the chair to carry it to Rose's room. Rose nodded slowly, trudging past them and up the stairs. Matthew snuggled up to Silas, opened his eyes, then yawned. Silas brushed his hand against the baby's downy head.

"Why are you giving your mama such a bad time, little fellow?"

Matthew gurgled in response.

Silas turned his attention to Frank. "Don't bother taking the chair up. Just make sure Rose gets into bed. I'll keep Matthew tonight."

For a moment, Frank looked like he wanted to say something, but then he nodded. "She deserves a night of rest."

The baby stared up at him, wide-eyed. Though his eyes hadn't yet developed into the same clear blue of Rose's, his dark hair, porcelain skin and tiny button nose were the very image of his mother.

As Frank went to make sure Rose was settled, Silas watched Matthew watching him. It seemed a shame that the boy would grow up without a father, but as Rose accurately pointed out about Milly's situation, Matthew had plenty of men to guide him. Still, as their eyes locked, Silas couldn't help but wish the little boy was his own. He hadn't been lying when he said he didn't need a son. But he'd be a perjurer if he had to say he didn't want the baby in his arms—desperately.

Could Silas and Rose find a way to build on the

friendship they had to create a family for both of their children? He pressed a kiss to the top of Matthew's head.

"I know your mama thinks it's not enough to marry for less than having it all, but I'm thinking that what we have here is good enough, don't you, little fellow?"

Matthew scrunched up his face like he was about to start fussing.

"All right, then. You win. I won't think any more about marriage, especially with your mama, unless it's the real deal. But I hope you know I'm always going to be there for you."

His answer seemed to convince the baby, who blew a bubble, then closed his eyes. If only Silas could be so easily satisfied, because as right as his answer was supposed to be, he didn't like it at all.

Chapter Eight

Rose woke to stillness unlike any she'd ever known. Rolling over in her bed, she reached for Matthew in his cradle. Her hands found only empty space.

Where was her son?

Her heart thudded in her chest as she sat up. She took a deep breath, trying to collect her thoughts. There had to be a reasonable explanation.

Jumping out of bed, Rose realized she was still wearing her clothes from the previous day. She'd been lying on top of her blankets with one of the spare quilts thrown over her. The dim echo of laughter from downstairs sounded against the stillness of her room.

Clearly she'd been more tired than she'd thought.

Had Matthew been fussing and someone… Rose shook her head. She'd have heard him. They'd have woken her.

Nearly tripping over her skirts as she raced down the stairs, questions ran through Rose's mind. Babies didn't just disappear out of their beds.

Except Rose couldn't remember putting him in his bed.

How could she have forgotten to put her son to bed?

And where would she have put him instead?

When she entered the kitchen, time seemed to have stopped, and it was like being in an entirely different place.

Silas sat at the table, bouncing a content Matthew on his lap and spooning something from a bowl into the baby's mouth. Milly sat next to him, contentedly eating her breakfast.

Liquid dribbled out of Matthew's mouth, which Silas very efficiently wiped away.

"What are you doing with my baby?" Rose rushed toward him, holding her arms out.

Silas smiled as he gave the baby more of the liquid. "Filling his belly. He was hungry. But he likes his porridge."

"I'll say," Maddie said, closing the back door behind her as she entered the kitchen. "I've never seen a little one take to food so quickly. I told you we should have been letting him try it."

Ignoring the older woman's chastisement, Rose grabbed her baby out of Silas's hands. She held him tight against her, pressing kisses against the top of his head.

Then she glared at Silas. "When he wasn't in his bed this morning, I had all kinds of horrible thoughts. You can't just take him. What were you thinking, taking him and not telling me?"

He had the nerve to shrug. "He was with me all night. You were so tired we thought it best to give you a chance to rest."

Silas stood up and reached out to wipe a stray bit of liquid from Matthew's face. "And we did just fine, didn't we?"

Oblivious to the turmoil in his mother's heart, Matthew giggled.

"But..." Rose blinked. While Matthew had been sleeping through the night, he still woke for an early-morning feeding. Though everyone else seemed oblivious to it, the tightness in her chest reminded her of the pressing need to feed the baby.

"He needs to eat," Rose said, turning toward the door.

"Oh, he's eaten plenty," Silas said, chuckling. "Maddie's right. This little guy has taken to eating porridge like a horse to fresh pasture."

"Ma-few eat like piggy!" Milly giggled as she banged on the table. "Me piggy too! More powidge, pwease!"

"I'll just go take care of him." She left the kitchen, carrying the baby up to the privacy of her room for feeding.

Despite everyone's words about how well Matthew had liked his porridge, he had no problem taking another meal. It wasn't until he'd been firmly snuggled against her for a few minutes that Rose finally felt like she could relax.

Though she knew everyone was just trying to help, Rose couldn't shake the ache in her heart. Did they all think she wasn't good enough to be Matthew's mother? That she couldn't take care of her own child?

Tears streamed down her face as she looked at the baby contentedly having his second breakfast.

A knock sounded at the door.

"Rose?" Silas called.

"I'm feeding the baby."

"I know. I'll stay here. I just wanted to be sure you were all right."

"I'm fine." Rose took a deep breath. She knew she sounded peevish, but with the tears still falling, she didn't need Silas thinking she was anything other than fine.

"I honestly thought I was trying to help. You seemed like you needed your rest."

His words sounded sincere, but it still felt like an insult that he didn't think she could manage on her own.

"Please, Rose, don't be upset. I can hear you sniffling in there."

Of course he could. Not only were the walls paper-thin, but Silas had always been able to sniff out her tears.

"I can take care of my own son."

"I know," Silas said softly. "And I don't know of anyone who is a more natural mother. But it's all right to have some help sometimes. I should have asked before interfering. I honestly thought I was doing you a favor. I'm sorry."

His immediate apology was a balm on her heart. People apologized to her all the time, but it always seemed like they were mostly afraid that if they didn't, it would only make her angrier. Like they were walking on eggshells. Silas seemed to be genuinely sorry he'd hurt her.

The trouble with forgiving Silas was that there was a part of her that still wondered, as safe as he seemed to her, could she truly trust him? She'd never expected him to break her heart the first time. Was it wrong of her to so easily hand it over now?

No, it wasn't her heart. Her friendship. She could rely on him as a friend, yes?

Friends did each other favors, right?

Rose wiped at her tears with her free hand. Matthew looked up at her and gave her a sleepy smile.

"I suppose there was no harm done."

The baby blinked, his dark eyes showing signs of lightening around the edges of his irises. People said that they thought his eyes were going to end up blue like Rose's, but until now, she hadn't been able to tell.

Everyone seemed to be a better expert on her son than she was. Like about giving him some of the food they ate. Her family had been saying she should let him try. But something in Rose had resisted.

Maybe she was being silly, but she'd thought it would be her to give Matthew his first taste of real food.

"Then why do you still sound so sad?"

Rose sighed. "I'm sorry. I suppose I don't like people making decisions about my son without talking to me."

"You mean like all the times you do things with Milly without asking me?"

She'd deserved that since she often took charge of Milly, and there had been that time when she'd purchased clothes for her that had upset him.

An apology was in order here, but she couldn't bring herself to say those words again so soon after she'd just done so.

"I…" She stumbled over the words on her tongue.

"I know," he said quietly. "We both overstep from

time to time. But we're both doing the best we can, so let's give each other some grace, all right?"

Some of the weight fell off her shoulders, and she looked down at her baby, who'd fallen asleep with a smile on his face, milk dribbling at the corners of his mouth.

"I just don't want anyone to think I can't do it on my own." She hadn't expected the admission to come out of her mouth, but having spoken it aloud somehow made her feel like she might have the strength to do it.

"You can't." His voice sounded as clear as if he'd been sitting in her room. "None of us can, which is why we all have each other. I thought that was the point everyone here keeps trying to make. So why are you so stubborn about understanding it for yourself?"

Because her circumstances were different. God might have forgiven her, but society never let her forget. And with each mistake, they shone the light of judgment on her. They'd said she deserved a baby who fussed all the time, who didn't sleep, and she knew that as Matthew grew, they'd be watching, looking for signs of his misbehavior to blame on her sin.

Rose closed her eyes to keep more tears from falling. Was she wrong to think that she might someday find a man who would love her as completely as the other men in her life loved their wives? Would there ever be someone who wouldn't hold her past against her, who wouldn't want her for her money, or, as in Silas's case, think her nothing more than the perfect mother for a child?

"Matthew's asleep. I don't want the sound of our

talking to wake him. The Garretts will be here soon, so I need to put him down so I can get Milly ready."

She couldn't see his face on the other side of the door, but she knew it bore an expression of complete exasperation. He expected an answer of her, but she had none to give him. If she shared what was on her heart, she was bound to get the same lecture she'd been hearing from Uncle Frank about her sins being forgiven. Which she already knew and accepted.

It was just the rest of society that couldn't.

And, like it or not, Rose was a part of society and had to live with the way people treated her. Which meant not letting her guard down, not even for a moment, not even here.

"I'll take care of it," Silas finally said. "I'd like to have a few words with them anyway. Frank says you haven't been to see the baby yet. Why don't you take advantage of the break to do so?"

Matthew sighed against her. After the momentary worry over his safety, she was loath to put him down. And she certainly wasn't going to leave him.

"Perhaps this afternoon. I won't leave Matthew, and—"

"I managed just fine last night."

"You'll be busy entertaining the Garretts. I won't antagonize them by forcing them to deal with Matthew, as well."

This time, she knew the silence on the other side of the door was because Silas knew she was right.

"They already hate me," she said. "I don't want to remind them of one of the reasons why."

Which is mostly how she tried to live her life these

days. Being helpful, but remaining in the shadows, keeping Matthew out of sight of the most disapproving people and making sure not to stir up trouble. Hopefully by the time Matthew got older, people's memories of the circumstances of his birth would have faded, and he'd be able to live as an ordinary boy.

"You know their anger is more about them than it is about you, right?"

Rose sighed, then looked out the window, giving her a view of the street. One of the carriages from the Rafferty was rounding the corner.

"The Garretts are almost here. You should prepare Milly."

"Fine." Silas sounded resigned, but he knew just as well as she that she'd played a role in angering the Garretts. After all, she'd stolen Silas's heart when she didn't have the right to.

"But Rose?" His voice was distorted like he'd turned away but come back again. "This conversation isn't over, and it will never be over until you understand that you're a part of this family, and just as you're here for everyone else, we're here for you, too."

Though it was nice that Silas considered himself part of the family, there was so much he still didn't understand. One more reason why, as much as she accepted that she'd been forgiven by God, the distance between her and her family members told her that she still had a great deal more penance to do.

Fortunately for Silas, Maddie had already anticipated the need to have Milly ready before the Garretts arrived, and he entered the kitchen just as they knocked on the door. Milly was dressed in one of the new outfits Rose had bought. Silas had to admit, his daughter did look rather pretty, and it was a far sight better than anything he could have chosen.

He'd been wrong to throw that in Rose's face. His words had hurt her, and he hated the wounded tone in her voice. Back when they lived in Ohio, that tone had been reserved for when her aunt had done something horrible or Rose had been fighting with Mary. She'd never directed it at him before.

But what was he supposed to do?

Things were different between them, and as much as he'd like for them to be back to how they used to be, or at least for their relationship to be as easy as it was, they couldn't go back. The part of him that wished they could do so warred with the other part that said their relationship held a lot more depth than it previously had.

Despite the newfound depth, he couldn't talk to her as easily as he once had. She'd put up a wall between them, and in those moments when he thought that he'd like to get past it, to be a balm to her heart, she seemed to double the bricks she placed in it. Years ago, he could have apologized, and she would have laughed, and they would have kissed, and...

The kissing was out, of course, but why did everything else have to be so hard?

He'd hurt her.

A thousand times that phrase rolled over in his mind, and no matter how many times she'd said she'd moved past it, the wall remained, reminding him.

And then today, when he'd hurt her again.

Silas pasted a smile on his face as Frank ushered the

Garretts in, directing them to the parlor. Milly clung to Silas's pants leg.

"I want to pway wif da kids." Her usual exuberant voice echoed with the kind of resignation someone so young shouldn't have learned yet.

"This afternoon. I'm sure Rose has something fun planned." He patted her head lightly, not wanting to mess up the careful hairstyle Helen had painstakingly done at breakfast before going to school.

Rose might have been worried about sleeping in today, but it had seemed like everyone had been happy to pitch in. The family at the Lassiter house worked in concert, each person having a role, yet able to fill in as needed. In some ways, it was exactly what he'd always imagined a family would look like.

Milly stuck out her lip in a pout, but she followed him into the parlor.

"Say hello to your grandparents, Milly."

"Hello." Her voice sounded hollow, wooden.

"You may kiss my cheek, Millicent." Mrs. Garrett gave them a regal look, and there was no warmth in her voice.

Silas tried telling himself that the older woman was guarding her heart, afraid he'd take Milly from her, but she'd never been warm.

Milly trudged to her grandmother, planted a kiss on her cheek, then turned and did the same to her grandfather. Mr. Garrett placed his arm around her, almost in a hug, and if it wasn't for the way his face softened at Milly's touch, Silas might have been tempted to rethink his desire to let the Garretts have a chance at spending time with Milly.

Then Milly turned and looked at Silas hopefully. "I go pway wif da kids now?"

"Not now," he said with a smile. Then he turned his attention to the Garretts. "What activity do you have planned for Milly today?"

Mrs. Garrett frowned. "I'm not sure what you mean."

"What do you intend to do with Milly this morning when you spend time with her?"

The Garretts looked as though he'd started speaking a foreign language, and not one they hoped Milly would learn.

"How did you intend to pass the time with Milly?"

They gave him a blank look.

"What did you do with Milly yesterday when you came to visit?"

Mrs. Garrett looked over at her husband. "We read a book to Millicent. Then we had tea, and I found her manners deplorable. She spilled her tea and had to be taken upstairs to be changed, which is when we left."

Deplorable manners. For a two-year-old. Silas couldn't even imagine what they viewed as such.

He knelt in front of his daughter. "Did you have bad manners yesterday?"

Milly shrugged. "I no hold cup wight."

Of course she didn't hold the cup right. She was two. Something that the Garretts had never seemed to understand about his daughter. He used to wonder if they'd gotten Annie as a full-grown human being because they always seemed horrified at what he'd come to realize was normal child behavior.

"I cannot fathom why Rose isn't teaching her proper deportment. Although I seem to recall that none of the

FREE Merchandise and a Cash Reward† are 'in the Cards' for you!

Dear Reader,

We're giving away FREE MERCHANDISE and a CASH REWARD!

Seriously, we'd like to reward you for reading this novel by giving you **FREE MERCHANDISE** worth over $20 retail plus a CASH REWARD! And no purchase is necessary!

You see the Jack of Hearts sticker above? Paste that sticker in the box on the Free Merchandise Voucher inside. Return the Voucher today… and we'll send you Free Merchandise plus a Cash Reward!

Thanks again for reading one of our novels—and enjoy your Free Merchandise and Cash Reward with our compliments!

Pam Powers

Pam Powers

P.S. Look inside to see what Free Merchandise is **"in the cards"** for you!

We'd like to send you two free books like the one you are enjoying now. Your two books have a combined price of over $10 retail, but they are yours to keep absolutely FREE! We'll even send you 2 wonderful surprise gifts and a Cash Reward†. You can't lose!

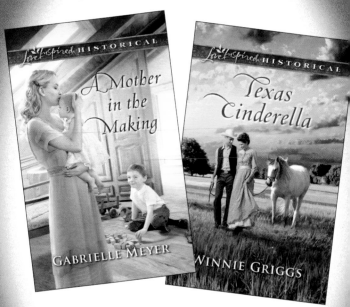

REMEMBER: Your Free Merchandise, consisting of **2 Free Books** and **2 Free Gifts**, is worth over $20 retail! Plus we'll send you a **Cash Reward** (it's a dollar) which is really the icing on the cake because it's in addition to your FREE Merchandise! No purchase is necessary, so please send for your Free Merchandise today.

Get TWO FREE GIFTS!

We'll also send you 2 wonderful FREE GIFTS (worth about $10 retail), in addition to your 2 Free books and Cash Reward!

Visit us at:
www.ReaderService.com

YOUR FREE MERCHANDISE INCLUDES...

2 FREE Books **AND** 2 FREE Mystery Gifts
PLUS you'll get a Cash Reward†

FREE MERCHANDISE VOUCHER

2 FREE BOOKS and **2 FREE GIFTS**

Please send my Free Merchandise, consisting of
2 Free Books and **2 Free Mystery Gifts** PLUS my
Cash Reward. I understand that I am under no
obligation to buy anything, as explained
on the back of this card.

102/302 IDL GLGZ

Please Print

FIRST NAME

LAST NAME

ADDRESS

APT.#   CITY

STATE/PROV.   ZIP/POSTAL CODE

NO PURCHASE NECESSARY!

© 2016 HARLEQUIN ENTERPRISES LIMITED. ® and ™ are trademarks owned and used by the trademark owner and/or its licensee. Printed in the U.S.A.

▲ Detach card and mail today. No stamp needed. ▲

HLI-N16-FMC15

Stone children had anything resembling proper manners. Their mother let them run wild, and then when she passed away, their behavior became even more so."

Mrs. Garrett gave a dignified snort. "This is why children need to have the right sort of influence in their lives. The Stones might have money now, but money cannot buy good breeding."

Silas could feel Milly tensing beside him. She'd grabbed his trouser leg again, hiding behind him. She might not have understood her grandmother's words, but she understood the intent.

"If you're to build a relationship with my daughter, then you're going to have to stop speaking of our benefactors in such a negative way." He reached down and patted Milly's head. "Milly is learning how to behave, and her manners improve every day. I couldn't be prouder."

Mrs. Garrett sniffed. Displeasure marred her features, the lines in her face deepening.

"Of course she is," Mr. Garrett said quickly. "We meant no offense. It's just that her um…er…her exuberance is, well, we simply aren't used to such an energetic child."

Fear shone in the older man's eyes. While Mrs. Garrett seemed intent on pressing her point, Mr. Garrett seemed willing to do whatever it took to keep Milly in their lives. The older man's tenderness gave Silas hope that they could somehow find a way to make this relationship work.

"All Milly really needs is to be loved," Silas said, reaching down and rubbing his daughter's back. His heart warmed as she looked up at him and smiled.

"But her manners!" Mrs. Garrett's face didn't soften.

"They'll come in time," Frank said, entering the room. "I'm sure it's difficult because your Annie must have been a remarkable woman and just as remarkable of a child. But we have to remember that all children mature at their own pace. Milly is still learning the joys of having other children to play with. She behaves well enough, and I can assure you that as she gets older, no one will look askance at her for her deportment."

Mr. Garrett patted his wife's hand as she murmured something under her breath.

"And I'm glad to find the two of you still here. I was so caught up in the excitement that I failed to invite you to join us at church tomorrow. We'd be pleased to have you as our guests."

It always amazed Silas how easily Frank managed to defuse difficult situations. Because for the first time since arriving, Mrs. Garrett smiled.

"That is very kind of you, Pastor. We would be delighted. It has been such a burden not to be at home with our church family."

He smiled at her like he hadn't noticed the guilt she'd poured on with her comment about their burden. "If there is anything we can do to make you more comfortable, please let me know. Many of our parishioners are missing home just like you, and we do our best to make them feel welcome."

For a moment, Silas felt bad for judging Mrs. Garrett so harshly. Truth be told, he'd been so interested in protecting Milly that he hadn't considered the other woman's comfort and how he could make things easier on her.

"I do appreciate your kindness, Pastor." Mrs. Garrett straightened, looking a bit more mollified.

"Well, then." Frank nodded at the Garretts. "I'll see you Sunday, if not sooner. I want to review my sermon notes, so if you'll excuse me."

"Of course," Mrs. Garrett said, looking almost pleasant.

Silas took a deep breath, then smiled at Mrs. Garrett. "It occurred to me that you play the piano very well. Milly loves music more than anything, so perhaps you could sing some songs together, or show her some of the notes."

He wasn't sure how well the latter would work, but at least he was trying to find an angle that reached Mrs. Garrett in a way that highlighted her interests.

"Well, I..." Instead of looking pleased, Mrs. Garrett looked flustered. "I haven't played since..."

Mr. Garrett patted her hand. "There, now, dear, it's all right."

Silas blew out a breath as he closed his eyes for a moment to collect his thoughts. He hadn't even considered that possibility.

"I'm sorry," he said slowly as he turned his gaze back on them. "I didn't mean to bring you more pain. I didn't realize you stopped playing after Annie's death. I just thought it was something we all enjoyed."

"It's true," Mr. Garrett said. "I recall we spent a good many happy times around the piano. It was good of you to remember."

The heaviness in Silas's heart grew. He'd spent so much time defending his loveless marriage that he hadn't given enough mention to Rose of the good times they'd had.

"I wouldn't want to forget. And I hope it is something Milly will someday remember."

He knelt beside his daughter. "Do you remember the songs we used to sing with your mother?"

"I wike to sing," Milly said with a smile. Then she pointed at Mrs. Garrett. "But she say I too loud."

All this time, Silas hadn't considered that the sound of Milly running through the house, singing, would remind Mrs. Garrett of what she'd lost. Annie had always been singing. She didn't have the best voice, and her songs were often slightly off-key, but she'd always sounded so happy.

Silas hugged Milly to him. "I suppose it's because it reminds her of your mama, and she misses your mama dearly. Your mama used to sing all the time."

"Miwwy wike to sing all da time. But I no want to be in da twouble."

"Will you sing us a song?" Mr. Garrett asked, his voice trembling.

Milly needed no further invitation. She belted out "Jesus Loves Me" with the biggest smile on her face. He'd never seen as much joy in his daughter as when she sang, but he realized as she started singing the chorus that Milly truly believed Jesus loved her. So, of course, the song brought her joy.

Tears streamed down Mrs. Garrett's face, and Silas watched as Mr. Garrett tenderly squeezed his wife's hand.

In this moment, Silas could almost believe that everything was going to work out perfectly.

Milly stopped suddenly, then ran over to her grandmother. "You no cry. Is happy song. About Jesus. Jesus wuvs you, Granmudder."

Mrs. Garrett picked Milly up and set her in her lap, holding her close. More tears followed the trail down the older woman's cheeks. For once Milly didn't squirm, but let the woman hold her tight as she sobbed.

But just as quickly as the emotion had overcome them all, Nugget burst into the room. "Milly! Will bought us a new ball. Want to come outside and try it out?"

Milly jumped off Mrs. Garrett's lap. "I go pway wif da kids, *now*?"

Mr. Garrett nodded, still clutching his wife's hand. Though today's visit had been short, it seemed to unlock something in everyone's hearts that would hopefully lead to progress in their relationship.

"Yes, Milly, you may go play with the kids."

Silas smiled as his daughter's face lit up and she ran out of the room.

He turned his attention back to the Garretts. "I'm truly sorry if this brought up any additional grief for you. I can't imagine the pain of losing your daughter. Annie was a good woman, and a good mother."

"But will Millicent even remember her?" Mrs. Garrett's voice still held the tears she'd been shedding.

"I do my best to help her," Silas said quietly. "We remember her in our prayers at night, and her picture is in Milly's room."

"And I often tell her how proud her mama would be of her," Rose said, entering the room. "I'm sure as she gets older, she'll treasure the stories you tell her about

Annie. I only wish I could have known her well enough to share some myself."

Silas didn't question the sincerity in Rose's voice. He knew from the brief times they'd spoken of Annie, Rose harbored no ill will toward his late wife. In fact, Rose had a deep compassion for her that stretched him in thinking of others with the same level of compassion.

The defenses on Mrs. Garrett's face came back up, and the scowl returned to her eyes. Rose seemed to sense the change in the older woman, as well.

"I meant no offense," Rose said quietly. "I merely wanted to give you comfort to know that we're doing everything we can to help Milly remember her mother. If there's anything you can think of that we might also do, I'd be happy to incorporate that into our routine."

"That's very kind of you," Mr. Garrett said, standing. "It's a difficult time, as I'm sure you can understand. We'll be going now, but perhaps we'll see you tomorrow at church."

He held out his hand to his wife, who used it as leverage to rise. As Silas watched Mrs. Garrett's strained motions, he realized that she no longer moved as quickly or easily as she once had. Had she injured herself? Or was she simply worn out from the grief of losing her daughter?

Mrs. Garrett turned her gaze to him. "Would it be possible for Millicent to have lunch with us at the hotel tomorrow after church?"

Possible, yes. A good idea? Silas sighed. If he said no, it would serve to strain relations between him and the Garretts further. But if he said yes, Milly's behavior was bound to shock them. Not that it would be bad, of course, but their expectation of how such a young child was supposed to behave was vastly different from what Milly could reasonably handle.

As he hesitated, Rose spoke. "I'm sure it would be a wonderful treat for Milly to dine in the hotel. However, we typically share a meal as a church afterward. You would be most welcome to join us, and you could see Milly interact with her friends. The Jacksons are typically present."

Silas fought the urge to chuckle at Rose's blatant use of the Garretts' snobbery to convince them to dine with the church. Not everyone at church participated in the meal, of course, but Frank's late wife had begun the tradition as a way of feeding the town's hungry. Everyone, including those who did not attend the church, was welcome. He supposed the Garretts wouldn't be impressed by the notion of sitting next to a down-and-out miner, but knowing Rose, she'd find a way to arrange it so they were seated with the Jacksons.

"That's a very kind offer," Mr. Garrett said.

"But unnecessary," his wife interrupted. "While it is good of you to include Millicent in your family activities, she needs to learn she has her own family, and I would like for the three of us to have our own family time."

The punch to his gut was harder than anything the most strapping lad had given him. But here was this frail woman, making him bleed in the worst way.

How many times would he be required to keep trying to include them, when they'd made it clear the only family unit they would accept was the three of them, without Milly's father?

Fine. Let them have it their way. It was only one supper. And perhaps, if the Garretts began to feel more comfortable with the situation, they'd be more willing to compromise, as well.

"All right," Silas said. "Milly can dine with you after church tomorrow."

Mrs. Garrett's satisfied smile told him that the war she was planning had only begun. His gut twisted, and Silas prayed he hadn't made a terrible mistake.

Chapter Nine

Silas didn't speak as he accompanied Rose to see Mary and the new baby. So far, all of her attempts at conversation had resulted in grunts and stony silence. Rose wasn't even sure why he'd come if he was going to be so disagreeable.

"Did I say something to offend you?" she finally asked, pulling the shawl around her shoulders a little tighter.

"No."

When he didn't elaborate, Rose didn't press the issue. It had never been so difficult to talk to Silas, but it seemed like the distance between them continued to grow. Especially after this morning's conversation.

"I'm sorry for how I treated you earlier. I shouldn't have been so hard on you. I know you were just trying to help with Matthew. You're good with him, and I don't give you enough credit for that."

Still, he said nothing.

She supposed it was for the best. What would their easy conversation accomplish? A deeper connection?

Letting him into her heart again? And then what? Rose could never love Silas the way she once had. She still wasn't sure she could love him at all.

As a friend, she supposed, but trusting him with her whole heart?

Rose sighed. Distance between them was a good thing, especially since she was in charge of Milly's care. Nannies didn't have deep friendships with their employers. Well, Polly had, but she and Mitch falling in love was different from Rose and Silas.

So why was she, once again, trying so hard to get him to open up to her, to feel something deeper than what he felt? Pursuing a deeper friendship with Silas was a bad idea, because once again, she'd be pushing for something that only she wanted. And truly, she didn't want that anyway.

What Rose wanted, what she needed, was a man who felt the same way about her that she did about him. Madly, deeply, passionately, in love.

Not a man who could kiss her with passion, declaring his love for her, then go off and marry someone else days later.

That wasn't love, but a baser emotion that led people astray. The trouble was, Rose had settled for those baser emotions too many times, and now she wasn't sure she'd know what love was if she found it.

But chasing a man and trying to get him to talk to her when he clearly didn't want to open up, that wasn't a situation where she'd find the elusive emotion.

They arrived at Mary's house, and Will opened the door as soon as their feet hit the porch.

"I'm so glad you made it! We were wondering why it took so long for you to come see the baby."

Joy radiated from every part of Will's body. Rose couldn't say when she'd seen a man happier to be a father, not even Joseph.

"Someone had to watch the children."

Will nodded. "I know. I'm sorry, I didn't mean to criticize. Our daughter is so beautiful, and I want to share her with everyone."

He ushered them in, and Rose felt a pang at what it must be like for a child to have such a proud father. Though she regretted nothing about having Matthew, she did regret that there would never be a man beaming with pride over his existence. Ben had died before Rose knew she was expecting, and even if he had known, she couldn't imagine that the man had enough love in him to be pleased with having a child.

Well, he might have been pleased if he'd been able to find an angle to take advantage of, but to love for the sake of love…

Rose shook her head. This visit wasn't about Rose's mistakes. It was about celebrating the arrival of her new niece.

"Does she have a name yet?" Rose smiled at her brother-in-law as he took her coat.

"We're still deciding," Will said. Then he looked over at Silas. "Did you have such a hard time coming up with a name for your little girl? Everyone said that if we had a daughter, I'd find myself more in love than I knew what to do with, but I had no idea. Between her and the amazing woman who brought her into the world, I almost want to burst."

Rose grinned. "So much for the tough lawman."

Silas chuckled. "Having a child will do that for you. And yes, coming up with Milly's name was difficult."

A dark look crossed his face, and then he sighed. "Annie had a younger sister, Millicent, who died of a fever when she was a baby. In their family, tradition says that they name the babies after a family member. Annie and her sister were named for their grandmothers. I knew if our baby was a girl, she'd be called Millicent, but when I met her…"

Silas shook his head. "Who names a baby Millicent?"

A smile filled his face, his eyes shining with love. "I took one look at her, and I called her Milly. Annie looked up at me and said it was perfect. I don't think she wanted to name her Millicent either, but she never went against her parents' wishes. She was always Milly to us."

Rose wanted to reach out and comfort Silas as he remembered the birth of his daughter. After last night's talk, she wondered if it also brought to mind their other child. Once again, she was touched by the tenderness he had for his late wife.

It also explained the tension between Silas and his in-laws when Milly's name was spoken.

"Milly is fortunate to have you as her father," Rose said instead.

Then she turned to Will. "Can I see the baby?"

He'd barely nodded when Rose started up the stairs to Mary's bedroom. Partially because she was eager to see the baby, but also because it hurt to be so torn in her conversation with Silas. His pain twisted her heart because she wanted to comfort him, but it also reminded her how stupid she must have been to think that he'd loved her nearly as much as she'd loved him. Why had she given her heart so easily?

When she opened the door to the bedroom, she spied Mary lying in bed, cuddling a tiny bundle.

"Rose!"

Mary smiled and gestured for her to come in. "I'm so glad you came. You won't believe how much she looks like Matthew."

When Rose was close enough to see the baby, the first thing she noticed was the same shock of dark hair her son had from birth.

"Oh, my!"

Mary held the baby out to her. "Say hello to your aunt Rose."

Rose took the baby and looked down at the tiny face. Mary was right. It was almost like looking at a feminine version of her son. She tickled the baby under her chin.

"Do you have your cousin's dimples, sweet one?"

The baby yawned as her eyes fluttered open, then closed again.

"I'm afraid not," Mary said with a smile. "That may be the one trait Matthew got from his father. I've seen Moses's dimples."

Rose nodded. Few people knew that Moses Jackson, the adopted son of Emma Jane and Jasper, was also fathered by Ben. Emma Jane had tried nursing Moses's dying mother back to health, and when the young woman passed away, she'd promised to care for Moses as her own. Though everyone in their circle was reasonably sure Ben was Moses's father, they'd all agreed that it did no one any good to reveal their knowledge. However, when Matthew was born, they'd discussed the possibility, once the boys were older, of letting them know they were half brothers.

Rose turned her attention back to the baby. "Well, I may be biased, but she is the most beautiful little girl I've ever seen."

"I won't disagree." Mary smiled, looking happier than Rose had ever seen her sister.

"Will says you're having trouble coming up with a name."

Mary looked up at her, her eyes filled with tears. "Not so much having trouble, as wanting people's blessings."

"Blessings?" Rose smoothed the baby's hair, noting how, just like Matthew's, it never wanted to lie down.

"I know things haven't always been good between us, and at times, they were pretty awful. But over the past year, I have come to love you deeper than I ever thought possible. I admire your strength, your courage and the way you have grown with the Lord."

A tear ran down Mary's face. "And Annabelle, dear, sweet, Annabelle. I can't imagine having a sister-in-law so dear to my heart. So Will and I want to call her Rosabelle. Rosabelle Faith."

Then she looked up at Rose with watery eyes. "Or Faith Rosabelle, if it makes you uncomfortable. But without the faith that brought us together, and without you and Annabelle, Will and I would not have the deep love we share. So what do you think?"

What did Rose think?

"I don't understand... I...I caused so much trouble for you."

"Without it, Will and I would have never fallen in love."

Rose's stomach started to hurt. "I humiliated you. And I—"

"You apologized, and I forgave you." Mary patted a spot on the bed next to her. "Did you really think I still held that against you?"

"No one lets me help or do anything anymore." Rose sighed. "It's like everyone's ashamed to be associated with me."

"Sit." Mary used the same tone Rose had heard her use when the children were acting up. Because as much as everyone said things were all right, they all still saw her as a child.

"Please," Mary said, her voice softening. "I hate that you think we're ashamed of you. Rose, what you've been through, the grace and strength you've shown is admirable."

"It was my choice. I did things that were wrong, and—"

"And you have repented, turning your life around and becoming an example of incredible faith and perseverance."

"Stop interrupting me." She knew her voice was shrill, but she was trying so hard to quell the horrible feeling in her stomach, like something inside her was going to explode.

Mary patted the bed again. "I'm sorry. I just don't like hearing you talk badly about yourself, but you're right. I should hear you out. Could you please sit, though? I do hate having to look up at you."

"All right." Rose sat, feeling awkward as her sister looked at her. Examined her, like she was some sort of criminal.

"Rose, you must believe that none of us have anything but the deepest love and respect for you. We don't ask for your help because it seems unfair when you have Matthew to care for and no husband to give you a break. We've offered to take Matthew from time to time, but you staunchly refuse. How can we add to your burdens when you won't let us help with the ones you already have?"

The lines in Mary's face had deepened, and the tears Rose had spied earlier grew thicker in Mary's eyes.

Her sister's words should have eased the tension in Rose's stomach, but instead, she only felt worse. Because they didn't line up with how Mary and the others had been interacting with her.

"You never told me," Rose said, not wanting to upset her sister anymore and tired of how their conversations always seemed to turn into arguments.

"I'm sorry. I thought I had." Mary took her sister's hand in hers. "I suppose I assumed things were all right between us, and when things seemed to go back to normal, it never occurred to me that you didn't realize the depth of our affection for you."

Mary sighed, and Rose could see in her eyes that once again, she thought Rose was being difficult.

"I'm sorry, I shouldn't have said anything," Rose said, focusing her attention back on Mary's baby. "I think Rosabelle is a lovely name, and I'm honored you'd want to include me in it."

Rosabelle made a soft cooing noise, reminding her of Matthew. "I should be getting back anyway. Matthew will need to be fed soon."

She tried to hand the baby back to Mary, but her sister shook her head. "No. You don't get to do that today. You want to know why we aren't close? Because every time someone says something you don't like, or you're not happy with, you use Matthew as an excuse."

Mary wiped at her eyes and looked down at her baby, then up at Rose. "You're right. We don't talk like we should, and yes, we've fallen back into the old habit of leaving uncomfortable things unsaid. So fine. Let's talk. Whatever it is, get it off your chest, because I won't stand for you continuing to think we're ashamed of you. That lie has no more place left in this family, do you understand?"

"Fine." Rose sighed as she adjusted the baby in her arms. "It just seems like, even though we apologized and said things were going to be better, they aren't. You have your life, and I have mine."

"I don't mean for it to be that way." Mary fiddled with the strings on the neckline of her nightgown. "I haven't done a very good job of trying. It's just hard, building a friendship with a sister you've known your whole life, when you should have been friends all along but don't know why you aren't."

And that was the part that always stung. Mary had always seemed oblivious to their differences. To the things that separated them.

"I'll tell you why," Rose said quietly. She looked

down at the baby sleeping peacefully in her arms, wondering if this little girl would ever face the same difficulty in her relationships with her family.

"It was always you and Joseph. Running around, playing your games, but never having room for me. Then, when Joseph went away to find Pa, I thought we could be friends, that you'd finally have room for me. But all we ever did, all we ever talked about, was taking care of the children."

The pain that had begun in her stomach now filled Rose's chest, making it hard to breathe. The words seemed stuck in her throat.

"You had your secret romance, and I had mine." Rose sighed. "Although I did try to tell you about Silas, once. You laughed and said, 'Silas Jones? Why, he's been promised to marry Annie Garrett for just about ever. I can't imagine why you'd think he'd ever be interested in you.'"

Her sister paled, and Rose knew that the very core of the problem between them was that wonderful season before Joseph had discovered their father's mine, changing their dreary existence into one of wealth. Back then, their only hope had been of marrying and finding someone to help them get out from under their aunt's thumb. For Mary and Rose, that had meant secret romances with men they'd thought were the answer to their prayers. But in the end, both sisters had ended up brokenhearted and alone, blaming each other for their heartaches.

"Rose, I had just assumed you knew. Everyone did."

Taking a deep breath, Rose looked at her sister. Hard. "But that's the problem. You assumed. You still do. I came to you after Silas and I had been kissing in the Forresters' orchard, and he asked me to run away with him. Instead of listening and then offering me advice based on what I said, you brushed me aside and repeated what everyone else was saying. But how did that help me, when I'd just offered him my heart, and I thought, he had offered his?"

Mary closed her eyes, but not before a tear trickled out and down her cheek. Then she opened them, and eyes so clear and blue they could have been a mirror of Rose's own stared back at her.

"You're right. I have no defense. I was so busy in my own romantic idylls that I didn't listen to what you had to say. We could have both saved each other a lot of grief had we talked to each other. And then, when Ben came to town last year, I should have been honest about our past relationship. I should have told you—"

"I wouldn't change it, so stop right there. Without my mistake with Ben, I wouldn't have Matthew. And he is worth every bit of scorn I receive for my behavior."

The baby began to stir, and Rose knew she would need to eat soon. "Rehashing the past isn't the point, anyway. It's just that I've never felt we were close, so to hear that you think of me this way doesn't make sense."

Mary nodded slowly. "Will says that I'm often quick to speak my mind, except when I think that people already know what I'm thinking, and then it's like dragging a mule through mud to get me to talk. My deepest desire is for us to be close. I want Rosabelle, Matthew, Catherine and all of the other cousins to be the best of friends. For you to be able to talk to me, and for you to be comfortable relying on us."

If she had ever been brave enough to admit to those thoughts, Rose would have said she wanted the same for herself. She used to watch as Mary, Annabelle, Emma Jane and Polly had sat in their little circle, talking and laughing, but when Rose joined in, they'd become quiet. Mostly, she'd given up on thinking she could be part of that friendship, and instead comforted herself with her regular visits to the Jackson household, where she'd take tea with Emma Jane.

"You and the other ladies don't always include me," Rose said softly, handing the now-fussing baby to her sister.

"Of course we do." Mary took her daughter and got her situated to eat. "When have we ever excluded you?"

Rose sighed. "Lots of times. You'll be talking and laughing, and when I come into the room, you stop."

"Like when? I can't think of such a time."

Rose could. Many times. "Just last month. For Annabelle's going-away tea. We were at Emma Jane's, and you were all laughing, but when I came in the room, you stopped. You whispered something to Annabelle, and then you asked me about the weather. The weather!"

Mary blushed. "It's not what you think. I had questions, about married woman things, and they were giving me advice. It wasn't meant as a slight. I just didn't think… That is… Well, you're not married, so it wouldn't have been appropriate to talk about it in front of you."

Now it was Rose's turn to be embarrassed. She could guess what kind of things Mary had wanted to ask about, especially with the way the other ladies giggled over their husbands sometimes. And, remembering

Helen's frustration at not being let in on all the secrets she thought she should know about, it occurred to Rose that while she had a child, there were still topics of conversation not appropriate for her ears.

"I'm sorry... I just..." She swallowed, wishing she hadn't brought up the subject at all.

"No, I understand. I have slighted you in the past, and though I've apologized, I can see where it would be easy to interpret things in the wrong way. I should have just let you know that's what we'd been talking about, but I was afraid you'd feel bad because you aren't married."

"And I should have just told you that it hurt my feelings and not let it fester." Rose let out a long sigh. "I can't believe you'd want to name your daughter after a sister who is so difficult to get along with."

Mary took Rose's hand in her free hand. "Because my sister is worth it. Because I hope that my daughter works as hard as you to reconcile broken relationships. But mostly, because I so admire you."

Tears filled Mary's eyes again. "I know you love Matthew, but I hate how some of the women in town treat you because of him. I could never walk with my head held high and a smile on my face the way you do."

Rose squeezed her sister's hand and let go. "Yes, you could. If you had to, for your daughter, you would."

Nodding slowly, Mary adjusted the baby in her arms, then turned her to burp her. Her sister was a natural mother, and it showed in the way she handled her baby. Not surprisingly, of course, since she and Rose had all but raised their younger siblings.

Then Mary turned and grinned at her. "Speaking

of reconciling relationships, how are things with you and Silas?"

With a long sigh, Rose shrugged. "Forgiving him isn't easy. I say I do, and I do, but then something comes up to remind me of how much I hurt, or what a scoundrel he was."

She shook her head. "But I also see what an honorable man he is, how good he is with Milly and even the affection with which he speaks of Annie. I know he's not a bad person, and I know he didn't intend to hurt me. But the hurt comes back anyway."

"Are you interested in him romantically?" Mary gave her a knowing smile.

For a moment, Rose sat there, picturing Silas in her mind. Remembering. "I don't know. Am I attracted to him? Yes. He's still the handsomest man I ever laid eyes on. However, I've learned that lasting love is about more than those feelings. I don't know if I trust him, or myself, enough to know that we have more than that."

"You've both grown and changed. You can't base trust on the past."

"True." Rose looked at her sister, older and wiser, wishing she'd been able to talk with her like this in the past. Maybe then it would have saved them all heartache. At least now, she had someone to talk to, even if it felt awkward.

"But part of me wonders. When he came back, he wanted to marry me for Milly's sake. He says he was wrong to assume, but sometimes I think, he's still thinking in that direction."

"Has he said anything to give you any indication of those thoughts?"

Rose sighed again, trying to think back to their conversations. "I suppose not. But the way he looks at me sometimes…" Then she shook her head. "I suppose I'm not making it easy for him. I try to talk to him, to be a friend to him. But it's different. We used to be able to talk about anything, and now it seems harder."

Then she looked at her sister, hoping Mary would be able to give her some wisdom. Hoping she wasn't wrong in trusting Mary with pieces of her heart she'd never entrusted to the other woman before. Talking to Mary about Silas was risky, but if she wanted things to be different between them, then she needed to act differently. Maybe if she started trusting and opening up to Mary, Mary would do the same for her.

"Sometimes I think I shouldn't even be trying to pursue a deep friendship with him. Can a man and woman truly be friends?"

That was the heart of all of her debates over the situation with Silas. Could she offer him her friendship, a gift not easily given, exposing her heart? Would she be able to resist falling in love with him again?

Mary looked thoughtful for a moment. "I think it depends. As an unmarried woman, friendship is how you learn a person's character and find out if you're suited for marriage. As a married woman…" She shrugged. "I'm friends with Jasper because he's married to one of my dearest friends, and he's my husband's best friend. But we don't talk about personal things. The only man I share my heart with is Will. He is my closest friend and the person who knows my heart better than anyone else."

None of which answered Rose's question about Silas

and their friendship. More importantly, what was safe to risk in a friendship with him.

Seeming to sense Rose's hesitation, Mary looked at her intently. "I suppose the real question is what you hope to gain from a deep friendship with Silas. If you're not interested in marrying him, is it fair to engage his heart when someday he'll offer it to another? And if you are interested in marrying him, then maybe you should just be honest with yourself about it, and see where it leads."

The question was designed to get Rose thinking about what she wanted. And while Rose could appreciate her sister's diligence in asking Rose to examine her heart, it didn't make the task any easier.

"But what if I don't know what I want?" Then she sighed. "Or if I'm just fooling myself to think that what I want even exists?"

She looked up at Mary, who bore an expression of such deep love and understanding that Rose wished she'd been more willing to talk with her sister before. So many times, she'd been afraid that Mary would think ill of her, but the respect shining in her sister's eyes told Rose that talking with Mary had done the opposite. Whatever happened between Rose and Silas, Rose and Mary's relationship would be stronger for it.

Adjusting the baby to free her hand, Mary reached for Rose, pulling her into a side hug that required Rose to lean against her sister. She breathed in Mary's warm honey scent and snuggled closer. How many times had she envied her younger siblings the fact that they could climb into Mary's lap and tell her everything?

Mary gave her a squeeze, like having Rose curled up

next to her was exactly what she'd wanted. "We pray, dear sister. We pray."

Tears filled Rose's eyes. "I've always wanted this."

"Me, too." Mary scooted slightly, encouraging Rose to cuddle even closer. "But I never knew how to reach out to you."

Resting her head against her sister's side, Rose said, "I remember reading in books about sisters snuggled in bed together, sharing each other's secrets. I used to wish that could be us, but all those years when we shared a bed, we'd just roll over and sleep, barely saying good-night."

The gentle touch of Mary's hand rubbing her back gave Rose more comfort than she could remember having. "I wished for that too. Sometimes, I'd lay there, rehearsing what I would say, but then I'd lose heart, and say nothing. I'm sorry I never found the courage to talk to you."

"It's all right. I never found the courage, either." She looked up at her sister, who smiled down at her.

"Yes, you did. Just now. And we're not ever going to stop doing this, all right?"

Rose laughed, struggling to sit up. "I think your husband might object to my coming over and spending the night with you in his bed."

"True. But when he's out of town on cases, you can come over with Matthew and spend the night. Will hates leaving me alone at night, so it'll be perfect. Not only can we have sister time, but our children will become close friends."

"I'd like that." Rose smiled at her sister, and for the first time she could remember, her heart was nearly bursting with love for the other woman, who looked so much like her, yet was so different.

"Now about that boy..." Mary grinned mischievously, and even though the matter of what to do with Silas felt small compared to everything else in her life, after this afternoon with her sister, Rose felt confident that the answer to her Silas troubles would come.

Chapter Ten

Silas started to follow Rose up the stairs, but Will held him back. "Mary wanted some time alone with Rose."

Though the sisters appeared to be getting along, Silas had seen enough of their fighting over the years. And the way Rose had been tensing up whenever Mary's name was mentioned lately, being alone with her might not be the best idea right now.

"I think maybe—" As Silas spoke, Will stepped in front of him.

"You're better off not thinking anything contradictory to my wife's wishes." Will grinned, but the look in his eyes was anything but friendly.

"Rose is a little sensitive right now, so I don't know if now is a good time for Mary to be getting anything off her chest."

"What's it to you if Rose is sensitive or not?"

The grin vanished from Will's face. Though he'd always known Will to be a reasonable man, there was no mistaking the threat.

"I'm not allowed to be concerned for her well-being?"

Silas kept his tone light, knowing that Will had taken on a strong brotherly role when it came to the Stone siblings. But Will's interest was more in Mary's comfort, not Rose's.

"Not when you've already broken the lady in question's heart."

The words packed a powerful punch, especially since no one, other than Rose, had ever directly confronted him about what he'd done to her. They'd all seemed to quickly forgive and move on.

"She's forgiven me."

Will shrugged. "A person can forgive, but it doesn't mean you get access to her heart to do it again."

Another punch to the gut, and one Silas supposed he deserved.

"I'm trying to help her." He took a deep breath. "Look, I know you're watching out for Mary and want to make her happy, but Rose is fragile right now, and I'm not sure anyone else sees it."

"So you're going to protect her?" Will crossed his arms over his chest. "Fine sentiment for a man who romanced a lady while engaged to another. When have you ever protected Rose?"

Another direct hit. "What happened between Rose and me is between Rose and me. I protected her plenty back then. Everyone was so caught up in everything happening to everyone but Rose that her needs got missed. So if I have to be the one to take care of them, then—"

Will shook his head. "I don't think so. What do you think that tells a woman, you taking up for her? You can't have it both ways. Either you're interested in her romantically or you need to take a step back and leave it alone."

"Just because I'm not interested in her romantically doesn't mean I can't care about her."

"Wrong," Will said. "If you really care about Rose, then you'll take a step back and let someone else do the caring about her. Anything else implies a more serious interest, and I will not see her getting hurt again. Rose has been through enough. More than anybody should have to, in my opinion."

For the first time, Silas saw through the other man's anger and noticed a deep compassion. Typically Will remained silently on the sidelines, watching over everything and not having much to say. And now Silas understood why. Will was the sentry, standing guard for the family and making sure they were safe.

"Sounds like you may have had this talk a time or two." Silas grinned at Will, finally understanding what he was up to.

"I might have done." He looked unapologetic as he shrugged. "I like to make sure the men who come sniffing around the ladies in our family understand that we will not tolerate hearts being trifled with."

Silas appreciated the protectiveness Will showed toward the women of the family. However, there was one area the other man was blind to. "But you have a vested interest in Mary's happiness, and I'm not sure that's always compatible with Rose."

Will nodded slowly. "I can see where you're coming from. When I first met them, I would have felt the same way. But things are different now. I may have a vested interest in Mary's happiness, but it seems that you're solely focused on Rose."

Clearly the two of them were standing on opposite sides of the fence. And Silas wasn't about to budge. Will had been right. Silas had failed to keep Rose's heart safe. He'd wounded her deeply, and he knew that. Some days he wondered if he could ever forgive himself enough to move on without always feeling responsible for the hurt he'd caused her. Now he had the chance to make things right by protecting her where no one else would.

"If I don't look out for Rose, who will?"

"Do you really think she needs to be protected from her sister?" Will was just trying to keep Silas from hurting Rose, but the other man was clearly hurt that Silas would imply that Mary would hurt Rose.

"No." Silas sighed. "I don't think Mary would intentionally hurt her sister, just like Rose never means to hurt Mary. But they don't always mix as well as everyone would like to think they do. And as much as Rose tried to make Mary and everyone else happy, she can't be anyone but who she is."

Which is what Rose had been doing with him. With Milly. He knew Rose loved Milly, but he also knew—no, not knew, but had just realized—that he wasn't dealing with the real Rose. No, the Rose he'd been dealing with, had been currently defending, was the woman he'd injured, who carried those deep wounds, but pretended she was fine while bleeding on the inside.

"I'm sorry," Silas said slowly. "You're right. I've been thinking so much about how hurt Rose has been by Mary, and wanting to protect her that I'd forgotten that

I'm likely in the same boat. I did hurt her, and while she and everyone else acts like it's fine, I'm not sure it is."

So how did he make it fine? How did he help them get past what he'd done? He could say that he wanted to make it up to her, had been trying to make it up to her, but how did you heal a broken heart?

Will reached forward and patted him on the arm. "And now you're starting to understand. If it helps, Mary knows things aren't right between her and Rose, but she wants to make it better. It's hard, because as you said, Rose pretends everything is fine when it's not."

Then he looked at him—hard. "I know you think we're all blind to it, but we see Rose's pain. It's just none of us know what to do about it. Rose blames herself for everything that happened. I suppose she did make some reckless decisions. We all have. Unfortunately for her, the consequences of her actions are more obvious and more long-lasting. I just wish we knew how to make her understand that we all love her just the same."

Something inside Silas shattered as waves of grief for what he'd done rolled over him. As much as he cared about her and wanted to make things right with Rose, he could never go back to a place where he could love her in such a compassionate way. Will was right. Either Silas had to make the move toward a romantic relationship with her, or he had to let her go.

"I'm sorry," Silas told Will, taking a step back. "You're right. For me to make things better with Rose, to make up for the things that have gone wrong between us, it requires a depth of intimacy that means pursuing a relationship with her. If I push any harder at making things right, I have to fully commit to loving her. As a man would love a wife."

The shattered pieces of Silas's heart clanged against each other, a cacophonous sound in his head that erased all rational thought. The truth was, Silas couldn't be that man for her. Mostly because in seeing how he'd wronged her, he'd realized how deeply unworthy he was of winning her heart. He'd had that chance, and though his motives weren't as ill as everyone would believe, he'd still messed it up.

Silas closed his eyes for a moment, praying that this time he was making the right decision. Then he looked at Will. "I don't deserve her. I can't even begin to approach being the kind of man she deserves. My mistakes…"

"Don't define you." Will looked at him just as firmly as he had when he'd been questioning him about his motives. "Just as we refuse to allow Rose to be defined by hers, so yours do not make you a bad man."

Slack-jawed, Silas stared at him. "Then what was all this about you protecting Rose from me?"

"Just making sure you don't make the same mistake again."

The trouble with Will's advice was that Silas had already made so many mistakes. And if he was honest with himself, he wasn't sure he could claim that he'd be able to steer clear of them in the future. Not when talking with Will was already making him wonder if he hadn't gone too far in entangling his heart with hers. Because the thought of not having Rose in his life was almost too much to bear. He'd lost her once. He wasn't sure if he could afford to lose her again.

Fortunately, he was saved from having to give any kind of answer to a man dead set on holding him accountable, because Rose came down the stairs with Mary, carrying a baby. Even without seeing the baby up close, he could tell that she had the same dark hair as her mother, her aunt and her baby cousin. Not shocking, and yet he was surprised by the longing that hit him hard in the gut.

He couldn't deny wanting Rose, couldn't deny wanting a family with her. But was it even possible?

Something was different about Silas, Rose thought as she saw him standing with Will when she came down the stairs. Or maybe it was her and the healing she'd found in her relationship with Mary.

"What are you doing out of bed?" Will said, rushing to his wife's side.

Mary groaned. "I just had a baby... I'm not dying." Then she turned to Rose. "You must promise to spend more time with me so he'll go back to work and stop hovering."

The simple request twisted Rose's heart in a way that nearly made tears of gratitude spring to her eyes. Everyone always wanted Rose's help with the work, but her sister asking for what amounted to emotional support felt...

How could all of her dreams come true so easily?

Silas coughed, and Rose realized there was one dream that wouldn't come so easy.

A husband. A man to share her life with. It was easy enough to tell everyone she didn't need one, but when she saw how Will treated Mary, loving and protecting her, the longing in Rose's heart was almost too much to bear.

Could a man love her like that?

Though she bore no personal shame for her mistakes, too many others would never let her forget. Could a man look at her with the same kind of love Will had for Mary, knowing her past? The men who'd tried to court her since her fall from grace all made their lustful intentions known, or they'd made the practicality of a marriage the forefront of the discussion. But none had taken a look inside Rose's heart and wanted it for his own.

Mary had asked about Silas, and Rose had no answer for her. Did Silas see Rose's heart? Or was it something else? Memories of a past they could never recapture, Milly's need for a mother, even Silas's need for companionship. But those things, they were not enough. Not when she knew that a woman could have all that and more.

The trouble was, how was Rose, who'd demonstrated such poor judgment about men in the past, to know when she'd found it?

"Are you ready to return home?" Silas asked, holding out his arm as though he already knew her answer.

Rose glanced up at Mary to see if Mary was ready to let her leave, and she nodded. "Yes. Thank you."

One thing that had become clear in Rose's conversation with her sister was that Rose needed to do a better job of guarding her heart. At least until Rose knew what she wanted out of friendship with Silas.

It wasn't fair, to him or to her, for her to so freely give her heart when neither of them knew if they had any kind of future together.

She gave him a polite smile, then hugged her sister one last time. Not in a goodbye forever way, but in a way that said they had so much more to look forward to. Then she hugged her brother-in-law goodbye, congratulating him again on little Rosabelle's birth.

Even hugging Will felt different, like she finally belonged as a part of his family. Mary had been right, she did keep people closed off, and it was time to do things differently. To be brave even when she wasn't sure she'd receive a favorable response.

Taking Silas's arm, Rose left the house, feeling like she'd left behind a lot of garbage she hadn't needed to carry around.

"Is everything all right?" Silas asked once they made their way to the street.

"It's fine," Rose said quietly, part of her wishing she could share her joy with him, but the other part questioning the wisdom of letting him become her confidant once again.

Losing Silas to Annie hadn't just been about the pain of falling in love, then finding her heart gone. In a lot of ways, during the loneliest time of her life, he'd been her best friend. Her only friend.

People had questioned why Rose had so easily run away with Ben. But they hadn't realized the depth of her loneliness. How isolated she'd been in a new place with no one she felt like she could confide in. She'd been carrying around so much hurt, and Ben had fed it, asking her questions, encouraging her to let it all out. Of course, Ben had his motivation for wanting Rose to talk to him, but she hadn't known it at the time. He'd used her pain to his advantage, and in the end, Rose had only been hurt worse.

So now, with all these wonderful things in her heart, how could Rose express them to Silas without becoming reliant on him? If they didn't end up married to each other, could Rose bear losing such a close friend again? But was Silas a man she could marry?

Rose continued walking, choosing to remain silent.

"What does 'fine' mean?" Silas asked, slowing their pace. "Is everything all right between you and Mary?"

Of course he would ask that. How many times had he listened to her tearfully recount the ways in which her sister had wounded her? Mostly because she'd felt left out or slighted or taken advantage of. Mary had never been cruel. But Rose had.

Rosabelle. Of all the gifts Rose had ever received, this was probably the greatest. For all the things Rose had done to her sister, wronged her and behaved selfishly, Mary saw past them and into Rose's heart. Her sister loved her.

"Yes," Rose said. And then, because it was the closest she could come to spilling all the delicious happiness of their newfound bond, she added, "They're naming the baby for me. And Annabelle. Rosabelle, they're calling her. She wanted my blessing."

Her heart overflowed with joy, but she kept it to herself, quietly celebrating the beauty of reconciliation, wishing she could share it with Silas, but reminding herself that things had changed between them.

"That's nice," he said, giving her a strange look. "It sounds like things are improving between you two."

"They are. Thank you for asking."

Not her most profound speech, and certainly confusing to Silas, who was used to her pouring out all of her thoughts and feelings, but in a way, it felt good to know that she could exert some control over herself and her emotions.

"You know you don't have to pretend with me," he said slowly, stopping, then turning to face her. "What's really going on? On one hand, you seem happy, but on the other hand, you're more distant than you've ever been."

One more thing that Silas would be the one to notice. He'd always been able to see through her, and he'd never been one to accept her excuses that hid her true feelings.

But perhaps it was good for them to get things out in the open. Especially now that she'd committed to living differently.

"Mary reminded me of the importance of guarding my heart around you. I'm too free with my thoughts and feelings. While I value you and your friendship, I need to be more careful of my emotions."

He looked like she'd just shot him. She'd seen a woman shot once, by one of Ben's men, and the image of the woman's face was still clearly imprinted in her mind. Now it was as though the woman's features had been transformed into Silas's.

"You don't really forgive me, do you?"

No wonder he looked so wounded.

But what could she say?

"I'm trying."

It was the only answer she could give, but even that seemed insufficient. Guarding her heart was one thing, but she did owe him a deeper explanation.

Rose took a deep breath, then looked up at him. "This isn't about how you hurt me in the past, but how I need to keep my heart safe for the future. I don't know if there is anything in store for us beyond friendship, and until I know the answer, both in my heart and yours, I can't open up to you the way I once did. It isn't fair to either one of us, and it certainly isn't fair to our potential spouses."

She'd expected him to argue with her, or at least act like her words came as a surprise. Instead, he nodded.

"Will told me something similar." Then he sighed. "But what are we to do? I can't pretend that I don't value your opinion, or that you aren't someone I rely on. Will I marry again? I don't know. But I do know that I will be loyal to my future wife, no matter what. Once I married Annie, I abandoned all thoughts of you. Why can't we stay friends?"

Rose took a deep breath. Never in all her life had she been one to end a relationship, but here, now, Silas's words made it clear exactly why they couldn't continue on as they had.

"Because the kind of friendship you're trying to build with me, the kind of friendship we had, will be devastating to lose again. You didn't just break my heart, Silas, you took away my only friend when I needed one the most. I won't be hurt like that again."

The only person Rose had ever slapped was her sister, and she regretted that action every day. Though she hadn't raised her hand to him, Silas bore the same expression Mary had the one time Rose had slapped her. They'd fought and Rose had said terrible things in a fit of anger and hurt, and in the aftermath, Rose had found no satisfaction. But this time, watching the waves of pain on Silas's face, Rose had no regret. Because as they slowly subsided, she saw the realization dawn on him that she was right.

"You were my closest friend, too," he said slowly.

"So it's not fair to either of us to continue. Not unless our hearts are turned in the direction of marrying each other. And I'm not sure that's possible right now." Without waiting for his response, she continued down the sidewalk the few doors to the parsonage.

They could have talked about it more, she supposed. But there wasn't much left to say. For the first time, Rose was saying what she wanted in a relationship, not gratefully accepting the crumbs she was offered. And even though letting go wasn't the easiest thing she'd ever done, Rose felt freer than she ever had.

Chapter Eleven

Silas couldn't argue with Rose's words. Or even her sentiment. How many times had he wished he'd had someone to talk to once things ended with Rose? He didn't have that same closeness with his wife, and he sometimes wondered if Annie knew and resented it. She'd known about Rose—not all the details, because he'd wanted to spare her that. But when they fought, Annie had often accused him of not loving her the way he did Rose.

And she'd been right.

He hated how that shame haunted him. How, despite his best efforts to be a good husband, he couldn't love Annie in the same way he'd loved Rose. He'd tried, and he would stand by the idea that he'd done his best by her. But even in the best moments of their marriage, he'd ached from the loneliness of not having anyone he could talk to the way he'd talked to Rose.

Could he do that again?

Now more than ever, his idea of marrying Rose to give Milly a mother seemed like the worst he'd ever had. Though he was working on his relationship with Rose, it wasn't the same.

He thought about his discussion with Will, and that to pursue the kind of deep friendship he'd once had with Rose, he would need to pursue marriage. To fully commit his heart to her and follow it to the eventual end.

Could marriage work between them?

Silas shook his head. Not when she was still trying to forgive him. Just as he was willing to give her his all, she needed to give him hers. Which couldn't happen if she still harbored mistrust in her heart.

He quickly followed her onto the porch. "Rose, wait."

She stopped and looked at him, a new hardness to her face he hadn't noticed before. "I told you, we can't—"

"I know. And I'm not asking you to. I just wanted to tell you that I understand."

Her face softened and her posture relaxed.

Silas swallowed and took a deep breath. "You weren't the only one who lost a valuable friend. We made a lot of mistakes."

His chest hurt, weighing on him heavier than any of the rocks coming out of the mine. "I made a lot of mistakes."

For a moment, she looked like she was going to speak, but he held his hand up. "No. I need to take responsibility for my actions. I know you made your mistakes, but I did you the greatest wrong because I should have been honest with you about what I was dealing with. I hid it from you because I was afraid you weren't going to talk to me anymore, and truth is, I couldn't face what I knew I had to do."

He'd never tried justifying himself or making excuses, but this seemed like the only moment he might ever have to give her the apology she deserved.

"I loved you, Rose. I meant every word I said to you, and I honestly intended to run away with you like we'd planned. But I stopped to give Ma a hug goodbye, and then Pa walked in the door, dejected because the bank wasn't going to give him an extension. I knew if I married Annie, all those problems would go away."

The emotions that played on her face were a mixture of hurt and understanding, but mostly unreadable. Nothing that spoke of the absolution he desperately wanted to receive.

"I took the coward's way out." He shook his head. "No, I wouldn't call it that. I thought I was being brave, marrying someone I didn't love to save them. I guess I took the easy way out. I didn't fight for what was right, and I didn't ask your opinion. So I immediately went to the Garrett place and did what I had to do."

He'd had to stop on the way to throw up. It had made him sick to think of not being with Rose, but that detail probably wouldn't serve any purpose. Not now. Not when Rose wasn't in a place where she could open her heart to him.

"I should have told you." Silas looked her in the eye. "I should have told you from the beginning that my parents were having trouble hanging on to the farm, and that Mr. Garrett had made it clear that if I married Annie, those troubles would be over. I'm sorry for the way my omissions hurt you."

Rose nodded slowly. "I'd heard as much. I should have asked you. Talking with Mary today, I realized that I've done a lot of assuming in my life. We all do."

Though she gave him grace, she hadn't accepted his apology. She hadn't offered him forgiveness. Then again, she'd said the words before, and while he knew she meant them, he also knew she was working through living that out.

She looked at him with the same unreadable expression she'd worn the whole time he'd tried apologizing.

"Had you been courting her all along?"

Nothing he said to justify his answer would make it better. "I'd been calling on her, yes."

Rose nodded slowly, her brow furrowed like it was when she was thinking deeply. "To what end?"

He'd spent those days desperately hoping that Annie would find some flaw in him, decide they didn't suit or confess that she, too, was in love with another. But mostly, they'd just sat on her porch, staring out at the farm, making small talk about the weather.

"To get to know each other, figure out if a match would work." Which made him sound like a terrible person. If a man had done that to Milly, he'd call him out.

"You have to know that I didn't touch her, didn't kiss her, didn't make any romantic gestures. Our first kiss was on our wedding day, and I took no pleasure in—"

"I don't want to know." Rose stopped him with the kind of glare she usually reserved for the most heinous of crimes. "I appreciate that you want to explain what happened. And I do understand. I don't fault you for doing what you think was right for your family. I might have done the same. I meant what I said about forgiving you. But it doesn't make my heart any less wary."

There wasn't supposed to be sympathy in her eyes.

She wasn't supposed to look like she cared about him. But she did.

"This isn't about you owing me anything over our past. But about me needing to live my life differently so I can have the future I deserve. And for you." Her shoulders rose and fell as she took a deep breath.

"If you'd truly seen me as the kind of friend you claim I was, you wouldn't have hesitated to tell me what was going on. I don't know how I would have reacted, but I do know that the kind of man I want is the kind of man who will always tell me the truth, no matter how unpleasant, and trust me to find a solution together. I know you think you loved me, and that I was your closest friend, but maybe you need to take a look at your definition of love."

She turned and reached for the door. "Please don't bother me again with your attempts at rehashing our past. I'm tired of having to live my life to justify my past, and I'd like to be free of this, as well."

Before he could respond, the door opened and Maddie came out, holding a wailing Matthew. Rose scooped him into her arms and dashed inside.

Maddie gave Silas a nod. "It's best you let things go between you and Rose. She doesn't need no man to make up for her past. Well, I don't think she needs a man at all. But if one wants her, then he'd best be prepared to fight for her future."

"How much of that conversation did you hear?"

Maddie grinned. "There ain't no secrets in these parts. Especially when you're doing all your talking on the front porch. So you mark my words. If you want

Rose, then you fight for her. And if you're not sure, then you leave her be."

That seemed to be everyone's warning.

So why couldn't he leave her alone?

He started to pass, but Maddie stood in his way. "I want your word. I won't have our girl hurt again."

Silas closed his eyes. Rose, the girl he'd spent so long loving and protecting because no one else seemed to notice her, now had so many protectors, he was being pushed away. He'd have liked to have been a part of that group, but Will's warning rang in his head.

"You have my word."

Maddie nodded at him. "Milly's in the back with Nugget. You should join her. Seems to me a man fighting to keep his little girl ought to be spending time with her instead of mooning over a woman he's not committed to."

Of all the blows that had landed on him all day, this had to be the worst. He'd been so focused on the situation with Rose, he hadn't given his full attention to Milly. The day was almost gone, and tomorrow, they'd be busy with church, and he'd agreed to let the Garretts have her afterward. Then he'd be back to work the next day, leaving just a few precious evening hours for him to spend with her.

"I'll get to it then."

This time, Maddie let him pass, and he went directly to the backyard where the children were all running around, playing some sort of game of tag.

Milly noticed him before he could call her name. She ran to him, her little legs moving faster than he'd ever seen them. With all the vigor her energetic young body held, she launched herself into his arms.

"Papa! I pway wif da kids!"

"Are you having fun?"

Milly nodded, her golden braids flopping around her head. She didn't have much hair, barely enough to braid, but she'd wanted braids just like the other girls, so somehow, Rose had found a way to make it work.

One more thing he admired about Rose. She'd given his daughter so much, and constantly sought out ways to meet her needs.

"You will pway wif us?"

"How do I play?"

Milly grinned. "Nugget! Papa will pway wif us!"

Nugget picked up a ball, then ran over to them. She briefly explained his role, which seemed to consist largely of him throwing the ball to them, but it didn't matter. The delight on his daughter's face would have made him willing to do just about anything.

Maddie had been right. Spending time focused on the situation with Rose took away from what was most important to him right now.

He picked up the ball and tossed it at the girls, who giggled and ran after it. This game was like nothing he'd seen before, and by the way Nugget explained things, likely something they'd made up on their own. Laughter rang out through the yard, and the girls brought the ball back to him, asking him to throw it again.

Silas threw the ball, and once again, they chased after it, their smiles contagious as he found himself feeling lighter than he had in a long time.

"What's all this commotion?" Rose stepped outside, carrying a now-smiling Matthew.

"Ma-few!"

Milly dropped the ball and ran toward them. "Ma-few pway wif us?"

"I think he's too little to play ball, but we can sit here and watch."

Rose sat on one of the chairs they had in the back for that very purpose. As she adjusted her hold on the baby, Milly climbed into her lap.

"I sit wif you and Ma-few."

There wasn't a prettier picture in all the world than the sight of his daughter on Rose's lap, tickling the baby in her arms.

"I wuv Ma-few."

Of all the things Silas wished he could give Milly, a baby brother or sister was the hardest to deny her. The trouble with Rose giving him permission to grieve the child he'd lost with his wife was that it made moments like these harder.

Someday, Milly was going to ask for a brother or sister of her own.

Milly leaned forward and gave the baby a big, wet kiss on the forehead.

"Matthew loves you, too," Rose said softly, giving Milly a squeeze.

Then Milly jumped down to go back to play.

"Papa! Is you's turn!"

Ignoring the gentle smile radiating Rose's inner beauty, Silas turned back to his daughter. He picked up the ball and threw it again.

So many things he wanted for the future—his and

Milly's. Though he would have liked to have given them all more thought, he had to remind himself that what he had now was enough. Even if he was tempted by the image of a certain raven-haired woman that kept popping into his head. Maybe someday he'd be able to pursue that idea. Maybe they'd both be healed enough to build a new foundation for their relationship.

Until then, he had Milly. And that was enough. It had to be.

Rose watched as Silas played with the children. The air was warm for November, but growing chilly, and soon they wouldn't be able to spend much time outside anymore. They'd been fortunate with such good weather so far, but it wouldn't last.

She pulled her shawl tighter around her and the baby. Milly's infectious laugh rang out and Matthew seemed to perk up. His head turned toward the sound, and she propped him up to get a better view. She hadn't been lying when she told Milly that Matthew loved her. Sometimes it didn't seem like a bad idea to take Silas up on his offer of marriage, even though he'd withdrawn it. Marrying him wouldn't be so bad. They did get along, and clearly they were attracted to one another. But was it the deep, lasting love everyone around her shared?

Rose sighed as she looked down at her baby, whose gaze seemed to follow Milly everywhere she went.

Would it be so wrong to settle for good enough for the sake of her son?

Milly darted by, then stopped. She ran back and swooped in to kiss Matthew's cheek. Just as quickly, she turned and ran off.

Silas joined Rose, falling into the chair next to hers. "She sure has a lot of energy."

"Yes. But she'll sleep well tonight."

A gust of wind hit, chilling her. "I should probably get Matthew inside."

"Don't want him to catch a cold," Silas said with a soft smile like he didn't quite believe her. Was he, like Mary, accusing her of using Matthew as an excuse to avoid being with him?

"The others should come in soon, too. They don't feel the cold because they're having fun, but soon we'll have little red noses, and if they turn into colds, it will be no fun for any of us."

He gave her a look that made her feel warm inside, but not in the way she used to feel. It wasn't one of desire or passion, or anything else she could name. Just warm.

"You're right," he said slowly. "But is it so wrong to not want this to end? I'm throwing a ball to my daughter and her friend, and though it seems so mundane, I can't help but want to hold on to the moment for as long as I can."

"There will be other moments," Rose said, standing.

Milly came running up to her. "Ma-few stay wif us."

Reaching down to give the little girl a squeeze, Rose said, "I think we should all go inside. We need to have something hot to drink and warm up."

"Maddie make cookies?" Blue eyes looked up at her hopefully.

"It's awfully close to supper," Rose said, knowing that in spite of her warning, Maddie was likely to still find the children each a small treat.

Nugget joined them, breathless and grinning. "We can talk her into one. I'll show you."

Without waiting for Rose, Nugget held out her hand to the little girl and they ran inside.

Rose glanced at Silas, who was shaking his head. "They are something else."

"They are. But I'm glad Nugget has Milly, with Polly and her family in Denver right now. It's good for Milly, too. I used to hate having so many siblings, but now I see how the children interact, and I realize that they need each other."

Rose smiled at him, noting that the usual pang in her heart over the lack of closeness with Mary didn't seem as strong. The childhood she didn't get didn't seem to matter as much now. Not when she could still feel the warmth of her sister's arms around her.

"Does it bother you about Nugget?"

Silas's question seemed to come out of nowhere, though Rose knew many still wondered what it was like to lose both parents only to find an illegitimate sister who was the product of one of her father's affairs.

"I can hardly cast stones, now can I?"

He put his hand on her elbow. "That's not what I meant. I was just wondering…" Then he sighed. "I don't know what I'm trying to say. Sometimes I marvel at how seamlessly your family has come together. You love Nugget the same as anyone else."

"Why wouldn't I?" Rose shivered again, noting the sun was getting lower over the hills beyond.

"Sorry, I don't mean to keep you. I guess I wonder, how easy is it to love a child not your own? I see you with Nugget and Milly, and you make it look like it's the most natural thing in the world."

What was he trying to say? That he would have a hard time loving a child that wasn't his? That he wasn't sure he could love Matthew? Rose clamped her mouth shut. Was this why she needed to guard her heart against him?

"You treat them the same," Silas continued. "As each other, as Matthew."

"Why wouldn't I?" She sounded defensive, she knew, but he seemed so incredulous that it felt like, well, like he hardly knew her at all.

"Not everyone would." His brow furrowed and he looked lost in thought for a moment. Turning his attention back to her, his gaze met hers.

"Milly is so happy here, with all of you." Silas looked away, his gaze focused on the mountains in the distance. "Could she find the same love and care anywhere else?"

Rose smiled at him. Of course he'd be thinking about Milly and how there were still so many uncertainties in their lives. The Garretts seemed resigned to the situation, but even she knew that they were barely tolerating it.

"We'll fight for Milly just the same as we'll fight for one of our own. Has there been any word from the lawyer you've been speaking to?"

Silas shrugged. "He says that I have the law on my side, but it would be best if we found a way to work things out with the Garretts."

"As it should be." Rose wanted to reach out and grab his hand to give it a squeeze, to let him know that she was on his side, no matter what. But it seemed too intimate a gesture, particularly given that she'd been so vocal in making sure he understood the lines they could not cross.

Instead, she smiled at him. "Come, let's see what the girls have talked Maddie into. I know I could use a cup of tea at the very least."

He nodded. "I know the Garretts have no legal grounds to stand on, but I can't help but worry about her. What will happen if she ends up with them?"

"She won't," Rose said, hoping her confidence gave him enough of his own to rely on. But the truth was, Leadville was a dangerous place, and none of them were guaranteed tomorrow. If something happened to Silas, as much as she hated to admit it, Milly would, indeed, end up living with the Garretts.

Unless, of course, Silas took a wife.

Could Rose stand to watch Silas marry another?

Now that was the question she wasn't ready to face. Her heart had almost not survived the first time. She might not be able to see him as her husband, but Rose wasn't stupid enough to think she'd be unaffected watching him court another.

Chapter Twelve

Silas left Milly every day to go to work, but watching her leave with the Garretts tore his heart in a way he hadn't expected. Would Milly be all right? Would they see some defect in her that gave them the ability to take her away?

Plus, this wasn't like letting Milly spend time with them in the parlor. They were taking her to the dining room in the hotel, a fine place, a place where the antics of a two-year-old wouldn't be welcomed.

"She'll be fine," Rose said in his ear. "The worst that can happen is that Milly will misbehave, and the Garretts will bring her home."

"No," he said quietly. "The worst that can happen is that they'll find some excuse to take her from me. I don't know why, but as well as things are going, I can't get rid of the feeling that something bad is going to happen."

"Welcome to being a parent." She smiled at him. Then she turned to greet Frank. "Uncle Frank, we have a worried father over here."

Frank clapped his hand on Silas's back. "Ah, yes. It is hard to let them go. But our Milly will be fine. You'll see."

Our Milly. Once again, he marveled at how quickly his daughter had become a part of the family. Not as a possession, the way the Garretts seemed to view her, but as someone they loved and cared for.

And yet, it didn't make him feel any better.

"Come," Frank said. "I'd like your help in moving some tables to get ready for supper, and I believe Rose was needed in the kitchen."

Rose gave a small nod as if to indicate her understanding, then headed for the kitchen. He couldn't help but watch the graceful way she moved, stopping to greet people she knew. But he also noticed how there were others she carefully avoided.

Did anyone else notice?

"She is something else, isn't she?" Frank asked.

Not this again. But how did Silas say so politely when it was only Frank's generosity that had given him any hope for being able to keep Milly?

"Indeed," Silas said, trying to tear his gaze from her but failing as an older matron grabbed her daughter by the arm and yanked her in the other direction so as not to cross paths with Rose.

How did everyone stand there and just watch? Surely he wasn't the only one who noticed the way people still treated Rose. He took a step forward, but he felt Frank's hand on his arm.

"It's not worth it."

"But it's Rose." He stared at the other man. "How can you let people treat her like that?"

Frank nodded slowly. "I've had a good many talks with Mrs. Davis. She's not able to comprehend that her own sin makes her just as in need of the Lord as our Rose. So what do I do? Do I shun her the way she shuns our Rose?"

He shook his head. "No. I believe the only way to change a person's heart is with love. To continue to love Mrs. Davis, even when our human minds cannot fathom why. That is why we have the strength of the Lord."

The conversation didn't seem to be about how people treated Rose, but about his own behavior toward the Garretts. Yes, he'd recognized the grief underlying their actions. But they'd been hard people to deal with even before Annie's death.

Silas swallowed. "How do you do that?"

"You pray. And you let the Lord guide you." Frank let out a long sigh. "It's not as easy as I make it sound. I have struggled many times over how to treat someone who mistreats me and my family, but I've learned the hard way that repaying evil for evil is the wrong way to live."

Silas stared at him. "Isn't that in the Bible?"

"More or less." Frank grinned. "Of course, if we just listened to Jesus in the first place, then learning the hard way wouldn't be necessary."

"I can't imagine you learning anything the hard way." Silas looked sideways at the older man, who still grinned.

"You'd be surprised. I've made more than my share of mistakes, which is why I can so freely give grace to others. I only give what I have been given myself."

Rose had given him a great deal of grace. Despite her

struggles to forgive him, she'd opened her heart to his daughter, who'd blossomed under her care. She might think she couldn't forgive him, but her actions indicated a level of grace that he wasn't sure he'd be able to give someone who'd hurt him. After all, Milly had barely left, and he was already questioning the wisdom of letting the Garretts have access to her.

Someone said something to Rose, and she started back toward them. At least this would prevent another awkward conversation about his intentions toward her.

Frank gave him another pat on the back. "I'm sure she's coming to remind me of something I'm supposed to be doing. I don't know what I'd do without everyone around here managing me."

"I'm sure you'd manage just fine." Silas grinned at the other man, who shrugged.

"Maybe, but I sure am grateful I don't have to find out." He gave Silas a measuring glance. "I hope you figure out things between you and Rose before it's too late. I know our Rose has her thorns, but it's the prickliest ones that produce the most beautiful flowers. There is nothing more wonderful than the love of a good woman. The two of you might be fighting it, but I pray you'll find your way together."

The expression on Rose's face told him that she'd heard every word.

"Uncle Frank! I thought you said that matchmaking was best left to the old ladies who had nothing better to do with their time."

Her flushed cheeks were supposed to be indicative of her fury, but Silas couldn't help but think they added to her charm and beauty.

"Who said anything about matchmaking?" Frank's eyes twinkled. "I was merely pointing out that with the way sparks are flying between the two of you, Silas needs to start thinking about making his intentions toward you clear."

Then he turned his attention back to Silas. "It's easy for a man to trifle with a woman's heart when no one's said anything about marriage and the future. But once a man makes his feelings known—"

"This is ridiculous." Rose's eyes blazed, the lovely blue shade sending sparks that could probably be seen for miles. "You think all it takes to keep a woman's heart safe is to promise marriage? Silas could promise to marry me right now, and I wouldn't believe it. You think he hasn't done so before? You don't think Ben promised to marry me before I ran away with him?"

She gave the kind of bitter laugh Silas didn't expect her capable of. "Men will say all sorts of pretty things to get what they want from a woman. But do they mean them?"

Rose shook her head, a few dark tendrils escaping from her perfectly coiffed style. "Not in my experience."

She shot Silas the same look she'd given him yesterday, filled with all the anger he deserved. "You can say you loved me all you want. But your actions showed otherwise. I will not allow myself to be taken in again. I can forgive you, and I have, over and over, but it doesn't mean I know the difference between your truths and lies. Which means I don't trust you, and I won't because I don't know what to trust."

Every word she spoke was like an arrow to a different place in Silas's heart. He'd apologized, tried to show his remorse for his actions, but even now, despite the progress they'd made in their relationship, it wasn't enough. The pain wasn't just about how he felt about the situation, but in knowing how deeply he'd wounded someone he cared about.

Squaring her shoulders, Rose turned her attention back to Frank. "I know you mean well, and I'm sure you're not the only person in this family to warn Silas about hurting me. But you need to leave this be. And you need to tell everyone else the same. My heart is not in danger here."

The tears in her eyes brought an ache to the very deepest part of Silas's heart. How could he have not seen how shattered she'd been by his thoughtless actions?

"I'm not sure I have a heart left to offer anyone." Rose brushed at the corners of her eyes with her fingertips. "I already gave it up—twice. The first time, I had it broken in a most cruel way, and the second, all the remaining pieces were burned to a crisp."

Rose gave him a look, not of the anger he deserved for what she deemed his cruelty, but of such deep sorrow, he wasn't sure he could bear the weight of the expression. But he deserved it. So he met her gaze.

"There is nothing but ashes left, and I cannot imagine what it would take for me to even consider offering them to someone else. I must be one hundred percent convinced of a man's honor first. If family is warning you away out of a misguided sense of your feelings, that's one thing. But if there is any genuine desire in your heart for me, then you'd best be prepared for the fight of your life. Because I will not be trifled with again."

Without a backward glance, Rose flounced off, head high and back straight. She paused when a woman stopped her, first putting a gloved hand to her mouth, then shaking her head.

"I think she was supposed to tell me that Mrs. Montgomery wanted a word with me, then forgot in the emotion of the moment." Frank's voice was tinged with humor.

"I never meant to trifle with Rose," Silas said quietly. "I had no idea my actions would cause her so much pain."

"I know." Frank patted his back gently. "We often say things without thinking, good things, reflecting what we feel in our hearts at the time, but sometimes they're best left unsaid. Anyone can see that you care for Rose, but if you don't know for a one hundred percent fact that you're going to marry her, you should make your feelings less obvious."

Less obvious. He thought he'd been doing a good job of it, especially because he wasn't certain they had a future together. "I just want to make amends for what I've done."

Frank gave him a long, searching look like somehow he could read the deeper meaning in Silas's words.

"Then keep your distance. Rose can't help but care for those around her, even when she thinks she's guarding her heart. She's more sensitive than she lets on, so until such a time comes as you are officially courting her, I ask that you put more space between you and her."

If Frank's expression didn't contain a great deal of compassion, Silas might have thought he was being chased away.

"I'll do better to watch myself," Silas told him, wondering what he was going to be able to talk to her about if they could only stick to safe subjects.

"I appreciate that." Frank clapped him on the back again as the woman Rose had just been speaking to approached.

"Mrs. Montgomery. So good to see you."

"Pastor." She gave him a small nod, then gestured to the young woman standing awkwardly behind her. A beauty, at least by most men's standards, but not enough to tempt Silas.

"You remember my daughter, Flora? She's been spending time with my sister, Bernice, in Denver."

"Yes, of course. Flora."

The girl nodded her head but didn't speak.

Frank gestured to him. "Have you ladies met Silas Jones? He's running the Stone mine in Joseph's absence. His wife recently passed away, and our Rose has been caring for his daughter."

"It is a pleasure," Mrs. Montgomery said, smiling at him. "I imagine your daughter must be the darling girl we see Rose with on our visits around town."

"Indeed, she is." Silas couldn't help the feeling of pride to hear another woman compliment his daughter, particularly given all the Garretts' nasty comments about how Rose's influence would ruin Milly's reputation.

"I was hoping you might have an idea of some gainful employment for Flora. I do think a young lady shouldn't spend all of her time idle, and since she's not welcome at the mission, I'm at a loss as to how to keep her occupied. Someone looking for a nanny, perhaps?"

Flora turned her attention to Silas, smiling and batting her eyes in a ridiculous manner. "I could help with your daughter. It has to be such a strain, your child being cared for by a woman who—"

"I do hope your next words are intended to be positive and encouraging, my dear." Frank looked pleasant enough, but everyone knew the underlying threat. "And you know you are most welcome at the mission, provided you can be kind to the other women there."

Flora's face reddened, and Silas realized that this method of deflecting criticism about Rose's circumstances probably worked better than most.

Mrs. Montgomery glared at her daughter, then said pleasantly, "I'm sure she only meant to say that it must be difficult to care for an infant and such a young child at the same time. I remember those days well, and if Rose ever needs some time to herself, I'm sure Flora would be happy to lend a hand."

The scowl on Flora's face told Silas she'd be anything but happy to help Rose, but she wasn't going to argue with her mother. Not when she'd already been called out for her bad behavior. Though Silas didn't know the other girl, he knew enough to know that he wasn't about to use Flora if Rose was unable to care for Milly.

"We appreciate that," Frank said with a smile. "I don't know of anyone needing a nanny at this time, but I'll be sure to let you know if I do. In the meantime, the mission has greatly appreciated all of the lovely blankets you've been knitting. I'm sure we'll always have a need for cozy blankets."

Mrs. Montgomery sent another glare her daughter's

way. "Thank you, Pastor. We are so grateful to be able to aid in the church's mission to serve the less fortunate."

Then she gave Silas a sly look. "And if you should ever care to join our family for supper, I'm sure you won't find a more welcoming table. Our cook prepares the finest pies you'll ever taste."

He should have expected that at some point, a matchmaking mama would seek him out as the future husband of her daughter. Though Leadville had a good many more men than women, general society agreed that most men weren't suitable for their daughters. They were too rough around the edges, and their positions gave little hope of a promising future for a young lady. Though Silas wasn't a rich man, his place at the Stone mine made him a better prospect than most.

"Thank you for the kind invitation, but, I prefer to spend my evenings at home with my daughter."

An easy enough excuse, but as he felt Rose's eyes upon him, he knew that there was another reason. The real reason he wouldn't be dining with the Montgomerys or any other family with marriageable daughters.

"Of course," Mrs. Montgomery said with the polite smile that told him she understood he had other reasons for refusing her invitation. "Just know that you're welcome anytime."

"I'm honored." Silas nodded at her, then looked over at Frank, who wore an amused expression that he was loath to find out the reason behind. "If you'll excuse me, I believe the ladies needed me to help them move a table."

As he walked toward the barn that housed the mission, Silas thought about his disinterest in furthering his acquaintance with the Montgomerys. True, Flora seemed rather unpleasant, but it was more than that. The thought of getting to know any other woman churned his stomach.

It was Rose who consumed his thoughts, and, though he hated to admit it, already owned a large chunk of his heart. Pursuing her meant risking his in a way he'd never done before. Frank and Will had made it clear that if Silas were to step up, he needed to give Rose his all—at the risk of being rejected outright.

The only way he'd ever heal the wounds he'd caused would be to put back together the broken pieces of her heart, mending it with his own. Could he prove his honor to her? Could he be the man she needed?

Succeeding meant taking Rose as his wife. Failure meant carrying around his own bag of ashes.

Rose sank into the chair, grateful that Matthew had finally gone to sleep. Though she was only gone a few hours, the entire household seemed to miss having Milly around. Which meant Matthew, used to her presence, had spent most of the afternoon fussing. She'd finally given in and fed him some of the mashed potatoes left over from lunch, which he devoured before promptly falling asleep.

She looked at the clock. The Garretts hadn't given any indication as to what time they'd be bringing Milly home, but surely it would be soon. Like Matthew, Milly was prone to crankiness when she didn't get her nap in time. Which should have happened nearly an hour ago.

Just as she closed her eyes, she heard footsteps on

the porch. She quickly went to the door, opening it as soon as the knock sounded.

"Rosey!" Milly launched herself into Rose's waiting arms.

"Did you have fun?" Rose hugged the little girl close, then looked up at the Garretts. "Was it a good visit?"

"We were pleasantly surprised at how well Millicent behaved." Mrs. Garrett sniffed as though she hated to give such praise. "Of course, as she gets older, she'll need better education in deportment, and I do think you should work with her on enunciating her words because sometimes she is rather hard to understand."

Then she looked over at her husband, who nodded. "But everyone at the restaurant thought her charming, and many greeted her as though they knew her. It seems Millicent is quite popular. She has a good many friends who seem to be of an acceptable social status."

High accolades indeed.

"Who did you meet?" Rose picked up Milly and held her in her arms. "I'm sorry, do come in. I was so happy to see Milly, I completely forgot my manners."

"No need." Mrs. Garrett waved her off. "We can't stay. We were invited to tea at the Montgomerys. I believe you're acquainted with them, yes?"

Rose wanted to smack the smirk off Mrs. Garrett's face. Of course she knew the Montgomerys. Hadn't Mrs. Montgomery been throwing Flora at Silas, since he was too new to town to know what a pernicious guttersnipe she was? Rose nodded her head. She was being unkind in her estimation of Flora, but Flora had never been kind to anyone that Rose knew of.

"Yes, they go to our church." But she wouldn't give

the Garretts or the Montgomerys the satisfaction of speaking ill of Flora.

"Mrs. Montgomery made mention of it." Then, with an evil smile that could only be described as contrived, Mrs. Garrett said, "She also mentioned that her daughter, Flora, is seeking work as a nanny. She would be delighted to care for Millicent should you not feel up to it."

Rose's face heated, and she closed her eyes for a moment to compose herself before looking directly at Mrs. Garrett. "I will always feel up to caring for Milly. And though I do hate to cast stones, since you're new in town, I feel obligated to point out that while you are concerned with my lack of reputation poorly influencing Milly's place in society, you should perhaps take the time to discover which homes Flora Montgomery is welcomed in. Very few good families receive her, so I'm not sure you'll find the situation an improvement."

Exactly the sort of thing Rose had just promised herself not to say. But it was the truth. And how could the Garretts possibly think to put Milly in Flora's care?

"I do apologize," Rose said slowly. "I hate to speak ill of anyone, and I have no knowledge of Flora's competence with children. But I do know that under Flora's care, Milly would not be able to visit her dearest friends, as Flora is not welcome in those homes."

Mrs. Garrett blanched, so Rose added pointedly, "Especially as it pertains to the Jackson mansion."

"I didn't realize." Mrs. Garrett looked at her husband, whose expression of defeat spoke volumes.

"The Montgomery family as a whole is one of the finest families in Leadville, and I'm sure you'll have a delightful time taking tea with them. Their cook makes fabulous lemon tarts."

Rose smiled pleasantly. She shouldn't have said what she did about Flora, especially since the reason the other girl was all but shunned in their society was how unkind she was to everyone around her, and her penchant for nasty remarks when displeased, but the last thing they needed was to have Milly under her care. If the Garretts wanted some fancy French nanny, that was one thing. But to have Milly cared for by Flora was another.

"I thank you for your concern," Mrs. Garrett said slowly, looking at her husband. "We'll be on our way, then."

"Good day." Rose smiled at her, then roused Milly, who'd fallen asleep on her shoulder. "Tell your grandparents goodbye."

"Goodbye," Milly mumbled, lifting her head briefly.

"It's past her nap time," Rose said by way of explanation. "She means no discourtesy. Will you be here to visit with her in the morning?"

Mr. Garrett coughed. "We were hoping for another afternoon visit. The chef at the Rafferty mentioned making special cakes for Millicent's tea."

"I'll give her an early nap so she's refreshed." Rose smiled, trying to sound efficient enough that the Garretts would put the idea of another nanny out of their mind.

"We would appreciate that," Mrs. Garrett said, taking her husband's arm before turning and walking away.

Rose sighed as she closed the door behind her. At least that visit was over with no real damage done. She shouldn't have been so harsh in her description of Flora, but she hadn't misrepresented the truth, either.

Milly had laid her head against Rose's shoulder again, and though she should have taken the little girl upstairs, Rose carried her to the parlor. It wasn't just the thought of losing Milly to Flora that bothered her. It was the thought of losing Milly at all.

How had this little girl become so dear to her in such a short period?

She returned to her chair, adjusting Milly so she could hold the sleeping child.

Milly lifted her head, then, as was her habit, twirled her fingers in Rose's hair. "I missed you, my doxy."

Rose stilled. "What did you just call me?"

"My doxy." Milly grabbed Rose's face with both hands then planted a wet kiss on her cheek. "That's what Granmudder calls you. The doxy. An' you're mine."

Milly eased back into Rose's lap, then rested her head on her chest, closing her eyes. "Granmudder not cuddle like you."

Rubbing the little girl's back, Rose blinked back tears, trying to focus more on the loving way Milly spoke to her rather than the horrible word she used. How was she supposed to even address it? They didn't use words like that in their home, even if they were true.

"Rosey?" Milly lifted her head and looked up. "Did you miss me?"

She planted a kiss on Milly's forehead. "Of course I did."

Matthew let out a small cry. Milly jumped up. "He go back to sleep. He no share you when I wif Granmudder, so is my turn."

The look Milly gave her nearly broke Rose's heart. "See? I know sharing. I teach Ma-few."

How, in such a short period, had Milly wound her way so firmly into their family?

Milly paused at the door. "Hi, Papa! The doxy is in there. I going to tell Ma-few go back to sleep. Is my turn wif the doxy."

She turned to go into the other room, but Silas picked her up. "What's this about a doxy?"

Milly grinned. "Is what Granmudder calls my Rosey. Is fun word to say."

Silas frowned, his brow creasing into furrows so deep that Rose could have planted an entire forest in them.

"It's fine," Rose said quietly. "She doesn't know any better."

"But she should." He looked down at his daughter. "*Doxy* is not a nice word. We don't call people that. Ever."

"Granmudder does."

The hall clock ticked the seconds so loudly it would have competed with thunder. Or perhaps it was Rose's own heart. How do you tell a child that someone she must respect has been insulting someone else she dearly loves?

"It doesn't make it right," Silas said softly. "From now on, I don't want you using names your grandmother calls people."

"So I shouldn't say Ma-few is a bass—" Milly's brow furrowed. "I not 'member the word."

"And you shouldn't," Silas said firmly. "Your grandmother shouldn't, either."

Milly frowned, then struggled in Silas's grip as she looked at Rose. "Rosey, I sorry I called you a bad name."

Tears filled Rose's eyes as she held her arms open for Milly. Silas let her down, and Milly came running to her. "I know you are, dearest. You didn't know. What matters is how much we love each other, and because we love each other, I know you'd never say something mean on purpose."

Big green eyes looked up at her. "But why does Granmudder?"

A lot of reasons the little girl would never understand. Reasons Rose didn't understand, except that Mrs. Garrett was hurting, but even that excuse was starting to wear thin. Except how many times had Rose herself said something mean to cover up her pain? How did one continue forgiving someone who continued to say hurtful things?

"Because your grandmother is really sad," Rose said softly, stroking Milly's hair. "And sometimes when people are sad, instead of saying they're sad, they say mean things. So in our house, when we're sad, we just say we're sad, all right?"

"Awright." Milly looked around the room, straightening. "Ma-few not crying no more. He went back to sleep all by his self."

She smiled and buried her head in Rose's chest again. "So I get time wif my Rosey." Then she looked up and glared at Silas. "Go 'way, Papa. Is my time wif my Rosey."

Silas shook his head and grinned. The smile sent

waves of contentment down Rose's body, warming her all over.

That was the trouble with how strongly she'd told Silas that they had no future. When he looked at her like that, she could almost forgive him anything.

But what did he really want from her? Her love? Or a mother for Milly?

However, with the sweet little girl playing with the tendrils of hair that had fallen from her bun, Rose was almost willing to give up on her own notion of true love to keep Milly with her always.

Chapter Thirteen

For the past week, Silas had been priding himself on the distance he'd been keeping from Rose. Not so distant that they never spoke, but he'd been careful to avoid speaking of things of a personal nature with her. He'd been asked to leave her alone, and though he hated treating her like a polite acquaintance, he couldn't figure out how else to act around her. Did he want to make amends? Desperately. But how did a man win the heart of a woman who'd made it clear it wasn't his for the taking?

No. That's not what she'd said. He'd have to work for it. But what did that mean?

How did a man court a woman when he couldn't court her?

And how did he fall in love with someone he respected, admired and felt drawn to, but could not explore any deeper feelings with?

Rose entered the room, carrying Matthew. The baby's eyes were shining, and he was smiling.

"Someone must have had a good nap," Silas said, reaching for the baby. "Come see Uncle Silas."

"Uncle Silas?" Rose gave him a funny look.

"Well, you refer to Frank as Uncle Frank, and I know it wouldn't be proper for the little guy to call me Silas, so why not Uncle Silas?"

In truth, he'd like to hear the little boy call him Papa, because just as Rose had been saying that Milly was as dear to her as her own, so, too, was Matthew to him.

"Uncle Silas it is." A pretty smile filled Rose's face as she handed Matthew to him. "He really likes you. I can't believe how well he's adjusted, thanks to your help."

Silas gave the baby a kiss on top of his head. "I just happened to have information that most people don't. You did the rest. You're a wonderful mother."

She turned away, her cheeks tinged pink.

He wanted to stop her and tell her that she had nothing to be embarrassed about, but how would his encouragement be taken? Instead, he focused his attention on the baby, making funny faces so that he would giggle.

"And you're an excellent father," Rose said quietly. "I know the Garretts are making noises about going back to Ohio again, but everyone here fully supports your right to keep Milly in Leadville."

They'd presented him with another offer—more money in exchange for having Milly return to Ohio with them, and this time, he'd be allowed to visit. As if that made selling his child any more acceptable.

"Thank you. My attorney says that they can only take her if I agree to it, but I hate that they keep trying. I told them I'll let Milly visit when she's older, but Mrs. Garrett seems only to care about having Milly all to herself.

Which she doesn't appear to appreciate during their time together."

Silas frowned, then looked at Rose, not wishing to hurt her, but knowing she'd find out soon enough. "I found out today that when they have Milly, they've also been having Flora Montgomery come to the hotel to help with her."

"What happened to the French nanny?"

"Didn't like the climate, I hear." Silas shrugged. "Apparently, Flora also speaks French, and the Garretts are delighted with her."

Pain washed over Rose's face. "Of course they are. I should have never said anything."

"What do you mean?"

Rose frowned, letting out a long sigh. "I'll admit, I wasn't thinking clearly. I was angry, and I told them that if they objected to my time with Milly, then they shouldn't consider Flora, because as bad as my reputation is, Flora is welcome in even fewer respectable homes. I should have known that they'd use Flora just to spite me."

"What's wrong with Flora?"

Sighing again, Rose plopped into her favorite chair. "That's just the trouble. And why I feel so terrible about saying anything in the first place. I feel like I'm guilty of the same crime we've all convicted her of."

Silas joined her on the nearby sofa. "I won't judge you. But I would like to know why you don't want Flora taking care of my daughter."

Her face softened as she looked at him. "No, you don't judge me, do you?"

Another expression flitted across her face, but it was gone before Silas could interpret it.

"Flora is the town's biggest gossip. Or rather, was. She's the reason everyone knows I ran off with Ben. Had it not been for Flora's big mouth, no one would have known. Obviously, people would have eventually learned of my downfall given the resulting child…"

She smiled at Matthew, eyes shining. "But she made it very difficult for a while. She was also the one to break the news of Emma Jane and Jasper Jackson's disappearance, forcing them to wed. I think she meant to humiliate Emma Jane, but Jasper is an honorable man, and because he had compromised her reputation, even though nothing happened, he married Emma Jane. Which only seemed to anger Flora even more, and she did everything she could to verbally tear Emma Jane down. Finally, people got tired of it, and countless others who'd fallen victim to Flora's tongue came forward."

Rose's brow furrowed. "She hurt a lot of people, and the ladies of the church got together and told Flora that if she couldn't be kind, she wasn't welcome at our events. Many people took that a step further, and now, no one even wants her in their home. Her mother sent her away for a while, but so far, Flora hasn't said or done anything to indicate she's changed. She still makes digs at me every chance she gets."

Shaking her head, Rose looked at him. "I probably said too much. I honestly don't wish to tear Flora down. I'm sure there are redeeming qualities in her, but the way she treats me, the way she treats others, I have a hard time finding them."

"I appreciate your honesty. I don't want anyone who

doesn't hold you in high esteem to be spending time with my daughter. It's bad enough that the Garretts are poisoning her mind—I don't need to add to it."

Rose nodded slowly. "All the same, at some point, Milly will learn what those words mean, and she will learn that technically—"

"Technically, those words should be out of use, and I won't allow you to accept them as definitions for you or Matthew."

He spoke with such force that Matthew started to fuss. Silas rubbed the baby's back gently. "It's all right, little fellow. I was just making sure your mama understood that we're not going to tolerate people saying bad things about you."

"Yet you can't erase what I did. No matter what words you do or don't use, I'm guilty, and that's all the rest of the world can see."

"But you've been forgiven by God," he said quietly. "At some point, you have to apply that forgiveness to every aspect of your life. You've made your peace with the Lord, so now you've got to choose to hold your head up high. When people continue to try to punish you for a mistake that God no longer holds against you, you don't have to let them."

Her eyes filled with tears and emotions he couldn't read filled her drawn brow. His own heart felt heavy. Burdened. For the first time, he understood Rose's struggle with forgiving him. She'd accepted God's forgiveness, but society still continued to punish her. As many times as she'd forgiven him, there was a small piece of her still trying to punish him, because, in her world, that's how it worked.

But that's not how forgiveness worked.

Until Rose figured that out for herself, there was no hope for a future between them.

Matthew leaned forward and reached for his mother. Rose took the baby and held him close.

"No one has the right to punish you," Silas said quietly. "But until you stop punishing yourself, and stop accepting the punishment everyone else lays upon you, you're never going to be free of the shame weighing you down."

Words Rose needed, but also, words he needed. All this time, he'd been punishing himself because he knew he deserved it after what he'd done to Rose. He'd been carrying shame when he'd already sought and received forgiveness. If there were amends to be made, he'd make them, but he had to stop torturing himself with jumping through the hoops he'd set up to make it right.

Tears ran down Rose's face. "But I did all the things people said I did. Even the things Flora said. She might have lied about everyone else, but she told the truth about me."

"None of those things are true about you anymore." Then he grinned. "Unless you're sneaking out at night to meet men at saloons."

"I would never!" A wide smile quickly replaced the immediate horror on her face. "I suppose you're right. All the things I did, I can't imagine doing now. Or ever again."

Silas took a deep breath. Maybe it was the wrong time, and maybe he was asking for too much too soon. But the parallel was too clear for him to miss out on the opportunity.

"I feel the same about my actions. I was wrong to court you when my family was in talks for me to marry another. If I court you again…" He shook his head. "No. Rose, I want to court you. I don't know if we've changed so much that we're incompatible, but honestly, I don't know that we knew enough about each other to know that we were compatible. Regardless, I promise you. When you're willing to consent to being courted by me, I will not court another."

She stared at him for a long moment. "And in the meantime?"

"You're the only woman I wish to court. But if that changes, you'll be the first to know."

Her posture relaxed, and she smiled at him. "I appreciate that. And you're right. About me punishing myself. And I suppose I've been punishing you, as well. I don't know how to move forward, and I don't know how to trust when trust has been broken. But I'm willing to try."

Matthew giggled and reached for her hair, managing to pull loose a wispy piece.

"You little rascal." She pried her hair free of her son's grip, looking more carefree than he'd seen her in a while.

He opened his mouth to ask her what trying meant, but Maddie entered the room, looking around like she'd lost something.

"Is something amiss?" Rose immediately stood, adjusting baby Matthew in her arms as she did so.

"Milly's not back yet. I thought they should have brought her home by now."

Silas looked up at the clock. They'd agreed to return by two, but it was nearly four.

"I'll go pick her up at the hotel. Perhaps they just lost track of time."

Silas's heart thudded in his stomach as he said the words. The Garretts were the most punctual people he knew. They wouldn't be nearly two hours late without a good reason. And for the life of him, Silas couldn't think of a single one other than the unthinkable.

When Frank entered the room, Silas looked at him. "When is the next train to Denver?"

The older man glanced at his pocket watch. "You go to the hotel. I'll get Will, and we'll head to the train station. Maddie, you get everyone to praying, will you?"

"Let's not panic," Rose said, her voice quivering.

"I agree," Frank said. "But we also don't want to lose time. If we don't find Milly before the Garretts get on the train, it'll be a lot harder and take longer to get her back."

Nowhere, in any of his nightmares, had he imagined this. Did he think the Garretts capable of taking Milly? Absolutely. But he'd also thought that they wouldn't be so sneaky about it. Even when he'd taken Milly, he'd warned them. Told them that if they didn't stop interfering with him spending time with his daughter, he'd take her and leave. But he'd been letting the Garretts have time with Milly every day.

So how could they do this?

Frank handed him his coat. "It's getting cold out there. Bundle up good."

As he buttoned up for the weather, he noticed Rose doing the same.

"What are you doing?"

"I'm going with you. I love Milly, too, and I'm not going to sit idly by while everyone else is out there doing something."

"What about Matthew?"

"I'm sure Maddie can manage."

The older woman was holding the baby, worry lining her brow, but she smiled down at Matthew. "And we'll do just fine."

He, Rose and Frank left the house, Frank immediately turning toward Will and Mary's, but Rose and Silas heading for the Rafferty.

They seemed to fly to the hotel and arrived before Silas had a chance to realize what was happening.

"Mrs. Rafferty is at the front desk," Rose said. "I'm sure she can help us."

She led him to where the woman stood watch over her customers.

"Good afternoon, Mrs. Rafferty." Rose gave her a smile. "I was hoping you could give us some assistance."

"Rose! Lovely to see you as always. What can I do for you?"

His daughter was missing, and they were exchanging pleasantries?

"We need to know where the Garretts are," Silas said, ignoring Rose's pointed glare.

"The Garretts?" Mrs. Rafferty said, her brow furrowed. "They checked out hours ago."

"Checked out?" Silas knew his voice was loud, but the pain burning his heart wouldn't allow him to be any quieter.

Rose rested a hand on his arm. "Did they say where they were going?"

Her voice remained calm, gentle, a contrast to the storm raging inside him. He tried to speak, but the pressure on his arm grew stronger.

"No, I'm sorry." She truly looked apologetic. But it didn't bring them closer to finding Milly. Silas struggled against Rose's grip on his arm, but her hand remained firm.

"Please, Mrs. Rafferty," Rose said gently. "They have his daughter. If there's anything you can think of that they might have said, or any indication they might have given about their direction…"

The older woman frowned, took off her spectacles, then rubbed her forehead. "They did seem in rather a hurry. Mrs. Garrett acted agitated and kept looking over her shoulder at the door. But it was just the two of them."

Silas's gut churned. What had they done with Milly?

Rose, however, remained calm. "Did you happen to see Flora Montgomery with them?"

"No." Mrs. Rafferty shook her head. Then she brightened. "But Flora was here earlier. And she did have a little girl with her. Flora said she was her charge, and she'd be traveling with the little girl's family to Ohio. I congratulated her on her new position. Flora seemed most excited to be starting a new life."

Silas felt like he was going to be sick. If they managed to get Milly to Ohio, chances of him getting her back were next to nothing. Why had they done this? Was having Milly all to themselves so important that they'd destroy all these lives? He'd worked so hard to find a way for them all to work together. So they all could be a part of Milly's life. But now…

Mrs. Rafferty let out a long sigh, echoing the pain in Silas's heart. "I know life has been hard for Flora lately. Her own doing, but I'd always hoped she'd find her way. I suppose going to Ohio…"

Then it appeared to dawn on her. "Oh, dear. Flora is a part of this?"

"I'm afraid so," Rose said quietly. "Is there anything you can think of that might help us find them?"

"Flora mentioned that she was going to say goodbye to her parents before meeting her employers at the livery. I thought it was a strange place to meet since the train is so much faster, but Flora said they were renting a wagon and driving to Buena Vista first. But I suppose, if they're eluding being caught, it makes more sense to take such an indirect route."

Then Mrs. Rafferty addressed Silas for the first time. "I am so sorry. I had no idea…but I hope that helps you. I wish I could do more. I'll be praying for you and the successful return of your daughter."

"Thank you," he tried to say, but the words felt stuck in his throat. Rose squeezed his arm again, and though everything in him seemed ice-cold, her touch was the one spot of warmth.

"I appreciate your assistance, Mrs. Rafferty."

Despite the turmoil in his heart, Silas couldn't help but notice the warmth passing between Rose and Mrs. Rafferty. The shame Rose felt from others only seemed to be from a select few, but many, like Mrs. Rafferty, seemed to care deeply for her.

As they exited the hotel, Rose turned to him. "Go

to the station and tell Uncle Frank and Will what we found out. Have them meet us at the livery. The proprietor is a friend of ours, so I'll talk to him and see what he recommends."

Once again, he appreciated the way Rose took charge of the situation and knew what to do. This was a more mature Rose than the one he'd known, and he couldn't help but be grateful for how she'd grown.

Without Rose, he'd have no chance of getting his daughter back. Even with her, he still had no idea how it was going to happen. Stealing a glance at her as she turned down the street toward the livery, he saw her lips moving. She was praying. Of course.

Once again, her example reminded him of how much he'd fallen short. But in this case, he could do better. Praying silently, he ran to the train station to get Will and Frank.

Chapter Fourteen

Rose walked into the livery, grateful that Wes, the proprietor, was out front, brushing one of the horses.

"Wes! I need your help!"

She quickly explained the situation, watching as Wes's frown deepened.

"I know the couple," he said when she'd gotten to the end of the story. "And I gave them a wagon to take back to Buena Vista. Amos Warner had used it to deliver goods last month, but he took sick, and his family came to get him. There was no one to take the wagon home, so I promised I'd keep it safe until I had someone who could bring it back. The Garretts seemed like the answer to a prayer."

He shook his head. "I never imagined they didn't have the right to take that cute little girl. I'm sorry. I should have asked more questions."

"You didn't know," Rose said, giving him an encouraging smile. "But I'm sure you can understand our need to get to them as quickly as possible. How long ago did they leave?"

"Their wagon pulled out nearly two hours ago. Should be easy enough to catch. Those draft horses of Warner's aren't very fast. They said they were hoping to reach Granite by nightfall, but I told them they'd most likely be sleeping by the road tonight."

"That's good news," Will said, sounding breathless from having to run all the way from the train depot. "Can you get horses saddled for Silas and me? I'm going to try to round up a couple other deputies to help, but I don't know which horses they'll need."

"What about me?" Rose turned to stare at him.

"You go home with Frank. It's going to be a long, hard ride. I think we can catch up with them before they reach Granite, but we'll definitely be spending the night out of doors. It's no place for a lady."

She stared at him long and hard. "Then I guess it's a good thing I've already lost that label according to society. There is no way I'm going to sit at home knitting while I wait for word of Milly. If you bring a bunch of deputies out to get her, she's going to be frightened, and more so if the Garretts resist."

"She has a point," Silas said quietly. Rose turned to face him. She hadn't heard him enter, but she should have known he'd have arrived with Will.

Will shook his head. "It could be dangerous, and I won't put Rose in any danger."

"Danger? From the Garretts?" Rose shot him another glare. "Both of them have difficulty getting around, and while I suppose they might have guns, I can hardly see them using one around Milly. Their sense of propriety wouldn't allow it."

Silas nodded slowly. "She's right. Mrs. Garrett doesn't know how to use a gun because she thinks it's unladylike, and Mr. Garrett is a terrible shot. He'd never risk using a gun around people, especially his wife and Milly."

"There's also the long and difficult ride, the fact that outlaws and bandits frequent that road, and the wild animals we could encounter. It's not safe."

Will stood with the posture of a lawman no one wanted to mess with. And, Rose supposed, his show of force probably worked with most people. But she'd never been most people.

"And if it were Rosabelle out there? Would you make Mary stay at home?"

Will blanched. There was no making Mary do anything, and he should have been smart enough to realize the same about Rose.

"It's not the same," he muttered.

"To me, it is. Milly's just as much mine as..." Rose's throat tightened as she glanced at Silas, who wore a pained expression on his face.

"I'm sorry," she said quietly. "I didn't mean to offend. I..." She hadn't realized the tears streaming down her face until she tasted the salt hitting the corners of her lips.

Silas's eyes filled with tears, as well. "You don't have to apologize. I'd do the same for Matthew."

Rose nodded, wiped the tears from her cheeks, and turned her attention to Wes. "I want a horse, too."

"If you won't stay for your sake," Will said, his voice solemn, "what about Matthew?"

She lifted her chin. "I'll carry him wrapped around me in a sling the way Emma Jane did with Moses. We've taken to wearing our babies like that at the mission so we have them close but our hands are free to work."

Silas shook his head slowly. "Maybe this isn't such a good idea. Will's right. I didn't think about the baby, but he can't—"

"I'm going and that's final." She looked from Silas to Will. "If you try to leave me behind, I will follow you. I know you two don't want me out there alone, especially since it's going to be getting dark soon. So you get what you need from the sheriff's office, I'll get my baby, and I will see you back here in a few minutes."

Rose turned and stormed out of the livery. Was it foolish for her to think she could take Matthew on such a journey? Perhaps. But what other choice did she have? She couldn't get the image out of her mind of how terrified Milly must be. And would be when a bunch of riders came upon them, and there was the inevitable argument between Silas and the Garretts. No, she had to be there for Milly.

When she entered the house, Uncle Frank had already rallied the rest of the family.

"I'm going to stay with you tonight until we get word. You don't have to go through this alone," Mary said before Rose could greet her.

"I'm going," she said forcefully, not giving anyone room to argue.

"But Rose, dear..." Mary didn't get much further because Rose stopped her with a glare. Mary nodded.

"I need to get some things for Matthew."

"Now Rose, you can't bring a baby," Frank said, frowning.

"I can't leave him alone, either." She brushed past them, into the parlor, where Helen was holding him.

Matthew immediately reached for her, smiling broadly. He couldn't talk yet, but she could almost imagine him saying, "Mama!"

She cuddled him close to her, kissing the top of his head. What would she do if someone took him? How hard would she fight? She could do no less for Milly.

The front door opened, and Will strode in. "You're not bringing the baby," he said, without preamble. "It's the only way you can go, and if you argue, I'm locking you in jail for the night."

"You wouldn't dare." She glared at him.

"Don't try me. It's bad enough you have to come, but in the dark, with the dangers we face, I refuse to put an innocent baby in harm's way. And if you were thinking clearly, you wouldn't, either. What would happen if the horse stumbled over a rock he can't see in the dark and throws you both?"

"It's a full moon."

"And at our pace, full moon or no, a horse can still trip and kill you both. I won't have it."

Everyone in the room remained silent, and Rose noticed that Silas had entered, as well.

"Please listen to him. The pain of losing a child… Don't do this to yourself. Don't do it to me." Then Silas looked around the room. "Don't do it to any of us. We love Matthew, and I can't put him at risk. I'll help Will lock you in that cell if it means keeping him safe."

Rose's chest burned. They were right, of course. But

what was she supposed to do? She couldn't not go after Milly. And Matthew, he needed her.

"But I can't leave him behind."

At their nods, she realized that had been their argument all along. Their plan to keep her home, as well.

"Yes you can," Mary said gently, putting her arm around Rose. "I have more than enough milk, and Maddie says that Matthew's been enjoying runny porridge. He'll be fine overnight."

Rose looked at her sister, unable to see through the tears in her eyes. "But I can't... I mean, I'm his... What if he..."

"I want to do this for you." Mary hugged her tight against her, sandwiching Matthew between them. "You'll never forgive yourself if something happens to him. And you won't be able to live with yourself if you don't go. Let me be the sister I've always wanted to be to you."

Mary pulled away, then took Matthew from her arms. "Come to your auntie, little fellow. Your mama's going on a trip tonight, but you'll see her in the morning."

Then she turned to her husband and smiled sweetly. "And someday you'll learn that we Stone sisters will not be thwarted in the pursuit of rescuing a beloved family member."

Will shook his head, a small grin at the corner of his lips. "I suppose it's foolish to even try."

Turning to Silas, Will said, "It's also foolish to fight the inevitable when it comes to these women. I may have had my reservations about you, but it's becoming clear where things are headed. You might as well face up to it and marry her."

"We're not getting married," Rose said, gritting her teeth. How like her family to turn this into some bizarre courtship ritual.

"Yes, you are." Will chuckled. "You're both willing to risk your lives for each other's children. Then there's the fact that you keep looking at each other like you've gone days without food and someone's just put a steak in front of you. You think we don't notice, but trust me. We're all counting down the days until the wedding."

"That's not love, that's lust." Rose glared at him. "And I've had more than my fill of that, thank you very much. So let's stop being ridiculous so we can go after Milly."

"Oh, I know the difference between love and lust," Will said flatly. "And while I lusted after many a girl in my youth, I was never willing to die for any of them."

He turned and gave Mary the kind of look Rose always wished a man would give her. "But I would die the most slow and painful death for my wife."

Grinning, he added, "And I will admit that I still lust after her. The way I see it, a good marriage has both."

Uncle Frank chuckled. "That it does. But Mary's right. The longer we stand around talking, the more quickly daylight fades, and it'll be that much harder to find them. I know they're headed for Buena Vista, but I can't see them getting even as far as Granite tonight."

"That's what we're thinking," Will said, turning his attention back to the task at hand. "If you wouldn't mind rounding up some supplies, I'm going to see if I can get some of the other deputies to ride out with us. We should catch up with the Garretts on the road, and in the morning, we'll head back. If it doesn't work out that way, I'll send a rider in the morning to update you on what's happening."

"Why not a telegram? You'll be close enough to Granite, then you won't lose a man."

Will nodded. "Good idea. In fact, I'll go by the telegraph office on my way and send a message to the sheriff's office in Granite now. They can be on the lookout for the Garretts, as well."

They finished making arrangements, then Will headed over to the sheriff's office, and Silas went with Uncle Frank to get the supplies they'd need for the trip. Rose went to change into her riding gear and give Matthew one last feeding before she left.

Mary followed so Rose could tell her what she needed to know about Matthew's care.

Only Mary wasn't interested in talking about Matthew.

"Will's right, you know. Your attraction to Silas shouldn't put you off. You should be encouraged that you have romantic feelings, as well as a deep love for each other's children. I know you're trying to keep things proper between the two of you, but the questions you ask about what level of friendship is appropriate speak to something deeper than lust. You two have everything you need for a successful marriage, so if not for your sake, perhaps you should think of the sake of the children."

Gently brushing the top of her son's head, Rose looked up at Mary. "I am thinking of Matthew. And it's for his sake that I want to be wise in the relationships I pursue, not marrying to give him a father, or respectability, but a real family unit, like I see with you, Joseph, Polly and Emma Jane."

"Maybe if you weren't being so stubborn about what happened in the past, you'd be able to see that you have that with Silas. All of us can see that he loves you, so why can't you?"

Because she wasn't sure she could trust herself in making that determination. "I thought he loved me once," Rose said quietly. "As many times as I've prayed, I'm not any closer to knowing how he genuinely feels. He told me today that he intended to court me, and that he would remain faithful in that courtship. But what is the true nature of his heart? Is it about the desire that everyone sees? Is it about a marriage for the sake of the children? Or does he truly love me, for who I am today, the sum of all my mistakes, and all the things that have brought me to this place?"

Matthew pulled away from his feeding, gazing up at her with a milky grin. Rose smiled down at him, then adjusted him to give him a good burping.

"I don't know," Mary said. "But I don't believe the way he looks at you is purely lust. You're right, though. You deserve to be fully loved, and I hope that when it happens, you can see it. Because sometimes, you seem to be so aware of your faults, that you're blinded to the wonderful woman I'm honored to have as a sister."

Mary's praise still felt odd to Rose, but her sister's smile was genuine. Mary had no reason to lie. But it didn't make it any easier for Rose to know how to feel about Silas.

At least one thing was easy. Watching the delight on her sister's face as she handed her her baby.

Chapter Fifteen

The ride was harder than Silas had expected. Will hadn't been joking when he said it was no place for a woman or baby. The sun had finally gone down a little while ago, and he was grateful for the full moon lighting the way. Even so, it was hard to see the road before them.

He glanced over at Rose, who seemed to be keeping pace just fine. She was an excellent horsewoman, something he hadn't known about her. Never had reason to, he supposed. Her family hadn't been able to afford much in the way of horses for pleasure riding back when he knew her before. Now he'd been too busy working, and she'd been too busy with her family for them to find out things like that about each other.

Maybe Rose had been right about him moving too fast. About them not really knowing each other, or knowing enough about each other for it to be love.

As they rounded a bend, Silas could see the faint glow of a fire. Will signaled for them to slow up.

When they gathered, Will said, "Could be the Garretts, but it could also be some unsavory types. I can't imagine bandits camping so close to the road, but it wouldn't be one of the dumbest things I've ever seen 'em do."

A couple of the deputies laughed at his joke, and one of them rode forward. "I'll go check it out."

Silas took advantage of the break to ride over to Rose. "How are you holding up?"

The moonlight glinted off her dark hair, and despite the fatigued expression on her face, she looked absolutely lovely. He knew he wasn't supposed to think of her in that way, but he couldn't help himself. Besides, it wasn't like she was dressed to impress him, or any man. Covered in dust and her hair such a mess from the wind that she'd be humiliated if he pointed it out, she was a vision.

The beauty he saw shining out from her reflected the strength of a woman who'd ride harder than most men, leaving behind a beloved baby. For his daughter that she loved as her own.

"A little tired, but I'll be fine." Rose smiled at him, exhaustion written all over her face.

"I'll admit I'm going to be sore tomorrow, but as long as I get Milly back, it'll be worth it."

"I feel the same way," she said, letting out a long sigh. "I didn't realize this would be so difficult."

He watched the lines deepen on her forehead. "Difficult?"

"I haven't ridden like this in, well…" Rose shook her head. "It doesn't matter."

The rider they'd sent to the fire came back, the

horse's hooves thundering as though it hadn't been ridden hard already.

"It's them," he called.

The rest of the riders needed no further encouragement. Will waved an arm, and they all spurred their horses, headed toward Milly.

Though the fire only appeared to be less than a mile away, it seemed like it took twice as long to breach that distance as it had to get all this way from town. As they drew closer, Silas could see the figures of three adults huddled by the fire, but not Milly.

Where was his daughter?

When they finally arrived at the campsite, Rose drew back, motioning for him to do the same.

"I think she's probably in the wagon. Hopefully asleep, so let's get to her first, before all the commotion wakes her up."

He followed her lead as she rode around to the back of the wagon, opposite to where the rest of the riders were headed. Will seemed to notice them breaking off, turning his horse their way. Silas shook his head and pointed to the wagon. Will nodded, then motioned for another rider to follow them.

They dismounted before they got too close, and the rider Will sent reached for the reins. "I'll hold the horses. You go get that little girl."

Quietly, Silas and Rose slipped to the side of the wagon. Silas noticed that Will waited to make his final approach on the camp until they started climbing in the wagon.

"She's here," Silas whispered, his heart thudding

in his chest louder than the hooves of the approaching horses.

Rose brushed past him, landing in the wagon with a thud. Silas looked over at the Garretts to see if they'd noticed Silas and Rose in the wagon, but by then, Will and his men had gotten their attention.

Though he got to Milly first, Rose wasn't far behind. He brushed his little girl's face with his hand, and her eyes blinked open sleepily.

"Papa?" Her little voice was the sweetest sound she'd ever heard. "What you doing here? Granmudder say you no want me no more."

Even in the dim light, he could see that her face was stained from having shed so many tears.

"Your grandmother lied. They took you without my permission. I'll always want you, Milly."

His daughter reached up and wrapped her arms around him. "I want my Rosey."

"I'm right here, my sweet," Rose said, coming alongside him.

As quickly as Milly had fallen into his arms, she leaped over to Rose and held her tight. "I no want that udder lady. She not my Rosey."

Milly twirled her fingers in Rose's hair. "Is okay if you doxy. You my Rosey. An' I love you."

Rose cradled his daughter to her chest, her shoulders rising and falling as though she were sobbing.

It wasn't proper, and Silas knew it went against how he agreed to treat Rose, but he couldn't help it. He wrapped his arms around them both.

Rose was indeed crying, but before Silas could say anything to comfort her, Milly spoke.

"Rosey, you no cry. I were good girl for Granmudder an' da udder lady. Now you wif me, and everything will be good."

Then she looked up at him. "Papa, why you cry? Are you sad to see Miwwy?"

"No." Rose shifted her weight, allowing him to take Milly in his arms. "I am very happy to see you, and that's why I'm crying."

"Crying for being sad. We happy. We no cry. If Granmudder hears us cry, she be mad. So no cry."

For the first time since seeing Milly, Silas remembered where they were. He looked over the side of the wagon, where the Garretts were talking to Will and his men. From the other direction, he saw another set of riders heading their way.

He held Milly close. "Sometimes people cry when they're happy. And I've never been happier in all my life."

Milly smiled up at him. "I happy, too. I stay wif you and my Rosey forever. No go wif Granmudder."

"You don't have to." Silas kissed the top of her head. Then he sighed. He didn't have it in his power to promise that Milly would have Rose forever. Who knew what the future held for Rose, and whether she would meet someone else who would take her away from this place?

The thought made him feel sick.

Rose gave Milly a squeeze. "You can have me as long as you need me."

Milly struggled out of his embrace. "Where Mafew?"

"He stayed home with his aunt Mary."

"But he no sleep if I no sing to him." She started to sing "Jesus Loves Me," but in true Milly fashion, sang it at the top of her lungs.

Which drew the attention of the Garretts.

"Millicent!" Mrs. Garrett broke away from the crowd of men and started toward them, but Will grabbed her.

Milly groaned. "Granmudder no like singing."

"You can sing all you like." Rose smiled at the little girl, then turned to Silas. "I'll stay with her if you'd like to go sort things out with them."

"No!" Milly went back to him, clinging to him. "No leave."

"We can go together," Silas said. "I want them to see how much taking her has upset Milly. They weren't just hurting me, but the little girl they claimed to love so much."

They climbed out of the wagon just in time to see the deputies putting handcuffs on Flora and the Garretts.

"What are you doing?" Rose asked.

"They're being charged with kidnapping," one of the deputies said. "We'll be taking them in tonight."

"It's not that much farther to Granite," another added. "There's been an increase in lawlessness in this area, and everyone will be safer in town."

"You don't mean we're going to jail," Flora shrieked. "I can't go to jail. I'm a Montgomery."

Will shook his head. "I guess you should have thought of that before you helped the Garretts kidnap a little girl."

Flora opened her mouth to speak, but Will turned away, his attention taken by some of the deputies needing to consult with him.

"We need to get moving," one of the deputies said. "We'll put the prisoners in the wagon, and…"

Prisoners. It was hard to think of Flora and the Garretts as prisoners, particularly since the three of them looked so downcast at the label.

One of the deputies drove the wagon, and two others sat with Flora and the Garretts. Silas and Rose climbed in with Milly, and the other deputies tied up their horses to follow behind.

Though Silas couldn't have imagined a better feeling than sitting in the wagon, Rose beside him, and Milly in his lap, every time he looked up at the Garretts, he felt downright awful. All he'd wanted was to get Milly back. Even though the deputies came with them, it hadn't occurred to him that they'd be looking at jail.

They'd done a terrible thing. They took his daughter. They tried poisoning his daughter against him and Rose.

But he also knew that they'd lost their daughter. A grandchild. And now, in their eyes, the only family they had left.

Did they really deserve jail?

He stole a glance at Flora, whose eyes were red from sobbing. Did she, a girl only listening to her employers, believing she was doing the right thing, deserve to have her life ruined?

But some sort of justice needed to happen.

What, then, was the answer? Silas closed his eyes and sent a prayer heavenward that God would clearly show him how to handle the situation.

Chapter Sixteen

Rose couldn't help but smile as she watched Milly fall asleep in her father's arms. No, not totally in his arms. Milly had wanted them both, and she'd ended up sprawled across both of their laps.

"She is something, isn't she?"

Rose smiled up at him. "You've done a great job with her."

"So have you." The tender look in his eyes warmed her to the toes. Not a bad thing, since the night air had grown cold. As it was, they were wrapped in blankets and still chilly. It had been a good idea to head to Granite tonight as opposed to spending the night on the road.

"Thank you," Rose said.

Silas adjusted his position, putting his arm around her. "Come closer. I can feel you shivering."

"That wouldn't be proper." Rose tried to straighten and move away, but he pulled her closer.

"We have chaperones. Even handcuffed, I'm sure the Garretts won't let me ravish you in the wagon. Plus, Milly's in the way."

He winked, and for a moment, Rose thought she recognized the boy she once fell in love with.

They'd aged, both of them, and though she liked the person she'd become, part of her missed the carefree way they used to be.

"You know what I mean," Rose said.

He gave her a look of mock horror. "You were thinking of ravishing me?"

"Silas." She swatted at him playfully but didn't resist when he pulled her closer.

"It's freezing. I know you don't want me to be so free in my affections, but I'd prefer not to have you die just so I can say I was being a gentleman."

She smiled and snuggled into him. "I know we said we aren't going back, but right now, you're sounding a lot like the old Silas."

"I feel more like that old Silas," he said. "I saw my worst nightmare coming true, and as I faced those fears, trusting in the Lord, I realized I didn't have to hold on so tightly. I've felt like I had the weight of the world on my shoulders, needing to do everything right, because otherwise, I'd lose the only thing I had worth living for."

Then a smile settled across his face. "I feel safe."

Feeling his warmth around her, Rose would have had to admit that she felt safe, as well.

Was it wise to allow herself to have feelings for him? To pursue a relationship that Mary said was obvious to everyone?

Rose looked across the wagon to where the Garretts sat. Though they had coats on, they lacked the warm blankets piled on top of Silas and Rose. Clearly the Garretts had traveled without thought to the weather and the fact that once the sun went down, temperatures dropped significantly. They'd only had a couple of blankets with them, and Milly had been wrapped up in them.

At least they'd given thought to keeping Milly warm.

When Rose and the rest of the party had set off, they'd brought a number of blankets, anticipating having to sleep out in the cold. She'd taken the blankets off her and Silas's horses, knowing they'd need them, but hadn't given much thought to what the others in the wagon might need.

"Let's put Milly under the blankets with us. Flora and the Garretts have nothing other than their coats. We can give them Milly's blankets."

Silas stared at her. "You're giving them Milly's blankets?"

"It'll be warm enough for her under ours. Weren't you the one who suggested we keep each other warm?"

She shifted, and they pulled Milly under the blanket with Silas. Then Rose picked up the blankets Milly had been using and carried them over to Flora and the Garretts.

"Here," she said, handing a blanket to the Garretts, then another to Flora. "You aren't prepared for the weather, and you look cold."

Mrs. Garrett ignored her, but Mr. Garrett took the blanket. "Thank you. My wife doesn't like to admit it, but she isn't well. It'll help to keep her warm."

Flora just glared at her. "I hope you don't think this changes anything. You might win people over by doing nice things for them in Leadville, but I know what you are."

Rose wanted to grab the blanket back and let the other girl freeze to death.

"No you don't," Rose said. "You don't even know me. Even before my scandal, you'd never said more than a handful of words to me."

Then Rose remembered her criticisms of the other girl. She didn't know Flora, either. Not really.

"But I do owe you an apology. I'd warned the Garretts against hiring you because they want Milly to be accepted into the finest homes and you're not welcome in many homes. It was wrong of me to divulge that information, both to them and to Silas. I don't know you either, and I don't know if you were qualified or not to care for Milly. I apologize for speaking against you."

Flora gave the nasty little smile she was famous for in town. "I don't know why you're apologizing. Obviously, your attempt at sabotaging me didn't work."

So much for trying to do the right thing. "All the same, I apologize. I shouldn't have said anything to begin with."

"Don't try to be a better Christian than me," she said, glaring. "You're already so deep in your sin that only the women on State Street are worse off than you."

Mrs. Garrett chuckled. "So true. A couple of blankets don't absolve you of your sin."

"My sin?" Rose looked at them, baffled. "Are you not on your way to jail for kidnapping a child?"

"Saving a child," Mrs. Garrett said smoothly. "Taking back what was ours to begin with."

The wagon hit a bump, and Rose started to fall backward, but Silas caught her.

"Milly was never yours." Silas glared at them. "I

can't believe that Rose is doing you a kindness and you still find fault with her."

Uncle Frank had told Rose early on that there would always be people who could never see past her sin. Silas had wanted her to let go of her shame, but couldn't he see how hard it was to do so when people never let her forget?

"And you refuse to see any of her faults," Mrs. Garrett said, glaring at Rose. "What kind of woman goes after a man who is practically engaged?"

Tears filled Rose's eyes. "I didn't know. I was too busy raising my siblings to have time for gossip, and Silas never told me."

"It's true," Silas said. "If you want to point the finger of dishonor at anyone, point it at me. I was the one who spoke promises of love to Rose. I was the one who hid the truth about Annie. I even shushed a girl in church when she started to say something to Rose."

Silas turned and looked at her. "I'm sorry. I just remembered that now. It was wrong of me, and it only serves to remind me of how deeply I wronged you."

Oddly enough, this new revelation didn't hurt as much as Rose thought it would. In fact, it served more to give her more sympathy for Silas and the depth of his guilt over his mistakes. The trouble with being aware of your mistakes was that it often served to make you feel worse as you saw every moment where you made a decision that was wrong, culminating in the one thing that so defined you, you could never go back.

"It's in the past," Rose said, looking at him for a moment, trying to see if he understood that she was trying as hard as she could to let it go.

"The past has a way of sticking with a person," Mrs. Garrett said. "So much so that I can't imagine Millicent will have a future if you continue to allow Rose to care for her. And what if you marry her?"

Mrs. Garrett looked at Silas with such disdain that Rose found it hard to maintain any sympathy for her.

"It's obvious that you're taking up where you left off, and if she truly is leading a respectable life, I can't imagine the pastor will let you carry on for too long without a wedding."

"We're not carrying on!" Rose felt the heat rise in her cheeks.

"Really? What were you doing on the other side of the wagon? You two seemed awfully cozy under those blankets."

The older woman's taunt was precisely why Rose hadn't wanted to let Silas get so close. And yet, the fact that she was turning something so completely innocent into something disgusting made Rose's skin crawl.

Flora's satisfied grin told Rose that as soon as the other girl got back to town, she'd be sure to spread tales of Rose's downfall—again.

"That way of looking at things is exactly why you're not fit to be around my daughter," Silas said, his voice full of rage. "I jokingly told Rose that her reputation wasn't worth freezing to death, but that's the only thing that would satisfy you, isn't it?"

"She is a loose woman!"

Mrs. Garrett's words echoed in Rose's head. That was all she'd ever be. Her ears burned and her vision blurred, making it impossible to hear Silas's response. Rose should have been gratified to know Silas was defending her, but anymore, she didn't know how much those defenses made a difference. No matter what she did, or how hard she tried to prove that she was a woman of honor, no one would let her live beyond those mistakes.

Silas had never imagined that Mrs. Garrett would actually think it preferable for a woman to die than to live with questionable morals. Unfortunately, in their world, the wrong woman's morals were being questioned.

"Rose is a good woman," Silas said firmly. "And she is wonderful with Milly. I don't regret a moment my daughter spends with her."

Mrs. Garrett grunted. "At the expense of my time with her."

"Is that why you took Milly?" Silas asked. "I gave you time with her, and if you'd wanted to see her more, all you had to do was ask."

"I shouldn't have to ask to see my own grandchild." Mrs. Garrett straightened, her haughty expression completely out of place with the handcuffs on her wrists and the deputies flanking her side.

"You wouldn't have to if you hadn't tried to keep me from her in the first place."

For a moment Silas felt like a hypocrite, mentioning the fact that he'd been the one to take Milly first. But he was her father, and they'd made all sorts of excuses to keep him from going up to the nursery to spend time with his daughter. Silas had at least attempted to include the Garretts in Milly's life.

"And now I don't know what to do," Silas said, his voice shaking. "You did everything you could to keep me from her, and I wanted to do the same, but I found it wasn't fair to Milly to keep her from the people who loved her. So I tried to compromise. But you were never willing to share, were you?"

The older woman appeared completely unaffected by Silas's words.

"You're not a fit parent," Mrs. Garrett calmly said. "We tried talking sense into that Leadville judge, but he wouldn't even listen to our case. Back in Ohio, we had a judge ready to sign papers."

Silas closed his eyes and took a deep breath. He'd been right in taking Milly from Ohio, right in going after them. They weren't going to stop unless they got to keep Milly.

"By what standard are you calling me an unfit parent? Milly is happy, healthy and progressing beautifully."

Mrs. Garrett cocked a head to one side. "She is ill-mannered, undisciplined, and your choice in nannies leaves much to be desired."

Silas's gut burned. Why did she always have to turn it back onto attacking Rose?

However, when he looked over at Rose to give her an encouraging smile, her face remained impassive.

"I am fortunate to have Rose as a nanny."

Even those words didn't change the expression on her face.

"Yes, it is your lack of fortune that is at issue, isn't it? You can't afford everything a growing young lady needs. Which is why you're living on the charity of the local minister and can only provide a woman of questionable morals for a nanny. Surely you can see that's not the best environment for a child. We can give Millicent everything. A good father would not deny her that."

His pride. They wanted to shred every remaining bit of his pride. But for Milly, he would accept it. If only it would have been enough for the Garretts.

"So why haven't you helped me instead of being my adversary? None of this would have happened if you hadn't taken away my livelihood and forced me out of my home. If you had Milly's best interests at heart, you wouldn't have tried separating us."

He had no regrets in taking Milly to Leadville. In the battle for his daughter, they'd fired the first shot. From a cannon. And they'd kept firing until he'd had the strength to finally find a way to build a new life with his daughter. Even when they came after her, he tried to find ways to get along with the Garretts, but here they were.

"I believe I did offer my French nanny. But no, you had to have that strumpet care for our precious girl."

"That's enough!" Silas was done with the niceties and trying to reason with the Garretts.

"You will not refer to Rose by any more of those names. I've tried being reasonable, even now. I tried to understand your point of view, but you're not willing to see mine. So here it is. If you want to see Milly, you will treat Rose with respect."

"How dare you?" Mrs. Garrett pulled against her restraints, and one of the deputies pushed her back.

"No." Silas turned to look at Rose. Her disinterested expression remained, though he could see the lines on her forehead deepening.

He returned his attention to the Garretts. "How dare

you? You continually insult a kind and decent woman, yet you act like you're the one being insulted. No more."

Pausing to take a deep breath, he felt it easier to breathe than it had been in a long time. Before he could speak again, Rose stepped forward.

"Silas, let it go," Rose said, putting her hand on his arm. "I love Milly. I told you, she's like my own. But you're never going to convince people like Mrs. Garrett that I am anything but that reputation. I promised Milly I'd always be there for her, and I will. But once we get back to town, I'll help you find a new nanny."

His chest ached as she said the words. Wasn't she listening when he'd just defended her?

She looked up at him, pain etched all over her face. "You asked to court me earlier today. Even if my heart were so inclined, I could never marry you. I refuse to subject you to the talk, and the doors that will close having me as your wife. You deserve better."

Removing her hand from Silas's arm, she looked down at Mrs. Garrett. "You win. Since I seem to be your biggest objection to Silas raising Milly, you can have no further issue with finding a way to work together in caring for her. I know you want Milly all to yourself, but Silas loves her, too. Let him be a father to her."

Taking a deep breath, she turned her attention to Flora. "If there is talk even hinting at impropriety between Silas and me, I promise you, you will have to go a lot farther than Denver or even Ohio to escape the repercussions of your actions."

Silas had no idea what those repercussions would be, but the look on Rose's face should be enough to scare anyone. Yet somehow she'd been scared into giving up Milly.

He grabbed for her hand, but Rose held it out of reach. "There's nothing you can say that will change my mind. I have to stop thinking about what I want, and instead, look to Milly and what is best for her."

One of the deputies leaned forward. "I know this is a private conversation, but I can't let this go on."

He looked up at her. "Miss Rose, what kind of reputation do you think you have? Because folks I know, they all say that you're one of the best women Leadville has. Who brings those babies to see the Widow Thomas every week, because she's stuck in that house of hers that she won't leave because she's convinced that someday her husband's going to come back? Who takes plates of food from the Sunday suppers to folks who can't make it?"

The wagon hit another bump, sending Rose into Silas. He steadied her, putting an arm around her. But she immediately pushed him away.

"I'm fine."

She turned and looked at the deputy. "I appreciate your kind words, and I'm truly grateful. But we all know there are those who will never let me forget what I've done. I've learned to live with that."

If it hadn't been for the strain in her voice and the tears in her eyes, he might have believed her. Though they made a big deal of the past being in the past and not knowing the person the other had grown into, Silas could still tell when Rose was lying.

But how did he convince her not to give up?

"We've reached Granite," one of the other deputies

said, and Silas turned to see the outlines of the buildings making up the town. Much smaller than Leadville, the town appeared to be mostly asleep.

Though he'd been eager to finally rest for the evening, he was loath to see the end of the ride and the end of his conversation with Rose. She might have said that there was nothing more to say, but he had plenty.

She might think there was nothing that could convince her to continue with Milly's care, but there had to be something. There had to be a way.

Chapter Seventeen

Rose's stomach hurt so bad, she thought she might be sick. Every argument the Garretts had made for taking Milly had been about Rose's unsuitability as her caretaker. Uncle Frank had been teaching her not to give in to the bullies, but this was more than bullying. This was a woman so desperate to keep a child away from her that she'd resort to kidnapping the child. But she hated the disappointed look on Silas's face.

They'd arrived at a house on the edge of town, owned by one of the deputies from Granite. Rather than putting Flora and the Garretts in jail with drunks and violent criminals, the deputy had offered his home for everyone to spend the night. The men were to sleep in one room, the women in another. But for now, they were all in the main room, discussing plans for the next day.

Rose couldn't concentrate on what was said, not with the way her stomach hurt. Not when the plans ultimately meant not caring for Milly. She turned to go to the room designated for the women, even though she was certain she wouldn't be able to sleep.

"Rosey?" A sleepy-eyed Milly, wrapped in a blanket, tugged at her skirt. "You no go 'way."

Rose knelt in front of the little girl, taking her in her arms. "I'm just going to bed, dear one. Would you like to come?"

"I no sweepy."

Cradling the girl in her arms, Rose smiled, until she caught Mrs. Garrett's glare. "Then you stay with your papa."

"You be here in morning?"

"I will. But we're going to find someone else to be your nanny."

"You be my mommy?" Those little blue eyes were so filled with hope, it made Rose's stomach hurt even more.

"I can't." How two words could cause her physical pain, Rose didn't know. But they tore at her heart in a way she'd never expected.

To think Silas had wanted them to marry for the sake of the children. By now, he should have realized such an action would only ruin Milly's life.

Milly placed her hands on Rose's cheeks. "But I wuv you, Rosey."

"This is an outrage!" Mrs. Garrett pulled against her restraints "Annie has been dead for less than a year and already her daughter is calling another her mother. You promised you'd keep Annie's memory alive, and here she has already forgotten her."

Tears streamed down the older woman's face. "You see? I had no choice but to take her."

"Everyone has a choice," Silas said coldly. "All you

had to do was talk to me. Let me know your concerns, and we could have worked through them together."

"I did tell you!" Another flood of tears came rushing down. Mr. Garrett tried reaching for his wife, but with his hands shackled, the gesture was almost lost.

Except Rose saw. The pain this couple was dealing with. Mrs. Garrett might have been the most vocal about their loss, but Rose could see the deep lines in the older man's face.

"How many times did I express my displeasure at that creature caring for Millicent? But you never listened."

"Did you even give Rose a chance?" Silas sounded just as forceful. "You accuse me of not listening, but did you?"

Then he turned to Rose, still cradling Milly in her arms. "Do you see how much Milly loves Rose? How much Rose loves her? Would you wish anything different for your grandchild?"

"Her mother," Mrs. Garrett sobbed.

Rose smoothed Milly's hair, then whispered in her ear. "Go give your grandmother a hug. She's sad, and it would make her feel better."

Milly hopped down, then went to her grandmother, placing both hands on Mrs. Garrett's cheeks as she'd done to Rose. "You no be sad, Granmudder. Is okay."

Though Milly probably had no idea what she was saying or doing, or even what Mrs. Garrett was sad about, she plopped down on the older woman's lap.

"Why you have deese?" Milly fingered the handcuffs.

"Because..." Mrs. Garrett started sobbing again.

Milly patted her cheeks again. "Is okay, Granmudder."

But it only made Mrs. Garrett cry harder.

Rose looked at the deputy who'd praised her. "Is all of this necessary? The handcuffs, the guards? They're grieving grandparents who only wanted to keep their granddaughter close to them."

"They kidnapped a child," he said firmly. "I know you've a good heart, Miss Rose, and you want to see the best in people, but grandparents or not, they haven't got the right to take her without her father's permission."

Then the deputy looked over at Flora. "And worse, they encouraged a young lady from a good family to join them in their plot."

Will entered the house, flanked by two other deputies. "You shouldn't be talking to them about the case. I don't want anything to interfere with getting a conviction."

Conviction. The word sounded so harsh to Rose. Though she had no love for the Garretts, she didn't think they deserved to be in jail.

"That sounds a little harsh, don't you think?" Rose said quietly, looking over at Silas.

"I've been thinking the same thing." Silas let out a long sigh. "I know technically this is considered a kidnapping, but could we chalk it up to a misunderstanding?"

The look of annoyance on Will's face was almost adorable, especially because ever since they found the Garretts, he'd looked at them like he wanted to kill them.

"Did they or did they not have your permission to take Milly?"

Will turned his gaze on the Garretts, the glare intensifying.

"It's not that simple," Silas said, also looking at them. "I don't want them taking Milly away, but I also don't want them to miss out on seeing her grow up."

"I don't want to miss out on watching her grow up, either," Mr. Garrett said, speaking for the first time since they'd caught up with them. He turned and looked at his wife. "I know you want her to come home with us, but I'd rather have a few afternoons here and there with her than to spend my last days rotting in a jail cell missing that sweet girl."

He patted his lap. "Come give your grandfather a big hug."

Milly crawled over to him, wrapped her arms around him, then gave him one of her big, wet kisses on the cheek. "Granfadder, I wuv you."

The old man's eyes filled with tears. "I love you, too." He looked up at Silas, then added, "Milly."

Rose felt her own eyes water at the sentiment. She remembered the story Silas had told about how Milly had gotten her name, and how the Garretts had refused to call her Milly.

She stole a glance at Silas, who appeared to be just as affected by Mr. Garrett's use of Milly's name.

What she wanted to do was go over to him and give him a hug and tell him that she supported him, that she understood his dilemma. But that was crazy. And would do neither of them any good. As much as she wanted to be there for him, it wasn't her place.

Silas hated the way Rose looked at him. Like she knew. He sighed. She did know. That was the trouble. She knew too much. If ever there was a woman who knew him, who understood him, it was Rose. Even now. Even with everything that had passed between them, and how they'd changed, she knew.

What he wanted most right now was to take her by the hand, sit on that front porch and figure out the best direction from here. He trusted her wisdom, and especially here in Leadville, she'd guided him in so many important ways.

How was he supposed to know what was right without her?

Will hadn't answered his question about whether or not this could all be considered a misunderstanding.

Silas turned his attention on Flora, whose eyes were red and nose puffy from crying. "And what was your part in this whole thing?"

"I wasn't..." She looked around, her gaze settling on Silas. "I didn't... They said she was being corrupted by Rose, and wanted to go home. They hired me to be Millicent's new nanny."

Silas felt Rose tense beside him. He reached for her hand and squeezed.

"Corrupted, how?"

Flora took a step back, immediately running into one of the deputies. "Well, everyone knows her reputation. She has a child to prove it."

Rose tried pulling her hand out of his, but Silas held her firm. "I'm curious, Flora. Who did she hurt with her actions?"

"What do you mean?"

"When she ran off with an outlaw. Who was hurt by that?"

For a moment, Flora didn't speak. Then she said, with just a touch too much smugness in her voice. "Her family. They were humiliated."

"No, we weren't," Will said, coming forward. "Everyone was disappointed by her actions, yes. But I can honestly say that I speak for the family when I tell you how proud we are of how well she's handled herself given the circumstances."

"There are many good families who won't receive her," Flora declared hotly.

"True," Will said. "But this situation has taught us about which friends we can count on, and those are the friends who matter. As for not being received, it seems to me that you're not welcome in a number of homes yourself."

Even without knowing her, Silas could see the pain in her expression. "That's just because they don't..."

Perhaps it was cruel of him to point out, but this young lady needed to learn an important lesson.

Silas gave her a sharp look. "Because they don't appreciate the way you've hurt people with your gossip? Tell us, Flora, how many people have you hurt with your thoughtless words?"

Tears streamed down her face. "But I only...that is, I..."

"Enough." Rose stepped forward. She looked at Flora, but it was too dim in the room for Silas to read Rose's expression. "I think the point Silas is trying to make is that the only person I hurt was myself. You've hurt a lot of people in our town, and for what?"

"I was just trying to help," Flora blurted. "All the sin and lawlessness in town and no one seems to care. If I pointed out the sins of others, it was to caution people to avoid being contaminated."

Rose took another step forward. Silas tugged at her hand to hold her back, but she pulled free from his grasp.

"Contaminated?" Her voice was calm. "Is that how you see me?"

Flora opened her mouth but didn't speak. Rose turned to the Garretts. "And you? Is that what you're afraid of? That my sin of…having relations with a man outside of marriage… If I spend time with Milly, do you think she's going to do it too?"

Silas wanted to laugh at how ridiculous it sounded. But Rose wasn't laughing.

She walked right up to Mrs. Garrett, kissed the old woman's cheek, and said, "There. Now you're a fallen woman, too."

Silence echoed through the group as they all stared at her. Rose shook her head as she picked Milly up out of her grandfather's lap and walked back to Silas. "Associating with me won't cause my sin to taint any of you."

Smiling at Milly, Rose said, "Would you tell your grandparents what I teach you about how to treat others?"

"I hafta be nice to dem, even when dey mean."

"Why?"

Even though his daughter was half-hidden by Rose, Silas could see the smile on her face.

"Because Jesus say to. Him wuvs us all. So we haf to wuv each udder."

Rose turned her attention back to Flora and the Garretts. "I might be, as you say, a doxy, but I have always worked with Milly to teach her about treating others with basic kindness. And you have done nothing but undermine those lessons with how you treat me, and anyone else you disapprove of."

Part of Silas wished he'd been the one to defend Rose. But as he caught a glimpse of the fire in her eyes, the other part of him was glad she'd done so herself. She was finally releasing the shame that had held her captive for so long.

He moved closer and put his arm around her. "Rose may not be welcome in some homes, but that is only because those people do not know her and her character. Those who know her know her to be a godly woman who seeks the Lord and encourages them to do the same. I cannot ask for a better example for my daughter."

Then he turned his gaze to Flora. "Those who do not welcome you into their homes do so because they know your character. Instead of helping others, you're hurting them, and no one wants to be associated with that."

Tears filled Flora's eyes. "My own mother won't take me on calls with her."

Rose nodded. "But if you showed repentance for your actions, and endeavored to change your behavior, I'm sure that would change. I know the other ladies at church would welcome you back if you did so."

Flora scowled, but Silas sensed a softening in her.

Will cleared his throat. "Did you know that the Garretts didn't have Silas's permission to take Milly?"

Flora looked around the room. "Well, I…" Her gaze

landed on the Garretts. "I'm just the nanny. And that's all I have to say until I speak with my father."

"Very well, then," Will said. "I'm sure you've all given us a lot to think about. I'll be speaking with Silas to sort out whether or not this was all a misunderstanding, or if kidnapping charges are warranted."

He looked over at Silas and nodded. "I'm sure you'll feel better if you sleep on your decision. Looks like that little girl of yours has already fallen asleep, and I'm pretty sure Rose will fall over if we don't get her to bed soon."

With a smile, Will held an arm out to Rose. "Let me take Milly. I'll help you both get settled. My wife will never forgive me if you take sick from lack of sleep."

Rose handed Milly over, looking more fatigued than Silas had realized. With emotions so high, it had been easy to miss. But now, she looked like she could sleep for an entire day.

"I've never been sick a day in my life," Rose said, rubbing her eyes. "But I do believe that you're right that I need some sleep. Good night, everyone."

Rose didn't look at him as she started to exit the room, leaving Silas feeling even more lost. What would he do without Rose caring for Milly? He could probably find any number of nannies willing to watch his daughter, even at the meager wage he could afford. But he'd meant every word he'd said about Rose and her character. And that was a rare gift he wasn't sure he'd find in anyone else.

He started to go to the room he'd been told would be where he was sleeping for the night.

"Silas, wait," Mrs. Garrett called to him.

Though his feet felt like his boots had been filled with lead, he turned.

"Please don't take Milli—that is, Milly, from us. You're right. We never gave the situation our honest effort. Rose..."

Mrs. Garrett's voice shook as she called out to Rose. Rose stopped and looked at the other woman.

"It's true," Mrs. Garrett said. "We never tried to get to know you. Any praise directed toward you, we ignored, and we found fault in everything you did. You just have to understand, Annie was everything to us, and to see someone trying to take her place, it was unthinkable."

The older woman sobbed, and Mr. Garrett attempted to comfort her through their restraints.

"I never wanted to take Annie's place," Rose said quietly. "And I would never want to erase her memory for Milly or Silas. From what Silas tells me, she was a good woman, a good wife."

With the kind of compassion Silas had grown to love about Rose, she looked down at the Garretts. "And obviously, a wonderful daughter. But you can't keep her memory alive by refusing to let anyone else live."

Even as exhausted as she was, Rose had still managed to find a way to handle the situation with grace and love. How could Silas not admire that in her? How could he not notice the depth of her beauty radiating out from her heart?

How was he supposed to let her go?

Chapter Eighteen

Sunlight streamed through the room as Rose woke the next morning. To say that every part of her body ached would have been an understatement, because she was certain that there were undiscovered parts of her body she knew nothing about, and they hurt, too.

She reached for Matthew, then remembered he was back at home with Mary. As grateful as she was that he hadn't had to endure last night's grueling ride, she wished she had him right now. Holding him gave her comfort when nothing else could. And she could use all the comfort she could get.

When she tried to sit up, she found the movement only made everything in her body hurt worse, if that was possible.

"Rosey!" The door flew open and Milly came running in. "Is time for bwekfast!"

Before Rose could react, Milly jumped on top of her. "Oh!"

At Milly's startled expression, Rose took a deep

breath, trying not to wince. "Here, sit by me." Rose patted the space beside her.

Silas poked his head into the room. "Milly! I told you not to disturb Rose. She needs her rest."

He must have noticed Rose's unusual position in the bed, because he darted in. "Rose? Are you all right?"

Even her attempt at smiling caused her pain. "I... Something appears to be... That is, I..."

How could talking seem so difficult? It felt like with every word, her ribs cried out for her to stop.

He shook his head slowly. "You've never ridden like that, have you?"

"Well, I suppose I might have...exaggerated slightly." This time, she made herself smile. "It didn't seem so difficult at the time."

She hated the way he looked at her like she'd somehow deceived him in telling him she could ride. She could. Just not the way they'd ridden last night.

"What's going on in here?" Will entered the room, giving Silas a stern look. "You shouldn't be in this bedroom."

"I only came for Milly," he said smoothly. "However, I'm glad I did. Apparently, Rose is having a hard time getting out of bed after yesterday's ride."

Giving Milly a squeeze, he said, "Go eat your breakfast before it gets cold. We'll take care of Rose."

Milly hopped off the bed and out of the room.

Will shook his head slowly, like he, too, was disappointed in her. "I knew I shouldn't have let you come."

But as her eyes filled with tears, he approached the bed and knelt beside her. "I'm sorry, Rose. I didn't mean to hurt you. It just makes returning home today more difficult. You can't ride in your condition."

"We can take the wagon," Silas said.

"The Garretts were supposed to be returning it to Amos Warner in Buena Vista. I can't in good conscience take it back to Leadville." Rose shook her head, ignoring the pain. "Just give me a few moments, and I'll be fine."

Will and Silas exchanged amused glances.

"I'm a seasoned rider, and my backside isn't looking forward to getting back on a horse today," Silas said with a grin.

Will coughed, and Rose bit back a grin. A man didn't speak of such things in front of a lady. But she and Silas were no ordinary man and woman.

"It's fine, Will." Rose smiled at Silas. "I don't suppose you have any ideas as to how to make it feel better."

Silas shrugged. "We could see if there's any liniment here, or we can send someone to the general store for some."

"You are not rubbing liniment on Rose!"

She'd never heard Will sound so protective.

"I wasn't offering." Silas took a step back. "I've done it for myself plenty of times. I was just suggesting it might help ease the ache in her muscles so she can get out of bed."

Then he turned his gaze on Rose. "I know it sounds like the last thing on earth you want to do, but the sooner you get up and moving, the sooner you'll feel better."

Rose nodded slowly, wishing even that effort didn't take so much energy. "I just need a little more time."

"Good," Will said. "You rest. Silas will get some liniment, and I will find a lady to come help you."

The last part he said with such a fierce look directed at Silas that Rose couldn't help but giggle.

"It's not funny. I know you think you're beyond propriety, but Rose, you are still a lady, and you will be treated as such."

Then he glared at Silas. "Or there will be consequences."

"Enough, Will." Rose gave him a stern look. "Silas cannot be faulted in his treatment of me. So stop threatening him."

"Fine. But I will not tolerate any hint of impropriety."

Rose groaned. "I'm already ruined, in case you've forgotten."

"Stop saying that." Will turned his glare on her. "I'm tired of you wearing your past like a shroud. I don't care what Flora and the Garretts think."

Obviously, her brother-in-law had spent more time listening to the family than he had spent dealing with people in town. "You don't understand," Rose said. "Other people—"

"Who?" The anger on his face was less directed at Rose than it was at whoever the people were. "Didn't you hear Deputy Elliott? People respect you, Rose. You're so busy listening to the negative things people have to say about you that you haven't been able to recognize what an important part of the community you are. There are far more people who see you in a good light than there are who think poorly of you."

"You don't have to defend me anymore, Will. I accept my position in society." Now, in addition to every other part of her body, her stomach ached. And her throat hurt.

"I never had to!" The vein throbbed in his temple. "Yes, there have been people turning their noses up at you, but mostly, they see how you serve others in the church, how you treat everyone with kindness and respect and how everyone can rely on you, no matter what."

His words burned, like the tears stinging her cheeks. "But I... Will, I have a child out of wedlock, and there are those in town who will never let me forget that."

"Maybe they would if you stopped using that as an excuse to hide. Maybe, if you stopped letting your sin define you, you'd be able to hold your head up a little higher and no one would question why."

Silas had said something similar. And yet none of them knew what it was like to walk around town, knowing people were whispering about her.

"I appreciate the sentiment," she said, looking from Will to Silas. "But neither of you understand the agony of walking into a place like the Mercantile and having people walk out as soon as they notice you."

Will shook his head at her. "That's where you're mistaken. Back when I lived in Century City, people thought I'd been part of a robbery. I couldn't go anywhere without the whispers that I'd killed a man. I hadn't, but even longtime friends abandoned me. You're surrounded by people who love you. So stop listening to the negative talk, and focus on the good things you're doing in our community."

Silas gave her an encouraging nod as if to remind her of how he'd been trying to tell her the same thing.

"But you were innocent, Will. I'm guilty. I did everything people think I did and more. You and Uncle Frank prettied up the role I played, but we all know I was selfish, vindictive, and God help me, I went willingly. Yes, I believed Ben's lies, but until you, Jasper and Mary came to rescue me, I was a willing participant in all the evil."

She turned her gaze on Silas. "I know you don't want to hear this. But you have to know—all of my sins I committed with full knowledge that I was doing wrong. And I enjoyed every minute of it. It's the consequences that are hard to live with."

"I don't care," Silas said quietly. "You're no longer that person. We've been through this, and I don't know how many times we have to tell you that those mistakes have no bearing on the woman you are today."

Will cleared his throat. "I disagree. Your mistakes have everything to do with who you are today. They've caused you to turn from being that selfish woman and to consider how your actions affect others. The woman who did those things would have never given up Milly, nor would she have refused Silas's offer of courtship."

And now, even Rose's heart hurt. Because if she were being honest with all of them, she'd tell them that she *did* want to be Milly's mother. She wanted… Rose shook her head. No, she couldn't allow herself to want that.

"Maybe so," Rose said quietly. "But I could give you a list of people just like Flora and the Garretts who will never see me as someone other than that former person. And I cannot burden another innocent child or her father with that prejudice."

She leaned back against the pillows and closed her eyes for a moment. So much inside her ached, and she couldn't tell the difference between the physical and emotional anymore.

After taking a couple of painful breaths, she opened her eyes to look at the two men. "If you wouldn't mind getting the liniment for me, I would appreciate it. I think I need a little more rest."

Silas looked like he was about to say something, but Will had placed a hand on his arm. Hopefully, it meant that Will had finally realized the futility of continuing to argue with her. Because as much as she believed she was doing the right thing, it was hard to face the disappointed looks from two men she respected.

On his way back to the house from picking up liniment for Rose, Silas ran into Will.

"I talked to Jim, the owner of the livery," Will said, pointing at a nearby building. "He's Wes's brother, and I've dealt with him a few times before. He'll take the wagon we brought and be sure it's returned to its proper owners."

"What about getting Rose home?"

"I stopped by the telegraph office. Frank's coming with a wagon, Mary and the babies. It'll mean spending another night here, but I think it's best for Rose. Jim is sending his wife over to help her for now, but I know Rose will be more comfortable in her sister's care."

"Good. Do you think Rose needs a doctor?"

Will gave him a long look. "Have you ever needed a doctor after a long, hard ride?"

"No." Silas shook his head. "I just thought…"

"You care about her."

"Probably more than I should, I suppose." Silas sighed. Between Rose chasing him off and her over-protective family, he didn't stand a chance with her.

"Like I told you before, that depends on whether or not you intend to marry her."

"And what if I did?"

Those words weren't supposed to come out. But Will didn't look surprised by them.

"It's not going to come easy, you know." Will stared at him like he was looking to see Silas's reaction. Like he thought Silas was going to run off the first chance he got.

"It hasn't been so far. And I'm still here."

"I'll talk to Frank," Will said. "Right now, I don't think she'll have you. Personally, I think she's making a mistake, but it's her life. Just so you know, I'll stand by whatever she decides."

With a wink, he added, "But I will do my best to guide her in the right direction."

Not the response he'd expected from the other man, not when Will had been so hard on him.

"I didn't know you approved."

Will gave another long nod. "Rose deserves a man who is going to love her fully, no matter what. The way I see it, you've stood by her and defended her when a lot of men would have already given up. Even now, when she's made it clear that she's not interested, you see through her defenses."

Her defenses. That was a kind way of putting it, because right now, he was starting to see that Rose's stub-bornness was the one thing that hadn't changed from their previous time together. Well, no. That wasn't true. If anything, it had gotten worse.

Will looked thoughtful, then added, "She's scared. And I don't blame her. She hasn't had an easy road, and I'd be lying if I said it would be in the future, but that's not how life works."

Giving a small shake of his head, Silas looked at him. "You think I don't know that? My wife and baby died. I lost everything. And just when I thought things were finally looking up, the Garretts came and tried to destroy it all. I'm not afraid of hard, but it sure would be easier to go through it with the love of a good woman standing beside me."

Will slapped him on the back, grinning. "And I think Rose needs a good man standing beside her."

Then his expression grew serious. "But now we need to figure out what we're going to do about the Garretts. Mr. Montgomery is coming with Frank to collect Flora, and I need to know if we're charging them with a crime or if you're going to say it was a misunderstanding."

Silas thought for a moment, examining the other man's expression for a sign of what he was thinking.

"I don't know," Silas finally said. "Part of me knows they were desperate, doing what they thought was best for Milly. They're grieving the loss of a beloved daughter and aren't thinking clearly."

Then he took a deep breath. "But what they did was wrong. If they don't face consequences, what's to say they aren't going to try again?"

"And Flora?"

Silas shrugged. "She was just going along with what

they wanted. Again, I'd like to see her face some kind of consequences, but nothing so severe as jail."

Will looked thoughtful. "I understand your dilemma. And I agree. I don't want anyone thinking it's all right to kidnap a child. If it were Rosabelle…"

His jaw hardened, and he blew out a breath. "I can't imagine what you went through, not knowing where Milly was. Honestly, I'd want blood."

Shaking his head, he grinned. "I suppose God isn't finished with me learning about forgiveness yet. When it comes to my family, I don't know if I'm capable of showing mercy."

This time, it was Silas's turn to clap Will on the back. "I think you'd do the right thing in the end, which is all I'm trying to do. The Garretts were my family once, and though Annie is gone, I'm not averse to maintaining that relationship for Milly's sake."

"You're a better man than me."

Silas gave a small snort. "I wouldn't say that. I just remember when I was a boy, all the things my grandfather taught me. I always wished I had more time with him before he died."

Looking at Will, he asked, "Did you know your grandparents?"

"No." Will gave him a thoughtful look. "But I remember my mother speaking fondly of my grandmother, and I always wish I'd had the chance to know her."

"How can I deny Milly that?"

Will looked thoughtful again. "It is hard to get to know someone behind bars."

Silas wasn't sure they'd last long behind bars anyway. Neither Garrett was in good health, and lately, he'd noticed Mrs. Garrett not looking well.

"I suppose I should speak to them. See if there is any hope of salvaging the relationship. If not, I suppose the only recourse is to press charges and let their future rest in the hands of a jury. I don't like it, but I also need to keep Milly safe."

Will nodded slowly. "Then let's go inside and talk to them. See if we can work something out. Otherwise, I'll need to have them transferred to the jail."

Jail. Such a harsh word. But what else was he to do?

They entered the house, and Flora and the Garretts were sitting in chairs, still guarded by deputies. The restraints had been taken off their hands, but it was clear they weren't going anywhere.

"Mr. Garrett. Mrs. Garrett. Flora." Silas looked at the three of them. Mr. Garrett appeared to be worn, accepting his punishment. Mrs. Garrett wore an expression of disgust, like she still thought she was in the right. And then there was Flora, her face blotchy from having spent the entire time since their capture crying off and on.

"I need to know how to proceed."

"Don't put me in jail," Flora wailed. "I cannot face such disgrace."

He looked at the woman, who appeared so young and fragile, barely older than a girl.

"But you said that sinners should be punished. You helped the Garretts break the law. And that means you should go to jail."

"Noooo!" Flora started sobbing again.

Silas cleared his throat. "What would you do in my position? Even without jail, it seems to me that you would go home and make it the talk of every parlor in town. Do you feel you deserve that?"

Tears streamed down Flora's face. "But how else will people know about the bad things others have done?"

"Do you want people to know about the bad things you've done?"

"No…" A loud sob burst out of her. "Please. It's bad enough that everyone is already shunning me. If they knew the truth about me, then I'd have no friends left at all."

Silas thought back to what Rose had said the night before. "And Rose doesn't deserve friends?"

"I was wrong," Flora said, sniffling. "I just…"

"You need to learn to see the world beyond yourself, to care about the feelings of others." Silas handed her his handkerchief. "Rose invited you to help out with the church ministry. Spend some time there. Learn about the people you've been turning your nose up at. Give it an honest effort, and no one will hear about this. But if you keep up your old ways, or I hear that you've said one bad thing about someone else, I will make sure that every person in town knows about what you've done. I will gleefully recount what it was like to see you in handcuffs."

He glanced at Will, who nodded. "And I'll back up his story. There will never be a bigger laughingstock in all of Leadville."

"All right," Flora said, brushing away the tears with the handkerchief.

"What about us?" Mr. Garrett asked, looking nervously at his wife.

Silas stared at them. What did a man say? "I'm torn.

Like I told Will, I understand where you were coming from. But I can't risk spending the rest of my life looking over my shoulder wondering if Milly's going to be taken from me again."

"I'm sorry," Mr. Garrett said.

"I know." Silas let his gaze rest on Mrs. Garrett. "But I suspect this wasn't your plan. I need to know that she's sorry."

Mrs. Garrett still didn't speak. Silas returned his attention to Mr. Garrett.

"I believe that you love Milly very much and would do just about anything to be with her. You've compromised when I think your wife would have preferred not to. So here's my offer—I want a written apology, detailing what you did, including the fact that you took Milly without my permission. You will not interfere with how I raise Milly, nor will you make disparaging comments about me or anyone I choose to bring into Milly's life."

His heart ached for the one person who had been most hurt by all of this. "You will also send a written apology to Rose for how you've treated her. And you will treat her with respect and dignity. You will not make any unkind remarks about her."

He looked around the room, noting the solemn expressions on the deputies' faces. Most of them were eager to put the Garretts in jail. They all had families. Children.

"I'll allow you to see Milly. But your visits will always be chaperoned by a person of my choosing. If they or anyone else reports back to me that you have violated my conditions, you will never see Milly again."

Mrs. Garrett finally looked up at him, tears in her eyes. "And if we don't agree?"

"I guess that's up to the jury."

His gut knotted as he gave those final terms. He didn't want to refuse them the opportunity to spend time with a beloved grandchild, but he'd tried. And he had to keep Milly safe.

"I agree to your terms," Mr. Garrett said. "You're being more than reasonable."

Silas took a deep breath, then looked over at Mrs. Garrett. "I need both of you to agree. It's pretty clear who's in charge here, and I'm not going to put Milly at risk."

Tears rushed down Mrs. Garrett's face, a great waterfall that seemed to go on endlessly. "But you can remarry, have more children. Milly is all we have left."

"You'll have no contact with her if you're in jail."

With a sigh, Silas gave them a final glance. "If the decision to cooperate is this hard, then it's not going to work. You'll be resentful and try to thwart me at every turn. I want you to have a relationship with Milly. I tried giving you that, but you tried to take more. Which leaves me at the terms I've offered you. Take them or leave them."

Silas closed his eyes and said a quick prayer, hoping he was doing the right thing. Hoping God would guide the Garretts in making the best decision for Milly. Or at least making it all right if they didn't.

"You have until the rest of our party arrives from Leadville to make your decision. If you can't, in good conscience, with a right heart and a good attitude toward cooperation, commit to my plan, you will be arrested."

His hands shook as he made his final plea. He didn't want the Garretts to grudgingly agree to his terms, then have things be a constant battle. He didn't want them to go to jail, either. But the outcome was no longer his to determine.

And somehow, he had to be all right with how it all turned out.

Chapter Nineteen

Rose was resting peacefully when the bedroom door opened and her sister, Mary, walked in, carrying a wailing Matthew.

"Mary! What are you doing here?"

"Bringing you a baby who only wants his mama. Even if we hadn't gotten that telegram, we were already loading up a wagon to come meet you."

Smiling, Rose held out her arms for her baby and set to work comforting him.

"I'm sorry he was so much trouble."

"It's not your fault. From what Will says, it was a good thing little Matthew wasn't with you on your journey."

"Of course you'd talk to your husband first," Rose teased.

"Of course." Mary smiled. "He took Rosabelle right out of her basket and refuses to let her go."

Her sister's expression changed to one of deep concern. "He says you're pretty sore from the ride."

"I can barely walk," Rose said. "I don't think I was this sore even after having a baby."

"Well, Maddie is in the kitchen, making up some kind of poultice or some such, and she'll be in to tend you."

"Thank you." Rose gave her a smile. "I am sorry for all the fuss. I didn't realize…"

"You love Milly like your own. What mother wouldn't go after her child?"

Rose's heart sank. "But she's not mine. And she won't be. I told Silas he'd need to find someone else to care for her."

"What would you do a fool thing like that for?" Maddie entered the room, carrying a strange-smelling pot.

"I won't have Milly tainted by my poor reputation," Rose said softly, adjusting Matthew in her arms. "It's bad enough Matthew will suffer for it. I won't do that to Milly."

"That is about the stupidest thing I've ever heard you say, Rose Stone, and I have heard you say some pretty stupid things." Maddie banged the pot with her spoon, then turned her attention to Mary.

"You go find what Milly's gotten herself into. I know the men think they're watching her, but you know how much that little girl likes mud. And those men don't know a thing about what's it like to have to wash a little girl's muddy dresses."

Mary shook her head, giving Rose a sympathetic glance. "I would stay because I have a feeling that you're about to get a talking-to that's going to hurt far worse than your body. But if you really believe that having you in her life hurts Milly, then I'm pretty sure you deserve it."

Maddie pulled up a chair and sat beside the bed. "I know they put liniment on you, but that stuff's best suited for animals. This here poultice will take away the sting."

She uncovered Rose and started smoothing it on her legs. Rose leaned back against her pillows and started to relax.

Until Maddie spoke.

"I'm told that you can't seem to accept that most people don't look down on you for your sin."

Keeping her eyes closed, Rose shook her head. "Not you, too. I know you mean well. You see me through the eyes of someone who loves me. But the people in town, they see me for what I've done."

"You're right, they do," Maddie said, kneading Rose's aching muscles. "They see how you help out at all the church functions. They see you doing good deeds for the people of Leadville. They see that you are the only one who can stand to give the Widow Thomas the time of day, bringing treats and the children to visit her. They see that you read to Mr. Bennett because his eyesight is failing. They see what a good—"

"Stop!" Rose opened her eyes and stared at Maddie. "I know you mean well, but so many others whisper behind their fans, turn and walk the other way when they see me coming, and I can't bear for Silas to be so dishonored."

"Silas, is it?" Maddie's voice was all sweetness, and Rose knew her mistake.

"Milly, too. Mostly Milly."

"You have feelings for Silas." Maddie's hand dug deep into Rose's thigh, hurting her.

"Ouch!"

"Gotta get deep in there. You aren't used to riding like that."

"I know." Rose sighed and kissed the top of Matthew's head. Everyone was right. She couldn't have done it if not for Milly.

Looking at Maddie, she said, "You're right. I do have feelings for Silas. He's a good man. I know what happened in the past was what he thought he had to do for the sake of his family. He is kind, patient, loving, self-sacrificing…"

"Not bad to look at," Maddie added, her eyes twinkling.

"There is that." Rose smiled. "But he's so much more. And more than I could have ever hoped for back when we first knew each other. He's changed for the better, and I am so proud to know him."

Mary was right in that this would hurt more than her body. Admitting her feelings for Silas, when she knew it would only cause him harm… It had been so much easier when she denied how much she cared for him.

"So why not pursue him?"

"Because he deserves a woman who brings him honor, not dishonor."

Her chest ached as she said the words. Could she stand seeing him with another?

Maddie removed her hands from Rose's legs. "So we're back to that, are we? Do you really think that the sum of who you are is your mistake?"

Rose turned away, not looking at her.

"Oh, no you don't. You look at me, and you listen. You listen well." Maddie stood over her until Rose turned to face her.

"What I'm about to tell you, well, I suppose it's common knowledge, but folks don't talk about it anymore. And I'd just as soon forget it myself. But you need to hear. Has anyone ever told you how I came to work for Frank?"

Rose shook her head.

"Do you know why we send gifts to Miss Betty's pleasure house every week?"

Rose shook her head again.

Maddie squared her shoulders. "Because Miss Betty and I used to be partners—that's why."

The words sounded as ill matched as ice cream and Christmas. "I'm sorry. I don't understand what you mean."

"I mean partners. Fifty-fifty. We'd both gotten so tired of living in tents and taking care of customers that we pooled our money and built that place. We were the first place of its kind to get a real building, and boy, were we raking in the money."

Maddie gave her a proud look. "Oh, yes. I was known as one of the finest madams this side of the Mississippi. When I was younger, folks would stop in the middle of the street and stare on account of my fine looks."

The image didn't make sense in Rose's mind. She tried to picture Maddie, one of the most respected women in their community, living that life.

And she couldn't.

"So what happened?"

Maddie sighed. "Catherine Lassiter happened. She

was the kindest woman you'd ever want to meet. I'd be in the General Store, no fancy Mercantiles and shops back then, and she'd greet me like I was the finest woman in town."

With a smile, Maddie patted her hand. "I do wish you'd had the chance to meet her. She had a way of making everyone feel like they were the most important person in the world."

Matthew cooed as though he'd met Catherine and agreed.

"I suppose, though, that is how she saw people. All equal in God's eyes."

Maddie reached for Matthew, and Rose let the other woman take her son. "One day, when I was at the General Store, and very obviously in the family way, she asked me if she might make a quilt for my baby. I told her she was mistaking me for someone else because no one would want to give a child of mine a quilt."

As Maddie cradled Matthew, she looked Rose in the eye. "And do you know what she said to me?"

Rose shook her head.

"She said, 'I know exactly who you are, Maddie Black. And that baby of yours deserves a welcome to the world like any other baby.' I was so ashamed, I ran away."

A tear trickled out of the side of Maddie's eye, and she wiped it with her free hand. "But Catherine, she started paying me visits, bringing me things for the baby, telling me that Jesus loved me, and therefore so did she."

More tears rolled down Maddie's cheeks, but she didn't bother with them, continuing her story.

"It took a lot of visits for me to believe her. Just when I started to think God might maybe care for a woman like me, my baby died. No one knows why. Those things just happen sometimes. I thought it meant God hated me. I was terrible to be around then, and Betty said I was scaring away customers. Catherine came and took me to the parsonage, which was smaller back then, but she gave me a room of my own, and she took care of me until I was right in the head again."

Maddie gave Matthew another kiss. "When I finally got it in my head that God loved me, I gave my whole life to the Lord. I walked away from my partnership with Betty, and I came to work for the Lassiters. And that's been my life ever since."

She turned her gaze on Rose, so warm it almost burned. "Folks pass through Leadville so much that most of the people who were around then are long gone. But there are those who still remember. Maybe some still hold my past against me, but I'd like to think that I've overcome the things I used to do."

She'd seen how people in town respected Maddie. Rose had never heard a word spoken against their housekeeper.

"Integrity," Maddie said slowly, "is not about doing something good once and a while but about doing the right thing over and over until it becomes the standard for one's character. People without it are always going to look down on you for one reason or another. But everyone else is going to forget that past mistake and see you for who you've become."

The same lesson Silas, Will and everyone else had been trying to get through to her, but she'd been too focused on the harsh judgment from Flora and the Garretts to believe them.

Maddie handed Matthew back to her. "Now, I am going to finish giving your muscles a good rubdown, and you are going to have some words with the Lord, asking Him to show you how He sees you. And when I am finished, I will hear no more nonsense about you refusing Silas and not caring for Milly because you want to protect them. If you don't love him, fine. I will be the first one to make sure you don't marry him. But if you love him, you'd best give it your all. I know a lot about what goes on between a man and a woman, and I can tell you that it is rare to find a man who loves a woman as deeply as Silas loves you."

So much to consider. Rose nestled Matthew in next to her and closed her eyes, pondering Maddie's words and asking God to show her the clear path.

Silas finished loading the rest of the supplies into the wagon they'd be driving back to Leadville. As it turned out, Wes needed some things from his brother, so they'd be bringing two wagons home, one laden with supplies.

He looked around for Will. They hadn't resolved what was going to happen with the Garretts, and he was starting to feel uneasy.

What if they couldn't work things out?

He'd already backed down on his threat, since he'd told the Garretts he wanted their answer when Frank arrived, but they'd all been so busy, he hadn't wanted to push. Now he wondered if he shouldn't have pushed anyway.

The door to the house opened, and Maddie came out.

She'd spent most of the time since they'd arrived yesterday closed in the room with Rose, not letting anyone disturb her recovery. Selfishly, he'd hoped to talk to Rose for a while, but everyone kept telling him to give Rose her space.

Plus, he missed holding little Matthew, but no one would take the baby from his mama.

Maddie said something to Frank, then walked over to Silas. "We're going to have Rose, Matthew and Milly ride with you in this wagon, and the rest of us will follow in the other."

"You're letting me ride alone with Rose?" Silas stared at her.

"You all have some things to talk about. Figured we'd let you have some privacy, but where we can see you, for propriety's sake."

Silas wanted to laugh because Rose was right in that everyone was entirely too focused on the appearance of propriety. But he also understood.

"Thank you. When are we leaving?"

The front door opened again, and Rose came out, carrying Matthew and holding Milly's hand. They looked like the picture-perfect family. He still didn't know how he was going to make that picture a reality, but he wasn't going to let Rose go easily.

She smiled at him, the color back in her cheeks, and once again, he couldn't help but think she was the loveliest woman he'd ever seen.

Will emerged next, followed by Mrs. Garrett, flanked by a deputy, then Mr. Garrett with a deputy, and then Flora, her father gripping her elbow tightly.

"Silas," Will said, standing between him and the

Garretts, looking official. "I believe the Garretts have something to say to you."

"I'm sorry," Mrs. Garrett said slowly. "I was only thinking of myself and our loss when we took Milly. I agree to your terms. We will cooperate with you in every way possible moving forward."

Then Mrs. Garrett turned to Rose. "I apologize for all the hurtful things I've said to you, and for not giving you a chance. Anyone can see that Milly loves you, and I, well, I suppose I feared that if Milly loved you, she wouldn't be able to love her mother, or us, anymore. But I was wrong. And I hope you reconsider finding her a new nanny because Milly needs you."

Milly. Three times she'd said Milly. If ever there was a sign that Mrs. Garrett was sincere in her apology, the fact that she so easily used Milly's name was that sign.

"Thank you," Rose said, looking the older woman in the eye. "I accept your apology, and I forgive you."

Then she turned to Silas, smiling at him. "As for my position as Milly's nanny, I'm not sure I can go back to that."

The smile on her face didn't ease the tension knotted in his stomach. There was no letting him down easy when all he wanted was Rose, and Rose in Milly's life.

"But I'd like to share my thoughts on Milly's care more privately."

Rose gave the others a smile, and Will nodded at her briefly before ushering the others into the waiting wagon. It wasn't until the wagon pulled away and waited at the gate that she turned her attention back on him.

In those agonizing moments, Silas tried to ascertain what Rose would have to say that would require such privacy. As much as he wanted to hope for something positive, he wasn't sure he could face the alternative.

Her shoulders rose and fell, and Silas thought he saw her shake the tiniest bit. "You asked to court me, and I refused. I was wrong. But I think, at least on my end, courting now is pointless."

Pointless. Silas swallowed the lump that formed in his throat. Will had said it wouldn't be easy. He wasn't going to lose heart. They had the whole ride back to talk.

"I'm sure you know that the purpose of courtship is to determine whether or not you'll suit in marriage. I've already decided."

Rose gave him another smile, then she bent down and whispered something in Milly's ear.

Milly's face brightened, bursting with so much joy he wasn't sure such a tiny girl could contain it all. She ran in his direction.

"Rosey wants to be my mommy!"

Silas caught his daughter in her arms and picked her up. "Is that so?"

"Yes," Rose said, nodding her head slowly, but Silas could tell her whole body was shaking.

"I thought the man was supposed to do the asking when it came to marriage."

Rose grinned. "I'm sure we all know that I don't do things the regular way. But you can ask me if it makes you feel any better. Besides, I don't know if you still want to marry me."

"Oh, I do," Silas said, bridging the gap between them with long strides. "Rose, will you marry me?"

"I will."

Silas bent down and kissed Rose, but as their lips touched, he felt Milly squirming in his arms. He looked down and noticed they'd pinned the children between them.

"It's all right." Rose batted her eyes at him the way she used to when they were younger. "We have the rest of our lives for that. Which will be starting soon. Because we're getting married as soon as humanly possible so that you don't have time to find another bride."

"Not a chance," Silas said, kissing her again, mindful of the children, and setting Milly on the ground. "I'm not letting you get away this time."

"Hey!" Milly tugged on his pant leg. "Dat's *my* Rosey!"

They pulled apart and looked down at the indignant little girl.

Silas knelt before his daughter. "If she's going to be your mommy, she has to become my wife. So you're going to have to share."

Milly appeared to consider his words for a moment. "Like wif Ma-few?"

"Exactly like that," Rose said, shifting the baby in her arms as she bent down to the little girl. "And with any other babies that happen to come along."

Her eyes twinkled as she looked up at Silas.

"You just asked me to marry you. Now you're telling me you want more babies?" He laughed as he shook his head. "You are something else, Rose Stone."

She grinned. "It'll be Rose Jones soon enough. Besides, didn't you tell me you wanted a large family because you disliked growing up without siblings? So let's get in that wagon and head for home. I've got a wedding to plan."

Knowing Rose, she probably already had it all planned out. And he wasn't going to argue. He'd waited long enough to make her his wife. While some might complain about the ups and downs that brought them there, Silas had nothing but gratitude for a journey that had made them both better versions of the couple that had originally fallen in love.

Epilogue

Three years later

Rose smoothed the back of Milly's hair one last time before her grandparents arrived. The Garretts couldn't handle Leadville winters, but they'd taken to coming for a visit every summer. At five, Milly had started learning to write enough that she could sign her name on the letters Rose regularly sent to them, updating them on Milly's progress.

"Mama! Stop messing with my hair!" Milly scowled at her as Rose stepped away.

"All right. I'm sorry. If you didn't like playing in the mud with the others so much, I wouldn't have to." Rose held up a leaf. "How did this even get there?"

Milly shrugged as the door opened.

"They're here!"

They'd barely entered the house, Silas following behind with their bags, when Milly barreled toward them. "Grandmother! Grandfather!"

"Milly!" Mrs. Garrett, rather, Constance, as she had

asked Rose to call her, wrapped her arms around her granddaughter.

"My, you've grown!"

"I eat all my vegetables," Milly said proudly. "And guess what?"

She looked eagerly at her grandparents. "You—" she pointed to her grandfather "—are *grandpère*. And you—" Milly pointed at her grandmother "—are *grand-mère*."

Then Milly turned and smiled at Rose. "Mama's new friend at the mission is from France. She is teaching me French. Mama says you will be so pleased."

"We are." Constance gave Rose a smile. "She is growing into a lovely young lady. Thank you for letting us visit."

"You're very welcome." Rose stepped forward and hugged both Garretts. "We're so happy you're here."

As soon as Rose finished greeting the Garretts, Milly took them by the hands and pulled them into the parlor. While Milly continued chattering at her grandparents, Silas came and put an arm around Rose. "She is something else. It'll be nice for her to talk their ears off for a change."

"That it will be." Rose yawned.

"Tired?"

She nodded. "Hope was restless last night. When I finally got her to sleep, Matthew woke up from a nightmare, so then I had to comfort him. It felt like I'd barely gotten to sleep when I had to get up this morning."

Silas kissed the top of her head. "I didn't even hear the baby. I'm sorry."

"It's all right. I managed."

With a grin, Silas nodded in the direction of the Garretts. "Speaking of managing, they seem to be doing fine with Milly. We could go upstairs for a while, and—"

"Silas Jones!"

"What?" His eyes twinkled. "I was just suggesting a nap."

Rose gave him a quick kiss. "I'm sure you were. But we've got family to catch up with, and Maddie will be serving supper soon. I think she's invited Flora, and I have no doubt that everyone else in our family will be straggling in at some point, as well."

Flora had made good on her promise to help out at the church, and to refrain from making disparaging comments about others. In fact, Rose had noticed her taking other girls under her wing and making sure they understood that in their society, gossip was unacceptable.

Silas let out a long exaggerated sigh. "All right."

As they watched Milly chatting animatedly with her grandparents, Rose couldn't help the joy rising up in her.

Though there were some who still whispered about Rose's fall from grace, most people had long forgotten that Matthew wasn't Silas's natural son. As Rose's standing in society grew, she'd come to learn of other women who'd also risen above past mistakes, and that Maddie wasn't the only former working girl who'd gained respectability. Proof that what you did in the past only defined you if you let it. Which was the only reason most people even knew of Rose's past. She'd found it helped the women they encountered in their ministry know that regardless of their mistakes, God could use them for something bigger.

In all of her girlhood dreams of becoming Mrs. Silas Jones, she'd never imagined that the reality would be so much better. The pain she'd suffered was worth the depth of love and respect she'd found with the man looking at her with such a loving gaze.

"What's that look for?" she asked, tucking her arm in his.

"Just thinking about how much I love you, and how grateful I am for all you do to make our family whole."

He nodded in Milly's direction, then turned his gaze back on Rose. He didn't have to say the words because she saw the love shining in his eyes.

"And I love you," Rose said softly as she reached up to kiss him again.

* * * * *

*If you enjoyed Rose's book,
pick up the stories of Rose's friends and family,
also set in Leadville, Colorado:*

*ROCKY MOUNTAIN DREAMS
THE LAWMAN'S REDEMPTION
SHOTGUN MARRIAGE
THE NANNY'S LITTLE MATCHMAKERS*

Available now from Love Inspired!

Find more great reads at www.LoveInspired.com

Dear Reader,

Some books are easier to write than others, and I'm going to go on record as saying this was one of the hardest. Bringing redemption to Rose was the easy part; the difficulty was realizing that the lesson about forgiveness was more than just her forgiving Silas for breaking her heart. Forgiveness seems to be an easy task, but as anyone who has struggled with forgiveness can tell you, it sometimes takes a lot more than saying, "I forgive you." Writing Rose's story forced me to look at places in my own heart where I'd been struggling to forgive, and I knew I couldn't do her story justice unless I was willing to take a journey through my own unforgivingness.

If you're like me, and there are things in your life that you've struggled to let go of, don't lose heart! I've learned that the regions of the heart where forgiveness needs to permeate resemble the layers of the earth. Some are thin, porous, and water has no trouble finding its way to the deeper layers. Other areas are thick, dense rock, seemingly impenetrable. But nothing is impossible with God's love, and ultimately, even the hardest of hearts can experience forgiveness at the very core.

Obviously, though I've poured my heart into this book, and shared a little about God's work in me in this letter, there is so much more I can say. If you'd like additional resources on forgiveness, please visit my website at danicafavorite.com and look for the section on forgiveness.

I always love hearing from my readers, so feel free to connect with me at the following places:

Website: danicafavorite.com.
Twitter: Twitter.com/danicafavorite.
Instagram: Instagram.com/danicafavorite.
Facebook: Facebook.com/danicafavoriteauthor.

Abundant blessings to you and yours,
Danica Favorite

WED BY NECESSITY
Smoky Mountain Matches • by Karen Kirst

Caught in a storm overnight with her father's new employee, Caroline Turner finds her reputation damaged. And the only way to repair it is to marry Duncan McKenna. But can a sophisticated socialite and a down-to-earth stable manager put their differences aside and find love?

THE OUTLAW'S SECRET
by Stacy Henrie

When Essie Vanderfair's train is held up by outlaws, the dime-store novelist connives to be taken hostage by them, seeking material for her next book. But she doesn't anticipate falling for one of the outlaws...or that he's secretly an undercover detective.

THE BOUNTY HUNTER'S BABY
by Erica Vetsch

Bounty hunter Thomas Beaufort has no problem handling outlaws, but when he's left with a criminal's baby to care for, he's in over his head. And the only person he can turn to for help is Esther Jensen, the woman whose heart he broke when he left town.

THE RELUCTANT GUARDIAN
by Susanne Dietze

On the verge of her first London season, Gemma Lyfeld accidently stumbles on a group of smugglers, catching them in the act...and they think she's a spy. Now she must depend on covert government agent Tavin Knox for protection. But how will she protect her heart from him?

———————

LIHCNM0117

REQUEST YOUR FREE BOOKS!

2 FREE INSPIRATIONAL NOVELS
PLUS 2 FREE MYSTERY GIFTS

Love Inspired® HISTORICAL

YES! Please send me 2 FREE Love Inspired® Historical novels and my 2 FREE mystery gifts (gifts are worth about $10). After receiving them, if I don't wish to receive any more books, I can return the shipping statement marked "cancel." If I don't cancel, I will receive 4 brand-new novels every month and be billed just $4.99 per book in the U.S. or $5.49 per book in Canada. That's a saving of at least 17% off the cover price. It's quite a bargain! Shipping and handling is just 50¢ per book in the U.S. and 75¢ per book in Canada.* I understand that accepting the 2 free books and gifts places me under no obligation to buy anything. I can always return a shipment and cancel at any time. Even if I never buy another book, the two free books and gifts are mine to keep forever.

102/302 IDN GH6Z

Name	(PLEASE PRINT)	

Address		Apt. #

City	State/Prov.	Zip/Postal Code

Signature (if under 18, a parent or guardian must sign)

Mail to the **Reader Service:**
IN U.S.A.: P.O. Box 1867, Buffalo, NY 14240-1867
IN CANADA: P.O. Box 609, Fort Erie, Ontario L2A 5X3

Want to try two free books from another series?
Call 1-800-873-8635 or visit www.ReaderService.com.

* Terms and prices subject to change without notice. Prices do not include applicable taxes. Sales tax applicable in N.Y. Canadian residents will be charged applicable taxes. Offer not valid in Quebec. This offer is limited to one order per household. Not valid for current subscribers to Love Inspired Historical books. All orders subject to credit approval. Credit or debit balances in a customer's account(s) may be offset by any other outstanding balance owed by or to the customer. Please allow 4 to 6 weeks for delivery. Offer available while quantities last.

Your Privacy—The Reader Service is committed to protecting your privacy. Our Privacy Policy is available online at www.ReaderService.com or upon request from the Reader Service.

We make a portion of our mailing list available to reputable third parties that offer products we believe may interest you. If you prefer that we not exchange your name with third parties, or if you wish to clarify or modify your communication preferences, please visit us at www.ReaderService.com/consumerchoice or write to us at Reader Service Preference Service, P.O. Box 9062, Buffalo, NY 14240-9062. Include your complete name and address.

LIH15

Gatlinburg, Tennessee
July 1887

As a holiday, Independence Day left a lot to be desired. Independence was a dream Caroline Turner wasn't likely to ever attain.

The fireworks' blue-green light flickered over the sea of faces, followed by red, white and gold. She schooled her features and made her way along the edge of the field to where the musicians were playing patriotic tunes.

"Caroline, we're running low on lemonade."

"Then make more," she snapped at eighteen-year-old Wanda Smith.

"We've misplaced the lemon crates."

At the distress in the younger girl's countenance, Caroline relented. "Fine. I'll look for them. You may return to your station."

It took her a quarter of an hour to locate the missing lemons. By then, the last of the fireworks had been shot off and attendees were ready for more food and drink.

The celebration was far from over, yet she wished she could return home to her bedroom and solitude.

A trio of young women approached and engaged her in conversation. As usual, they wanted to know about her outfit, whether she'd had it made by a local seamstress or her mother had had it shipped from New York. Before they'd exhausted their talk of fashion, a stranger inserted himself into their group.

"Excuse me."

Caroline didn't recognize the hulking figure. Well over six feet tall, he was as broad and solid as an oak tree and looked as if he hadn't seen civilization in months. He was dressed in common clothing, and his shirt and pants were clean but wrinkled. Dirt caked the heels of his sturdy brown boots. His thick reddish-brown hair was tied back with a strip of leather. While he appeared to have a strong facial structure, his mustache and beard obscured the lower half of his face. His mouth was wide and generous. Sparkling blue eyes assessed her.

"Would you care to dance?" He spoke in a rolling brogue that identified him as a foreigner.

Don't miss
WED BY NECESSITY by Karen Kirst,
available wherever Love Inspired® Historical books
and ebooks are sold.

www.LoveInspired.com

LIHEXP0117

Turn your love of reading into
rewards you'll love with

Harlequin My Rewards

Join for FREE today at
www.HarlequinMyRewards.com

Earn **FREE BOOKS** of your choice.

Experience **EXCLUSIVE OFFERS** and contests.

Enjoy **BOOK RECOMMENDATIONS**
selected just for you.

PLUS! Sign up now
and get **500** points
right away!

Earn
FREE
REWARDS
Join
Today!
HarlequinMyRewards.com

MYR16R